MISSING IN ACTION

His name is Tobias Godwin Porter the Third. Toby for short.
He is heir to a fabulously wealthy and aristocratic American
dynasty. He is tall, slightly built, with a genius I.Q. and a
black belt in karate. And he is the best friend that Matt
Eberhart, former U.S. ace fighter pilot, has ever had.

Now Toby is missing somewhere in the Southeast Asian
jungle—along with a rumored slave army of American G.I.s
who had been given up for dead for almost twenty years.

And now Matt is going to bring him back alive or die
trying—on a blood-soaked odyssey into the dark heart of
the mystery called—

THE CHINESE SPUR

Thrilling Fiction from SIGNET

THE CHINESE SPUR

BERENT SANDBERG

A SIGNET BOOK
NEW AMERICAN LIBRARY

TIMES MIRROR

PUBLISHER'S NOTE

This novel is a work of fiction. Names, characters, places, and incidents are either the product of the author's imagination or are used fictitiously, and any resemblance to actual persons, living or dead, events, or locales is entirely coincidental.

Copyright © 1983 by Peter Lars Sandberg and Berent & Woods, Inc.

SIGNET TRADEMARK REG. U.S. PAT. OFF. AND FOREIGN COUNTRIES
REGISTERED TRADEMARK—MARCA REGISTRADA
HECHO EN CHICAGO, U.S.A.

SIGNET, SIGNET CLASSICS, MENTOR, PLUME, MERIDIAN AND NAL BOOKS are published by The New American Library, Inc., 1633 Broadway, New York, New York 10019

First Printing, April, 1983

1 2 3 4 5 6 7 8 9

PRINTED IN THE UNITED STATES OF AMERICA

To Gladys and George Brooks,
Who never believed all the
Prisoners of War held by the
Communist forces were returned.

To their son, Lieutenant Commander
Nicholas Brooks, United States Navy, MIA Laos,
1970–1982.

And to the rest.

Chapter
ONE

We were in the cockpit of a Rockwell Sabre 75, cruising at 40,000 feet over the Strait of Malacca, between Singapore and Kuala Lumpur. I was in the left seat. Terry Melbourne was in the right. Sun splashing through the windshields. Visibility so good we could see west across the lush jungles of Sumatra all the way to the offshore islands in the Indian Ocean, and east across the Malay Peninsula to the rippling South China Sea. Behind us, the eight-place VIP cabin, with its elegant bar, galley, seats, and sofa, was empty. No one else aboard.

"Do fighter pilots always check the instruments so often?" Terry asked. I was going over them for maybe the tenth time since our takeoff from Singapore's Seletar Airport twenty minutes ago. Terry, an international celebrity from Australia and the sister of an old friend, was an accomplished pilot herself. It was not surprising she had noticed my concern with the gauges.

"Just getting reacquainted is all," I lied. "It's been a while since I've flown the Sabreliner."

"My father was like that," she said. "He flew fighters for the RAAF as if he'd been born in one; but he was always careful. Now that you've had a good look, what have you decided about the plane?"

"I've decided the plane's a beauty," I said. "Just like the sister of the man who owns it."

"Oh balls," she said.

"Retired fighter jocks are always pretty smooth," I said.

"You fighter jocks," she said. "You're all of a stripe."

I had retired from the United States Air Force several years ago, owned and lived on a small horse farm in Virginia now. To keep my flying skills as current and sharp as I could, I did free-lance work as a pilot-reporter for a number of international aerospace and defense magazines. A couple of months ago, I had flown the German Alphajet. Before that, the British Hawk, and Swedish Saab 105.

1

So here I was in a Rockwell Sabre, eight miles over the Strait of Malacca, checking the gauges yet again: RPM, EPR, Oil, EGT. I tried to do it less obviously this time, not wanting to alarm Terry with the faint niggle I had that something about this particular airplane might be wrong. After twenty years of flying, you develop a sixth sense like that. It doesn't always prove out, but if you're careful, you don't ignore it.

"Everything fine?" Terry said with a twinkle.

"Everything fine," I said.

And it was. All gauges were good; engines thrumming in perfect synch; the world below, brilliant in colors of blue and green.

The environment was familiar. I had had three combat tours in Southeast Asia. My last assignment had been as air attaché at our embassy in Phnom Penh, Cambodia. I had lost my wife, Diana, there; had all but lost my son. Those were the bad memories. I had flushed them out of my brain by drinking a lot of whiskey for a while. I had never found a way to flush them out of my dreams. They came to me at night in visions of fire and blood: every night during the first couple of years; much less often now.

I had good memories of my Cambodian tour as well.

Graham Melbourne, Terry's older brother, was one of these.

He had been an officer then with the Australian Secret Intelligence Service. We had tried to win the Cambodian war together for a while, Graham, Toby Porter, some tough Khmers; a handful of people from a half-dozen countries, who went on believing a long time after the rest of the free world had stopped.

Now a civilian, Graham owned his own company, a firm based in Singapore that sold used but classy business jets throughout the five ASEAN countries.

Two weeks ago, at an ungodly hour of a crisp October morning at my farm in Virginia, I had received an unexpected phone call from him.

"You're calling from where?!" I had shouted, still half asleep. Our connection had sounded like bacon frying.

"Singapore! My sister is on for holiday! She says she wants to meet you!"

"In Singapore!"

"Yes! The tickets are on me! All arranged!"

"I remember your sister's picture! I've forgotten her name!"

"Terry! She won the Cosmos/World thing several years ago!"

"The Cosmos what?!"

"World! Put a stick to it, Matt! We've got the champagne on

ce! You should plan to stay at least two weeks! I expect Campbell to pop in sometime while you're here!"

"Campbell?!"

I changed the phone to my other ear, fully awake now at the mention of my father-in-law's name. He had recently been promoted to Special Assistant to the Deputy Director of Operations for the CIA. "Popping in" wasn't his style.

"Can you leave in the morning?!" Graham yelled through the poor connection.

"Is it some kind of emergency?!" I yelled back.

"Bloody Christ, no, Eberhart! It's a reunion! Pull your thumb out and get aboard, will you?! Would you like to chat with Terry?! She's standing by!"

"Yes!" I shouted. "No!"

"I should warn you! She has a nasty thing for any Yank fighter pilot over six feet tall!"

"Good God," I said.

"How's that?!"

"That's odd!" I said.

"Will you come?!"

"No!" I said. "Yes!"

And so, as my old friend Graham Melbourne would have put it himself, I had pulled my thumb out and gone.

Terry had her Australian commercial pilot's license and had logged over a hundred hours in Rockwell Sabres, demonstrating the sleek jets for her brother's more important clients. I had flown the USAF version of the same plane—the T-39—out of SAMSO in Los Angeles. With these credentials in order, Terry had agreed today to let me take the pilot's position. I loved her for that, and for some other things too.

Graham, who had orginally intended to go up with us, had begged off at the last minute. He said he had overlooked an essential appointment with the Indonesian tea merchant whose plane this was apparently destined to be. I think all Graham really wanted to do was give Terry and me some time alone in the air. His approval of our budding affair had been unqualified.

"Give the bird a full flight check while you're up, will you?" he said. To an Australian the phrase could have more than one meaning. He grinned when he said it.

"Will do," I promised.

"See you for cocktails, then."

"Bye, Gray," Terry said.

"Bye, kid. Take good care of Eberhart here. *And* the bird."

Terry returned her brother's smile.

"Eberhart will have to fend for himself," she said. "We'l both look out for the bird."

I thought Graham had carried the years well since we ha known each other in Phnom Penh, and he seemed relaxed enoug as he walked away, a tall, good-looking, red-haired man in gray tropical suit. Terry and I watched him go, standing by th civilian flight line at Seletar, holding hands.

"He's worried about something," she said.

The remark surprised me.

"If so, it doesn't show," I said.

"He wouldn't let it. Not in front of you."

"Any idea what it might be?"

"Something to do with your father-in-law, I think."

"Campbell?" I said. The last ten days had been the happies and most carefree I had known since before the Vietnam War. Terry and I were having so much fun together, I had completely forgotten Graham's reference to Campbell's popping in.

"A couple of weeks ago he was calling Gray a lot—from Bangkok," Terry said. "Gray would get very excited, then suddenly very cryptic, as if he thought the calls were being monitored."

"Did you ask him what Campbell was calling about?"

"Yes. Gray said it was confidential. Sort of patted me on the head. I am the kid sister, you know."

"Pretty terrific sister," I said. She was all I wanted to think about.

She smiled, tightening her grip on my hand.

The electricity had been working for the two of us from the moment we had first met, on the night of my arrival in Singapore. It had taken three days for us to spar with each other and establish our respective ground; three more to test-fly the relationship; one to discover it worked in bed. The rest had been gravy. The more we got, the more we wanted.

Terry was sitting primly now in the copilot's seat, black toreador pants and green silk blouse. A wicker picnic basket she had just fetched from the galley rested on her lap.

"Hey," I said. "That's supposed to be for when we get to Sentosa."

Anticipating that event, I had worn Levi cutoffs and a polo shirt, and had put two bottles of Piper Heidseick to chill in the galley fridge. Sentosa was the name of the island lagoon off Singapore where we planned to go swimming after our flight.

Terry looked at me as if to say, "Bugger off, Yank. I'm hungry." She had no lipstick on, or any other makeup, as far as I could tell. "Putting on side," as she liked to phrase it, was something a woman was required to do while reigning as a current Miss Cosmos/World. One year of that had been enough for Terry. In the years since, she had reverted to the more natural person I suspected she was inclined to be. Her auburn hair, once shoulder-length, was now cut attractively short; eyes wide-set and amber, flecked with gold; figure lithe and tall. She was in her early thirties, had seen a lot of life and had never, from the way she talked about it, been overly impressed.

"Sentosa is that way," she said, gesturing behind us. "By the time we put this plane through its paces, get back to the airfield, and drive to the lagoon, I'll have died from malnutrition."

She poked around inside the basket. The food packages had been wrapped in linen. There were cubes of Szechuan smoked duck, barbecued ribs, butterfly shrimp, and egg rolls—all put up personally by a chef I had gotten to know at the Raffles Hotel.

I watched as Terry popped a cube of the duck neatly into her splendid mouth.

"Want one?" she asked. Around the duck, the question sounded more like, "Wan won?"

"I'll settle for a cigarette," I said, shaking one out of my pack.

"Filthy habit," she said.

"You're right. I'll be giving it up pretty soon. Actually I've been giving it up for quite a few years now."

She bit into a piece of barbecued rib.

"No luck?" she asked.

"Some. When I'm on the farm, I hold it to three a day: two during the cocktail hour, one after supper. I can usually stick to that."

"Remarkable self-control," she said. She popped my lap belt, slipped her hand into the pocket of my cutoffs, rummaged there for my lighter.

"You're distracting the pilot," I said.

"I can tell," she said.

She lit the cigarette for me, put it between my teeth, returned the lighter to its pocket. She kept her hand there, moving it in an interesting way.

"Now listen, pal," I said, smiling at her. "We've got work to do here. Your brother Graham wants every system on this bird checked out, top to bottom.''

"*Which* bird?" she said.

"You Aussies," I said. "You're all of a stripe."

"According to Singapore Control," she said, "there's absolutely no traffic within two hundred miles at this altitude. Not so much as a cormorant."

"That may well be true," I replied. "But we're sitting in three million bucks' worth of airplane that doesn't belong to us. I know *you* know we've got to keep that in mind."

Old Eberhart: A twenty-year man, always attentive to duty.

"Of course," Terry said.

She unfastened her seat belt and went aft to put the basket away in the galley. I finished my cigarette. When she came back, she paused behind me, leaning down, kissing me softly on the neck, just below the ear. As she did, I could feel the gooseflesh rise, all the way down my bare legs.

"Now you're not going to be dull, are you?" she murmured. She had slipped a cartridge of Ravel's "Francesca da Rimini," a favorite of ours, into the quad sound system.

"Oh hell, I thought.

I had already engaged the autopilot.

She kissed me again, twice, same place as before. I reached up, pulled her to me, kissed her on the mouth.

"Do I taste like a barbecued rib?" she asked.

"More like a smoked duck," I said.

She laughed happily, walking back again to the empty cabin. There was more rising around me now than my gooseflesh. By the time I joined her, she had unbuttoned her blouse to her waist and had struck one of the poses that had made her famous in the fashion magazines from Bombay to Brazil: back arched, one leg forward, head nestled fetchingly in hand.

"Anybody for the five-mile-high club?" she said.

I took a double breath. That's the kind when you inhale twice without exhaling in between.

Then, trusting to our luck, Singapore Control, and the Collins autopilot, I took Terry in my arms.

We were alone in the world we had created, private and perfect.

Nothing was going to interfere.

Chapter
TWO

Anyone who has kicked around the Far East for a while will recognize the work of Hawper's of Singapore. They are best known as interior designers for custom yachts, but they've left their mark in a lot of the pricier shops and office buildings as well. Graham Melbourne had commissioned them to redecorate the interior of the Sabre 75.

They had used steamed and pressed teak to frame the furniture in the aft cabin. The sofa was covered with a Kelantin silk gold weave, more appropriate to the conversation room in a Malaysian palace than bolted into a plane. Balinese dancing maidens, carved in ebony and Sawa wood, decorated the cabin walls. The door to the head was teak, with rosewood overlays. The galley was hidden behind lacquerware lattices inlaid with mother-of-pearl. Hammered copper, depicting scenes of fighting elephants, set off the windows on both sides of the cabin. Each window featured Polaroid glass and an electrically controlled woven-cane shade.

All very plush, and not such a bad place to spend some time with Miss Cosmos/World, especially if her name happened to be Terry Melbourne, and the two of you thought you might be in love.

We kicked and fumbled out of shoes and shirts, cutoffs and toreador pants. We both knew we weren't going to spend a lot of time on the sofa-by-Hawper. Our urgency, fueled by desire, carried massive overtones of guilt due to the unattended front end of the airplane.

We turned the cabin stereo up full and, as a safety precaution, piped in Singapore Control on the UHF. With this arrangement, any transmission from them would cut out the Ravel.

They say the pulse of love beats faster whenever there is risk of discovery. I'm not so sure about that, but I can vouch for the fact it beats faster when there is even a minimal risk of plowing

7

into a cormorant—or worse—at 40,000 feet over the Strait of
Malacca.

Still standing, we reached for each other, drawing quickly
together in a breathless, knee-buckling embrace, sliding toward
the couch, then onto it, our body heat increased and given back
by the sensuous silk of its covering, the two of us immersed in
the taste and feel and scent of our combined arousal, Terry's
husky whisper urgent in my ear: *I need you, Matt, I want you,
here, like that, now hurry, hurry . . .* The two of us joined in a
single thrust, becoming one with each other and with the pulsing
music, mindless and encapsulated as the small sleek jet shot like
a silver needle through a blue clarity of sky.

I was still lying on the sofa when the UHF came up. Terry
was standing next to me. She had just pulled on the bikini briefs
she wore under the toreadors.

"Nine Victor Alpha Sierra Echo, this is Singapore Control, do
you read?"

The controller's accent was Chinese with Australian overtones.
He sounded as if he had gotten his training at Sydney Center,
which he probably had. Flat on the sofa, I reached over my head
for the microphone attached to the intercom system. Before I
found it, Terry had darted to the cockpit and grabbed the mike
for the right seat. I heard the exchange through the cabin speakers as I pulled on my cutoffs. Terry's voice was professional
and, I thought, a little on the breathless side.

"Singapore, this is Alpha Sierra Echo, go ahead."

"Oh, hullo, Terry; thought it was you. You're coming up on
Puffer Intersection. When do you want clearance for your airwork,
over?"

"Hullo yourself, Lee. We'll do a one-eighty at Puffer, then
vector one two five for my usual place south of Bandar. Keep us
on the scope."

"Okay, Sierra Echo. Report Puffer and I'll clear you to flight
level three eight zero in your turn."

"Thanks, Lee. Sierra Echo out."

Terry rushed back to the cabin in a blur of pink-and-tan skin,
snatching up the rest of her clothes. I think if Lee could have
seen her as they talked, he might have swallowed his microphone.

"Take your time," I said, pulling my shirt over my head and
slipping into my sneakers. "I'll get the left seat."

As I switched off the autopilot and resumed control of the
plane, I felt a mingled sense of relief, satisfaction, and a fair

amount of residual guilt. In the parlance my father had used when I was a kid growing up in Montana, Terry and I had just gotten away with something, out behind the barn.

When she returned to her seat, fully dressed again, she blew me a kiss, then was all business.

"After we turn at Puffer," she said, "I'll call off the checks and you perform them."

Our TACAN navigation equipment was set on Channel 94. It was picking up the Batu Arang transmitter, twenty miles north-west of Kuala Lumpur. The needle showed we were on the 275-degree radial; the distance-measuring-equipment digits said we were fifty-five nautical miles out from the station. This meant we had reached Puffer Intersection, an electronic point in space used for aerial navigation.

"Turn starboard to one two five degrees," Terry said. "When I get clearance, descend to three eight thousand."

She picked up her mike, and keyed it.

"Singapore, Alpha Sierra Echo, over."

"Sierra Echo, this is Singapore, go ahead."

"We are at Puffer in a right turn. Request permission to leave flight level four zero zero for three eight zero, over."

"Sierra Echo, you are cleared to flight level three eight zero. Call when level, Terry."

"Roger, Lee. Sierra Echo out."

To lose altitude rapidly in a jet fighter, and in executive jets like the Rockwell Sabre, the pilot normally throttles back the engines while thumbing a switch that actuates the speed brakes. These brakes consist of one or more hydraulically operated doors which, when actuated, open into the slipstream and create sudden and tremendous drag, thereby quickly hastening descent. When a jet is shut down and parked on a ramp, normal procedure is to leave these doors open. It had struck me as odd, during our preflight inspection, that Graham had left them closed. Though they were not critical to the operation of the plane, I wanted to be sure they worked.

I was about to thumb the speed-brake switch on the left throttle when Singapore came back up.

"Nine Victor Alpha Sierra Echo, make a shallow descent. You have traffic at your three-o'clock position climbing out from KL, acknowledge."

I relaxed my thumb from the switch and eased both throttles rearward until the two RPM gauges on the instrument panel read 75 percent power from each engine.

"Sierra Echo acknowledges traffic," Terry transmitted as she peered out of the right quarter panel window. "I have a tally, Singapore. Will call you reaching three eight zero."

"Thank you, Sierra Echo. Singapore out."

I held a standard 30-degree turn throughout. As the directional gyro on the horizontal situation indicator approached one two five, I began my rollout. In a few seconds, I was on course and level at 38,000 feet. I brought the throttles up to standard cruise at 92 percent.

Singapore acknowledged Terry's call that we were level at three eight zero. She grabbed a knee board, pencil poised over the first check sheet.

"Okay, love," she said. "Push them up a hundred percent. As soon as the engines and airspeed stabilize, I'll call the numbers."

I firewalled the two Pratt and Whitney JT12s, then answered her queries, left engine first, then right.

"Free air temperature?"

"Minus forty-one Celsius."

"Indicated airspeed?"

"Two twenty-two."

"EGT?"

"Three-eighty degrees."

And so on, through fuel flow, EPR, cabin altitude, and differential pressure.

At Terry's request, I throttled back to 90 percent and we did it again. Then we did a complete systems check, radio, navigation, radar—everything short of flushing the john in the head.

Thirty minutes later we were abeam Bandar. Terry called Singapore and got permission for all-altitude airwork. She checked off the maneuvers she wanted me to perform, and I fed her the results. We did slow flight, tight turns, max-Mach descents, and lazy eights to check control response.

"How about we break for some loops and barrel rolls?" I said finally.

"You fighter pilots," she said. But I could tell she shared my enthusiasm for the flying, the day, our nation of two.

"*Hah!*" I shouted happily, as we thumped through the entry jet wash when I pulled through the bottom of a loop.

"*Double hah!*" Terry replied, after taking control and pulling one through of her own.

"Very nice!" I said. "*Damn* nice!"

We were so pleased with ourselves we leaned over and kissed each other at the top of the next loop.

Then it was time to get serious again.

We leveled at 14,000, where we would begin our check of the regular and auxiliary hydraulic systems. These raised and lowered the landing gear, and opened and closed the speed-brake doors.

I watched Terry pencil a final note on her page, then turn to the next.

"The maximum gear-down speed is one-eighty knots," she said. "Slow down to one-sixty, Matt, and cycle the hydraulics."

"Roger," I said.

I reached out my right hand and pulled the two throttles toward me.

Then, as I thumbed back the speed-brake switch on the left throttle, our private and perfect world exploded.

Chapter
THREE

The explosion had gone off somewhere underneath the plane, as if we had been hit by a surface-to-air missile. In the first seconds after the blast, we were whirled and caught in the midst of a kaleidoscope, where down was up: too stunned, too disoriented to react. I could feel a negative G pull and a sharp wrench at my waist. Then, through the top panels of the cockpit, where only blue sky should have shown, I could see the azure waters of the Strait, and the tree-root patterns of mud fanning out from the estuaries of the Malaysian rivers that fed into it.

Both engines had flamed out; the tree-root patterns were revolving. The force of the explosion had blown us upside down and into a deadly inverted spin, something the Sabre had never been stressed or certified for. We were going to have to break the spin fast, or crash. I knew it. So did Terry.

I hung from my lap belt, eyes painfully gritty with dust and dirt from the cockpit floor. Maps and let-down charts were plastered to the ceiling. To my right, I could see Terry trying to force her arms against reverse gravity and the centrifugal forces from the spin long enough to turn our radar transponder to the emergency code. She finally managed it. The wind noise up front was little more than a hiss; but from the aft cabin we could hear a loud roaring sound where something had ripped a hole through the floor, or an escape hatch had blown out. Our airspeed indicator read just over 200 knots. The altimeter was passing through 11,000 feet, and unwinding rapidly. Our vertical speed indicator said we were losing 3,000 feet per minute. In the brief moments since the explosion, neither of us had said a word. I was still badly disoriented.

"Verify spinning to the right!" I shouted.

"Turn needle in full right deflection!" Terry shouted back.

I held the control yoke neutral with hands that wanted to fall up, and pushed full left rudder.

Nothing happened.

I held the controls that way while the plane spun yet another full turn. We were losing precious altitude. Again, nothing happened. In desperation, I pulled the control column back into my lap. The movement seemed to aggravate the spin for a half second, then, abruptly, the rotation stopped. I quickly neutralized the controls.

We were still hanging from our belts, upside down.

"Get ready to do a multiple airstart!" I yelled.

"Ready when you are."

The Sabre was still inverted, spin broken, nose pointed down. We needed plenty of speed to turn the engines over for the start. I decided the safest way to pick up that speed was to roll out and dive. The liability would would be a loss of altitude. We were already coming through 7,000 feet.

As I rolled out and held the nose down, I shouted for Terry to begin the airstart procedure. The miscellaneous clutter that had been pinned to the ceiling fell like outsized confetti around us. The biting pressure of our lap belts eased off as we came right side up. As soon as we were, I turned east toward the distant coast of the Malaysian Peninsula. The coast was lined with mangroves, and looked to be well beyond glide range. Terry quickly checked the throttles in idle, master switches on, fuel-tank selector to crossfeed; then she flipped the airstart switch for the left engine.

All of this was taking place in a very few seconds. Our warning-light panel was lit up like a Christmas tree. Tiny sensors in each failed system screamed their problems. The only electrical power we had operational came from two 24-volt Ni-Cad batteries. Scarcely two minutes had passed since the inflight explosion itself. The Strait below was calm and sparkling. In the distance to my left, I could see in miniature some coastal traders, and what looked to be a Malaysian navy patrol boat plying the shore. I wanted to believe they had picked up our emergency signal and were ready to assist if we went down in the Strait; but I knew better than to count on that. There was no guarantee our transponder was working; and visually at these distances we wouldn't look much larger than a small gull diving toward the sea.

I cracked off a fast "Mayday" on the UHF, giving our position, but heard no response.

The waters of the Strait were coming up fast. In the cockpit, we could hear each other breathe.

"There's no ignition," Terry said. "She's not going to start."

"Try the starboard engine," I said, altering our course slightly in the direction of the boats I had seen. She put the airstart switch to the number two position. The RPM gauge moved up.

"EGT increasing!" she said. "We've got a light-off!"

We were happy about that, until we saw the temperature needle shoot past 700 degrees.

"Ah, shit," Terry said in a flat voice. "We're getting a hot start."

She hadn't finished speaking when I heard a loud rumble from the rear of the plane where the engine was mounted along the fuselage.

"Cut it!" I shouted. "Hit the fire extinguisher!" I yanked the throttle back. We were still carrying enough jet fuel to blow us all the way to Bangkok. Terry had already slapped the airstart switch off. She reached up and pulled the now-illuminated fire-extinguisher handle connected to the burning engine. We heard the whooshing sound of the high-pressure bottle discharging its foam into the hot section.

"EGT decreasing! Fire's out!" she said.

I eased my grip on the yoke. We were coming through 2,000 feet, on a fast, descending glide. Terry twisted quickly in her seat to look into the aft cabin. I heard her swear. The roaring noise back there had never let up. It sounded even louder now. I knew by the taut look on her face the news was bad. She said the floor hatch had been blown out by the explosion. That meant we had a three-foot hole in the bottom of the plane.

"Swell," I snapped.

"We're going to have to ditch," she said.

"That's right."

"Christ," she said. "With that hatch open, we'll sink like a brick."

"Go back to the cabin," I said. "Pop the window exit plug; then strap yourself into the nearest seat, facing aft. As soon as we stop moving get out fast."

"Not without you," she said.

"I'll be right on your heels," I said. "We'll meet on the surface."

She shot a glance out her side window as she unstrapped from the copilot's position and stood up. The water was clear, and bright with sun.

"Lots of sharks down here," she said.

"Nothing for it," I said.

"Enjoy the ride?"

"Damn right," I said. "Now move it!"

She smiled her terrific smile, as if in spite of the fact our world had been blown away, we had somehow managed to win.

"On the surface, then," she said, speaking rapidly. "I'll have the life cushions. Don't keep me waiting."

As she hurried past me, I wanted to take her in my arms, say the hell with the rest of it; but I wasn't built that way, and neither was Terry.

I heard the increase in air noise as Terry removed the window plug. We were below 1,500 now. Our angle of glide was ten degrees. In less than thirty seconds we would impact the Strait at over a hundred miles per hour.

The instant we did, the hole in the Sabre's belly would start scooping water like a bucket on a wheel.

Chapter
FOUR

In the brief time I had before touchdown, I turned the plane parallel to the oily, breeze-stippled swells of the up-rushing surface. I was holding a hundred knots airspeed on the final glide. My pulse was pounding; I had the coppery taste of combat in my mouth.

Take it easy, I thought. *You've done this before.*

But never with a hole in the floor of the plane.

I banged the flap switch down, prayed our electrical motors were still working, felt a stab of relief as the flaps extended and our glide speed eased off. I wanted the gear down too, so it could help absorb the shock of the landing, but our primary hydraulic system was shot, and right now I didn't dare take my hand off the control column long enough to fiddle around with the backup.

The reflection of the sun was blindingly bright off the surface of the water. Looking into it was like looking into a camera flash: small rocket bursts of white and red, a loss of focus. I needed my dark glasses. They were on the bar, next to the sofa-by-Hawper where, less than an hour ago, Terry and I had made love. I needed Terry herself, in the right-hand seat, working the emergency gear. I needed the hatch cover in place and five minutes to take another pass.

All dreams of what might have been.

No time for any of it to come true.

Individual pieces of flotsam were now visible on the surface below: chunks of what looked like cork, each the size of a door; slats of wood like barrel staves; black globs of petroleum hawked from the bilge of some renegade tanker . . . all coming up very fast.

I began to flatten my glide, checking automatically to be sure my lap belt was secured. It was, but in that relaxed, easy time before the explosion, I apparently hadn't bothered to hook my shoulder harness to it.

Christ, I thought, tightening my grip on the yoke. Sweat was stinging my eyes; the muscle in my right calf had started to twitch.

There was no replay of my life in the final seconds before impact. Only fragmented memories of old recurring nightmares, of a dreamlike fiery crash where, as a young lieutenant, my head would slam into the instrument panel, gray brains splattering, life gone in an instant.

No time left to hook the shoulder harness up. All I could do now was try my best to ease the crippled Sabre down while the oldest survival instincts I had were screaming at me to let go of the yoke and try to protect my head with my arms.

I came in over the water tail low, held it off for a long second or two, then felt us hit with a spine-jarring jolt and a sound like a depth charge cracking off. The yoke slammed forward; we skipped back into the air. I tried to keep the nose up and wings level with controls that had no effect. Behind me I heard Terry's sharp exhalation of breath as we hit the surface of the water again with a final concussive slam.

Then, time came to a halt for me, and I went to another place.

For a while, it was all family, most of them dead now: my father during World War II on an OSS mission with J.R. Coyle and Campbell Cooke; my mother a few years after that of heartbreak and cancer; my wife, Diana, cut in two by steel fragments from a 500-pound bomb dropped over Phnom Penh; my son, Brian, all but killed in the same incident, comatose for over two years—Walter Reed, the Swiss clinic, Nurse Whiskey at his side, the respirators, the laser treatments, the continual rising and falling of hope. . . .

But Brian's alive, I reminded myself. *He's out of the clinic now. He's out of his wheelchair a couple of hours a day, clumping around like the Tin Man, with his aluminum crutches and stainless-steel braces. He's alive. In Paris. With Coyle and Dominique.*

I smiled. The thought was a good one; something to hold on to. My own life had become jumbled and funny.

I couldn't figure out where I was. A shrill, hissing sound enveloped my head and hurt my ears. There was the tart smell of an ocean around me. Something plucked at my waist. I seemed to be lying in a chair, on my back, like an astronaut on a launch pad. The chair was bobbing up and down. Through a vague lattice of cobwebs, I thought I could see the sun.

"Matt!" a woman's voice called.

"I'm okay," I croaked, thinking it was my mother, knowing it couldn't be.

"Wake up!" the voice said. It came from another planet.

"I am awake," I told it impatiently. *"I'm okay."*

Things slid into focus then: sights, sounds; perceptions becoming sharp and identifiable.

The Sabre was sinking tail first, bobbing in swells, its nose just poking above the surface. I was still in my seat, facing skyward. Heavily compressed air, trapped in the cockpit, was whistling out of cracks in the side panels. I could see waves breaking over the nose of the plane. We were sinking fast. Terry was next to me, immersed in water to her shoulders, floating parallel to the floor of the plane, trying to unfasten my lap belt. When she saw I had come around, she spoke sharply to me.

"Matt! Work the buckle!"

"Okay, okay," I said. I unfastened it with fingers that felt half hinged and sore. She helped me fumble out of the seat and flop into the water beside her. The water seemed warm and comforting. Debris from the cabin was still popping up around us. The light in the cockpit was fading, the remaining air fetid and heavy.

"Hurry up," she said. "Get some air. We'll go out through the bottom hatch."

I started to cough as water slopped into my mouth; then craned my neck, took a last deep breath, held it. I still wasn't functioning well; I made no effort to move. Terry slid down my body, took hold of my legs, began to tug and pull. She was strong. I felt as if I were being yanked through a storm sewer.

She brought me down into the vertical cabin, toward the canted galley and bar and sofa-by-Hawper, through a lazy drifting assortment of half-buoyant objects that couldn't seem to decide whether to go up or go down. I could feel the pressure change in my ears. The right side of my forehead stung. I wanted to cough again, knew I couldn't. My chest felt as if someone had parked a bus on it.

Terry moved me into position next to the hatch opening. I put one hand on the lower edge. The edge was sharp and jagged where the explosion had ripped it. I gestured for Terry to go first. She shook her head slowly, auburn hair like some special Sargasso weed in a turquoise sea. I let her help boost me through and up. She broke the surface just after me, gulping air.

I kicked off my sneakers, treaded water with limbs that really weren't responding, spluttered in the sunlight. Two life cushions floated fifty feet away: dull-green biscuits, out of reach.

"Can you hold on here while I get them?" Terry asked. Her voice was anxious.

"I think so," I said, treading away, cobwebs clearing.

"It would be a nuisance to lose you now."

"I'm pretty hard to lose," I said.

"You've got a lump on your forehead. It's oozing blood."

"I've got a hard head," I said.

She flashed me about half of her old smile, then stroked off to get the cushions. She had skinned out of her toreador pants sometime earlier, and was doing a crisp Australian crawl in her silk shirt and briefs.

"Put your arms through the loops," she said when she had brought the biscuits back.

I did, floating effortlessly then, the life cushion buoyant under my chest. She tore one of the sleeves off her blouse, tied it around my forehead, covering the place that was oozing blood.

"You're thinking sharks," I said.

"It crossed my mind."

"I've read if they come close, the best way to deal with them is to whack them on the nose."

She did her best to look amused, got on the other cushion, held onto my polo shirt so we wouldn't drift apart. Bubbles were still cascading to the surface not far away: air trapped in the sunken plane still leaking out. A couple of tin canisters from the galley popped up and immediately began to bob away on the breeze.

"She's leaking fuel," I said, pointing to a pale-yellow viscousness on the surface where the bubbles were rising.

"We must have ruptured a tank when we crashed," Terry said.

"You did a helluva thing down there," I said.

"I threw the cushions out and dove after them as soon as the plane came to a stop. The tail was already under. I could see you were unconscious. I pounded on the windscreen, but you didn't move, and the cockpit was settling. . . ."

"How did you get back in?"

"I dove down along the bottom of the plane and went through the blown-out hatch. I really didn't think there was going to be time; but I couldn't leave you. It sounds silly when I say it."

I looked at her. Her face was drawn with concern, hair plastered to her skull, eyes red from the salt, one sleeve of her blouse gone. She gave a wobbly grin. I pulled her close enough to kiss. It was an uneven, snatching thing, but it was good.

"Thanks for getting me out of there," I said.

"I love a chance to excel."

"You Aussies," I said.

"Any idea what caused the explosion?"

"Just a hunch," I said. "Nothing solid. Let's table that for now and deal with this. How far offshore do you think we are?"

She shaded her eyes with one hand, squinted toward the distant coast of Malay.

"Ten miles," she said. "Perhaps less. It's hard to tell."

"That's a long way to paddle these cushions," I said. "The breeze is against us. So's the current. Those tins that popped up are almost out of sight, going the wrong way. Take a look."

As I spoke, she gripped my arm.

"Matt," she murmured, without reference to anything I had said. "We do have a shark."

I shot a glance back in the direction of the shore, saw a single triangular fin cutting the surface, cruising lazily a dozen yards away. Before I could say anything to Terry, it was joined by another. The sight produced an instantaneous, gut-wrenching, primordial fear.

"Christ," Terry breathed.

"Better get rid of your brightwork," I said, trying to hold off the panic I felt. "Your watch. Bracelet. Anything shiny. Give them to me. I'll put them in my pocket."

She did that.

"There are three now," she said, keeping her gaze fixed on the growing cluster of fins. "Jesus, Matt," she said, "I can't handle the sharks."

"Let's move toward the fuel slick," I said. "Use a breast stroke. Very slow. Don't break the water with your kick."

She had hold of my arm, fingers digging into my flesh. There was a look of naked terror in her eyes.

"Hang on," I said. "I'll take care of the swimming. You hang on to my shirt."

I angled us off toward the place where the bubbles were rising from the sunken Sabre, keeping one eye on the fins that cruised in an idle way as if these sharks were only curious as to who we were and what we were about. There were four of them now. Their aimless fins rose a foot and a half above the surface, gray and leathery, water evaporating from them in the sun and breeze. My gut was churning; I was breathing too fast.

The water around the bubbles was gassy and oily from the jet fuel. I slowly frog-kicked our cushions around the widening slick, hoping I could put it between us and the sharks. No good. They followed, circling as we circled, not quite keeping up, but not falling far behind either. I remembered films I had seen of their feeding frenzies—how as soon as they had the taste of blood in their mouths they would eat anything that moved, including themselves.

Terry had reached the edge of panic. I could sense it in the shallow way she was breathing, and the death grip she had on my arm. I was close to the edge too: loaded with adrenalin, needing to act, not knowing what the hell I should do.

A gull soared over us, cocking its head to look down, shrieking its lonely call. The water felt tepid around my legs. Somewhere in the distance, I heard the sound of a ship's horn.

I scanned the horizon. One boat in sight, to the north. It looked as if it might be coming toward us, but it was still far away—small, like a child's toy.

Maybe the sharks would go away after a while.

Maybe they wouldn't.

There were five of them now. Closer than before. Bobbing on my cushion, I fished in the pocket of my cutoffs, found my cigarette lighter among the jewelry Terry had given me, brought it to the surface. It was a standard butane lighter: good for a thousand lights. All I wanted was one.

I held it up and spun the spark wheel with my thumb. Nothing happened.

"What are you trying to do?" Terry said. She was watching me and the sharks at the same time.

"Torch off this fuel slick," I said. "There's a boat out there. If we put up some smoke and flame, there's a good chance they'll see it."

"Will it drive off these sharks?"

"It could. Give me a hand. We've got to move ourselves upwind of the spill."

"I can't," she said, but she began to.

"Slow and easy," I said.

We held on to each other with one arm, quietly stroked with the other. We could smell the sharp stink of the fuel. I had the lighter between my teeth. Water slurped against the front of the cushions as we circled around.

"Okay," I said when the slick was finally downwind of us.

"Keep us right where we are. Let me know if anything changes with the sharks."

I tried the lighter again. It didn't work. I moved the butane feed up to full and blew hard on the wheel. This time I got a spark, but no flame. I kept working at it, blowing hard, thumbing the wheel. The size of the spark began to increase.

"Where are the sharks?" I said.

"About halfway downwind of us at nine o'clock," Terry said.

"Coming this way?"

"Moving back and forth. They're closer now than they were."

I blew on the lighter again and worked the wheel. This time a jet of flame shot up. As soon as it did, I snapped it off.

"We can't go straight flame to fuel," I said. "The flash point's too high—not like gasoline. We'll have to heat it first. Peel this bandage off of me. It's the only thing we've got that's half dry. Drape it along the top of the slick. Load it up good with fuel."

Terry did what I told her to do. She seemed as relieved as I was that we weren't simply going to hang on to our cushions, with our legs in the water, waiting for the sharks to make the first move.

When the fuel-soaked strip of silk was ready, I held it up in front of us; she cupped the lighter flame under it. It took a few seconds for the fumes to heat up; then a tongue of flame slowly ran to the top and the silk burst into fire.

"Get back!" I told her. *"Get farther upwind!"*

She moved away from me. I held the flaming silk next to the fuel on the rolling surface of water. The fuel flattened out in a twelve-inch radius, began to turn brown and heat. When it caught, I lost the hair on my arm as I backpedaled away. The fire took hold. In seconds, it had spread several feet; then, as the air over the surrounding fuel heated, it all went up like a giant canister of napalm, spreading thirty yards in front of us, super-heating the air, sending up a sheet of fire under a cloud of black greasy smoke.

We joined cushions again and held on to each other, staying as close to the inferno as we could stand. Terry's face glowed in the light. She looked more like herself again.

"Those sharks went packing," she said. "As soon as the fuel touched off. Sorry I got nervy about them."

"Boat on its way," I said, pointing north.

She squinted at it, looking provoked.

"Wish I hadn't dropped my slacks," she said.

Chapter
FIVE

We were picked up by the *K. D. Mutiara*, a 130-foot hydrographic survey vessel under the command of Captain Dato' Rahman of the Royal Malaysian Navy. The ship was spanking clean, the crew well disciplined. Two of them held a blanket for Terry as she came over the top of the boarding ladder. There weren't any smirks, smiles, or comments that they were rescuing a celebrity. Captain Rahman was a stocky man with a full, neatly trimmed mustache. His officer's whites heightened the permanent tan he had acquired during his years at sea. He spoke precise English with an Oxfordian accent. Terry and I stood just outside the wheelhouse, close to the starboard rail, small puddles of water collecting at our feet.

"My radio officer picked up a transmission from Singapore Control," Captain Rahman told us. "They said they had lost radar and radio contact with a private airplane over the Strait, somewhere west of Bandar. We've been keeping a lookout, but it's a very large area. Frankly, when we saw the smoke, we feared the worst. It is a pleasure to have you aboard, Miss Melbourne. And you, Colonel Eberhart."

"Pleasure to be here," I said, brows arching in surprise. "Did Singapore Control give you our names?"

Captain Rahman smiled.

"I've been in the service of the RMN for over twenty years," he said. "My father was an officer before me. He was killed not long ago by pirates in the Gulf of Siam. Since then, I've made it a point to be careful about whom I pick up at sea. One of the air controllers at Seletar described you for us. I take it you didn't have time to switch to the emergency code on your radar transponder?"

"We switched it on as soon as we knew we were in trouble," Terry said. "We were just coming through eleven thousand feet. I remember—"

"Things were pretty dicey then," I said, cutting her off. "We were trying to break out of an inverted spin. It could be we fouled something up.''

Terry gave me a withering look. Captain Rahman, who I suspected didn't miss very much, smiled his smile.

"What was it that caused you to crash?" he asked.

"We're not sure," I said. "We were running some standard hydraulic checks when we lost both engines. We tried a multiple airstart and developed a fire. There was an explosion. . . ."

I shrugged, as if there was nothing more to say. Captain Rahman seemed satisfied.

"As you know," he said, "there are regular procedures that must be followed after an accident of this kind. With your permission, we can facilitate some of these while we make way for Singapore."

I said that would be fine with me. Terry, wrapped in her blanket, nodded her head. Captain Rahman said his sonar operator had already determined that the sunken Sabreliner would not pose a hazard to navigation. He would contact the necessary authorities so they could meet us on our arrival in port. He concluded by saying that the ship's doctor could examine us for evidence of drugs or alcohol.

"We're *not* irresponsible," Terry said.

As she said it, I remembered the two of us on the sofa-by-Hawper: low grades there for responsibility, but not something I would trade.

"These tests are only a formality," Captain Rahman replied. "Best all around to get them out of the way. I suggest we start with that, then show you to my quarters, where you can wash up and change clothes. The men have just been on liberty in one of the ports in Sumatra. They always come back with a variety of costumes to give to their families. One of my officers will find something appropriate."

"I'd like to call my brother, in Singapore," Terry said. "He likes to monitor the UHF. He could have heard we were in trouble. I don't want him to worry."

"When you're ready, I'll have my radioman contact the marine operator," Captain Rahman said. "Is there anything else we can do for you?"

"I'm hungry enough to eat a piece of the deck," I said. "Is there a chance we could get some food?"

"Our cook will prepare a tray and send it to my quarters," Captain Rahman said. "Please make yourselves comfortable there. We should dock in Singapore at eighteen hundred hours."

Terry and I thanked him again for having come to our rescue. He said it had been his very great pleasure.

We took our turns in the sick bay with the ship's doctor. He took blood and urine samples, checked the lump on my forehead, painted it with some Merthiolate, and slapped on a small gauze bandage. Aside from some singed hair, jet-fuel rash, and salt-scoured eyes, we were in good shape.

Terry showered first, in the captain's cabin, got into the white muslin blouse and flowered sarong one of Rahman's men had brought for her, then hurried off to the radio room to call her brother. I got into the shower and stayed there for a while, humming a snatch of "One Fine Day" from *Madame Butterfly*, trying to keep my bandage dry. The stall wasn't much bigger than I was, but the water was hot and there was plenty of it. I was still kicked up from the adrenaline high I'd developed during the crash and I wanted to stay that way: in the combat mode; ready for whatever might develop once Terry and I were back in Singapore.

"You've got some explaining to do," she said, when she came back to the captain's cabin from making her call. I had gotten into the clothes Rahman's man had provided for me: natty pair of white ducks, black safari shirt, pair of leather sandals with a cane weave.

"Did you get through to Graham?" I asked.

"No. I tried his office, the apartment, the mobile phone in his car. No luck. I left a message with his answering service. He's probably out tearing around someplace. You still have some explaining to do."

She was sitting on a couch with a bamboo frame and royal-blue cushions, facing a rectangular window that presented a view of the sea. Her hair was still damp from the shower, lips chapped from salt and sun. When I realized she was shivering, I found the control for the cabin air conditioner and turned it from medium to low. Then I sat down next to her on the couch.

"Sorry I cut you off in front of the captain," I said.

"I'm sure you had an excellent reason."

"I didn't think we needed to raise unnecessary questions in his mind as to why our transponder didn't work."

"Why didn't it?"

"I'm not sure. I'd like to find out. There are a lot of things about what happened up there that I'd like to find the answers to."

"The explosion went off just as you began the hydraulic checks, am I right?"

"Yes. I thumbed the speed-brake switch on the left throttle and *bang*. It was instantaneous, like firing a gun."

"There are fuel lines that run near the speed-brake area. Could there have been some kind of vapor buildup from a small leak, touched off by a spark?"

"I don't think so. The speed-brake switch itself is electric, and there's an electric solenoid that opens the hydraulic pressure valve; but the action in the speed-brake well is all mechanical. There's nothing there to create a spark."

Terry thought for a long moment, her tanned forehead wrinkled in a frown as she puzzled things out.

"Then we were sabotaged," she said finally. "It was some kind of bomb, rigged to go off when you worked the switch."

"That's my hunch. Right now I'd bet the farm on it."

"But why?" she said. "Why would anyone want to kill us?"

"I don't know."

"I did have a run-in or two during the year I held the Cosmos title, but nothing really serious. There were the usual people who were jealous of me, some disappointed suitors—but nothing dramatic; nothing to bring about anything remotely like this." She looked at me. "Is there anything that might relate to you?" she said, as if she thought this was much more likely. I'd already done some deep-down thinking about that.

"As a mercenary, I ran a covert mission into Cambodia a few years back," I said. "A couple of West Germans got pretty badly burned by it. There's a chance in a million this ties to them, but I don't think so. I'd be easy to get too many other ways. How about Graham? He was scheduled to go up with us today."

I saw a flicker of apprehension cross Terry's face, replaced almost at once by a refusal to consider the possibility I had raised.

"Gray's been out of Intel for years," she said. "He has practically no competition in his business; he's liked and respected by everyone who knows him. No," she said. "No. I can't imagine anybody doing this to Gray."

I knew her well enough now to catch the trace of doubt in her voice in spite of the effort she had made to speak with assurance. I wanted to ask her again what it was she thought Graham might have been worried about in his dealings with my father-in-law, Campbell Cooke, in the days just prior to my arrival in Singa-

pore. I wanted to ask her if she thought there could be any
connection between that relationship and the sabotaging of the
plane. Campbell was now one of the most powerful men in the
CIA. His operations regularly took him around the globe and
could involve him at any time with forces who would think
nothing of boobytrapping an airplane if it happened to serve their
particular needs. Before I could sort out a way to bring this up
with Terry, she spoke again.

"The transponder could have been jiggered too, couldn't it?"
she said.

"My guess is it was," I said. "For insurance in case anyone
survived the explosion. Whoever did it had to have access to the
plane, and must have known our flight plan."

"I don't suppose it would have been all that difficult."

"Not for someone who knew what he was doing. I saw at
least a dozen mechanics hanging around the flight line. It could
have been any one of them—or someone dressed to look like
one."

Terry gazed through the captain's window, across the dappled
waters of the Strait. She looked tired and irritable, as if she
thought there was no excuse for this unwelcome intrusion into
our lives, as if she thought the two of us should be at Sentosa
Lagoon right now, swimming in champagne. I felt that way
too. We were quiet for a long time.

"Gray will know what to do about this," she said finally.
"Gray always knows what to do."

The captain's steward brought us platters of skewered beef and
chicken bits garnished with a hot peanut and pepper sauce. He
also brought a silver ice bucket filled with a half-dozen bottles of
Tiger beer. We ate and drank in silence. I felt dehydrated from
our time in the water; the hot sauce fired my thirst. I tried to
settle for two bottles of the beer and wound up having four. I
kept going over things in my mind, trying to come up with
answers that wouldn't come.

"When Graham called me at the farm," I said, "he told me
we were going to have a celebration, reunion, something like
that. He said he had the champagne on ice."

"He does," Terry said. "A whole fridge full in the servants'
pantry. That's where I got the Piper Heidseick I gave you to
bring on the plane."

"I've been in Singapore over a week. How come no celebration? It's the kind of thing I figured we'd do when I arrived."

"Your father-in-law is due in any day. I think Gray's been waiting for him."

I stood up and began to pace around the cabin. I could feel the effect of the beer, pulsing at my temple.

"No," I said, "there's something wrong here, something missing. I should have picked up on it before, Terry, but I didn't. I was just too happy just being with you. You know, I really haven't seen that much of Graham since I got here. He met me at the airport. We've had cocktails together. But he always seems to be off somewhere. Now I'm remembering something else. When he called me at the farm, he said you were in Singapore on a holiday. That isn't true, is it."

"No," Terry said. "It isn't. I've lived in Singapore for almost a year now—ever since our mother died. Gray only told you I was here on holiday to be sure you would come."

"You mean right away."

"Yes. Otherwise he thought you might put it off."

"And that bit about your wanting to meet me?"

"*That* was your father-in-law's idea," she said. "Gray assured me it was."

"If Campbell wanted me in Singapore," I said, "why didn't he just ask me to come?"

"He's your father-in-law. I wouldn't have a clue."

"Was he the one who paid for my plane tickets?"

"No, that was Gray, I think."

"Are you sure?"

"Yes. Gray told me he had paid for them."

"Okay, how about those phone calls you told me about—the ones Campbell made to your brother from Bangkok? You said Graham would sound excited, then get cryptic, maybe because he was worried about a tap. Any idea at all what the calls were about?"

"No."

"Nothing sticks? No catch phrases? Code words?"

"Matt, I never really listened in. All I got was a general sense. The last call came when we were driving to the airport to pick you up. Gray took it on the mobile phone. He told your father-in-law that Papa Wolf was inbound. I took that to be a reference to you."

"That was the call sign I used during the war," I said. "Both Graham and Campbell would know it. Anything else?"

"When Gray hung up, he looked anxious again. As if he had been hoping for good news from your father-in-law, but the good news hadn't come. When I asked him if things were all right, he gave me a sort of ironic smile and said, 'The rabbit's halfway out of the hat, kid. We've got him by the ears this time. All it takes is patience. A bloody *lot* of patience!''

The reference meant nothing to Terry, nor was there anything else she could remember. We went over it all again, then lapsed into separate silences: she sitting on the captain's sofa; me standing in front of the window, watching the green, mangrove-clotted coast of Malaysia slide by, less than a mile now, off the port rail.

"Toby Porter," I said finally.

"What did you say?" Terry asked.

"Toby Porter. Does the name mean anything to you?"

"No. Should it?"

"Not really. I was just thinking out loud."

It was nothing more than a hunch, with so little to back it up I labeled it as such and put it away.

Chapter
SIX

Mutiara means "pearl" in Malay. Captain Rahman told us this about the name of his ship as he put us ashore at the Singapore Naval Port. We were met dockside by a representative from the civil aviation department, police, and customs officials.

Terry had lost her purse in the crash. Her passport was at the apartment she shared with her brother. This presented no problem, since she was recognized by several of the authorities on sight. My passport was in my room at the Raffles Hotel. The soggy cards in my wallet—particularly my USAF ID—satisfied the authorities I was indeed who I claimed to be. The police asked us to stop by their station on St. Andrews Road in the morning, passports in hand. The civil aviation man, impressed with the details Captain Rahman had already taken care of, asked us to come to his office sometime during the next twenty-four hours to fill out an accident report. I was glad to have that much time. I wanted to have a chance to talk with Graham privately before Terry and I made any official statement as to what had happened in the air.

"Did you reach him?" I asked her. She had tried again, this time from the harbormaster's phone.

"No," she said. "I'm starting to worry."

"Let's grab a taxi," I said. "We can stop by the Raffles, see if he's showed up there for cocktails. If not, we can try the apartment."

"The harbormaster says news of the crash has already been on the telly: the fact a private plane went down in the Strait; two survivors picked up; no other details."

"Doesn't take them long, does it," I said.

"At least they haven't got my name. If they did, they'd be piling all over us."

"Come on," I said. "Let's grab that cab."

We pulled up to the stately Raffles just as the evening trishaw tours were assembling. A gaggle of chattering tourists was milling around the three-wheeled cycle rigs, each rig powered by its own guide. I asked our driver if he would wait for us while we went into the hotel. He became visibly upset, wringing his hands, certain we were going to stiff him for his fare. Terry finally agreed to wait in the taxi while I went in to look for Graham. She said she felt silly wearing a sarong. I said she looked terrific wearing a sarong; it was hard to imagine anyone wearing it better.

I went in and checked for messages at the main desk. There were two. One had been called in from the States by Dawson Jones, the ex-jockey who had been helping me run the farm since late spring. He wanted me to know a horse deal that had been pending had finally gone through.

The other message was a telex from my father-in-law. It read:

MATT: ETA SELETAR 0800 TOMORROW.
MEET YOU BREAKFAST AT RAFFLES.
TRIED TO REACH GM NO LUCK.
TELL HIM NEGOTIATION SUCCESSFUL.
            CAMPBELL

I went up to my room on the off chance Graham might have slipped a note under the door. He hadn't. No sign of him out by the pool, where, in the Palm Court, candle-lit tables had been set up for supper. I tried the Long Bar, which in its time had watered the likes of Joseph Conrad and Somerset Maugham. No Graham. I bought a pack of Barclay's at the tobacco shop and made my way again through the gaggle of tourists to rejoin Terry.

"Did you try calling the apartment?" she asked.

"No," I said. "I didn't think to. I probably should have. There was a telex from Campbell. He's coming in tomorrow morning. He said to tell Graham things had worked out. Maybe we'll have that celebration soon."

Terry did not look convinced.

"Ask the driver to hurry, will you, please?" she said.

"I will," I said, "but it's rush hour. It's going to take some time."

Our driver seemed resigned to the fact this was not going to be his lucky day. He had taken our measure by the cut of our clothes and assumed at once we were a couple of eccentrics. When I asked him to step on it, I used my command voice and fixed him with a steely red eye. He dropped his head so far between his shoulders he looked like a rifle sight hunched over the wheel, muttering imprecations that certainly included a long line of my ancestors.

We headed northwest on Orchard Road. We saw the multiracial jam of people, rich and poor, crowded into the parking lot across from the market called Cold Storage. In the lot, now empty of cars, scores of tiny carts and hot-wagons had been set up by the mini-chefs of Singapore. They offered Chinese, Malay, Indian, and Indonesian appetizers: succulent morsels that were purchased quickly and chopsticked into hungry mouths. On-site health inspectors ensured the food was safe to eat.

Singapore was like that. Trash on the street was seldom seen—toss a cigarette into a gutter and the fine was $250. There was practically no crime—thieves were thrashed with six-foot poles. Prime Minister Lee Kuan Yew ran his small island nation as a very tight ship. I tried to keep this in mind as our dyspeptic driver threaded his way through the early-evening traffic. Singapore: the Switzerland of the Far East. One of a fast-vanishing breed of cities where you could still walk the streets at night in safety.

Graham's apartment building was located on Chen Lung Road, four blocks past the British High Commission office. Our driver pulled in with a not-so-inscrutable flourish, hoping, no doubt, to cadge a tip. When I paid him off, he examined the soggy

Singapore dollars I gave him as if this were absolutely the final affront. I couldn't help smiling.

"It's a long story," I said. "You probably wouldn't believe it anyway."

"Have nice day, you," he said through clenched teeth, speaking of a day that was already gone.

The apartment building was a modern, fifteen-story high-rise with a white marble facade. The facade was perforated with offset windows and recessed balconies, giving it the effect of a computer card standing on end. The walls of the lobby were mirrored, the decor tasteful contemporary.

Terry asked a uniformed building superintendent if her brother was in. The superintendent said he didn't know, that he had just come on duty. Terry asked him for a spare key—her old one residing now with her purse at thirty fathoms in the Strait of Malacca.

Graham's apartment was on the tenth floor: 3,500 square feet of opulence, complete with a day staff of servants to look after the cooking and cleaning. I had visited it before. The master suite included a large living room and balcony, huge bedroom, small library, dining area, kitchen, and pantry. Adjacent to this, off the living room, was a self-contained bedroom suite with full bath and dressing room, pullman kitchen, small sitting area, and separate balcony.

The smaller suite was Terry's. When her mother had died, she and Graham had become the last surviving members of the Melbourne clan (the father had died of a heart attack in the 1960s; a middle brother had disappeared years earlier on an archaeological dig in the Yucatan).

After the mother's death, Graham, whose business of brokering executive jets had been extremely successful, had asked Terry to join him in Singapore as a demonstrator pilot. Graham had been divorced twice, and had no children; Terry had never married. They were twelve years apart in age, seemed to have a relationship based on mutual respect and family ties. As far as I could tell, they treated each other like a couple of old friends, with Graham sometimes inclined to come on with the authoritarian role, and Terry very much inclined to ignore him whenever he did.

We rode the self-service elevator to the tenth floor, where Terry led the way in long, swinging strides down the corridor to their corner apartment. Here, she had trouble fitting the superintendent's key into the lock.

"Damn," she said, "I'm shaking like a leaf." There was a faint odor of hair spray in the corridor. As she started to reach for the doorbell, I caught her arm.

"Let me give the key a try," I said quietly. She looked at me, the corners of her mouth drawing down, her eyes shading toward the same expression of fear I had seen when she had spotted that first shark in the Strait.

"Something's wrong, isn't it," she said.

"Maybe not," I said. "But I don't see why that key shouldn't work. It's not new, and the number's right."

She gave it to me and I tried to push it into the lock. When I couldn't, I squatted in front of the door and checked the keyway. The hair-spray odor was stronger here; a sticky substance was hardening around the lockplate.

"What is it?" Terry said. Her voice was shaky. In my own head, a warning bell had started to clang.

"It's what somebody does when they're inside an apartment where they don't belong," I said, "and they want advance notice when the owner returns. It's a trick Graham would know, but there's no reason why he should use it here."

I held my lighter flame to the key. When the key was warm enough to melt the substance that had been sprayed into the lock, I inserted it and felt the tumblers turn.

I told Terry she should wait in the hall. She shook her head. I could see there wasn't going to be any arguing with her. We pushed into the dusky apartment, shoulder to shoulder.

There was a single light on in the living room. It came from a celadon lamp lying upturned on the floor next to a long sofa. The room resembled the track of a tornado: a swathe of destruction several yards wide that had disrupted everything in its path, tables, chairs, bookcases, lamps. The swathe began at the point where we were standing and diagonaled across the living room through the open library door.

I don't think Terry caught the muted click of a latch closing from the kitchen-pantry area. She was totally focused on the scene in front of us.

"*Graham!*" she shouted. "*Gray! Are you here?!*"

She bolted for the library, following the path of destruction. I ran for the kitchen. It was dark. I lost several seconds groping for a light switch. When I finally found one, I turned it on. There were small, bright drops of blood on the white-tiled floor, some smeared where I had stepped on them. The drops led to the utility stairs off the pantry.

I wrenched the door open, paused on the landing, listened at the stairwell. The well was blind: no way to see down. Several flights below, I heard a pattering and swishing sound. I ran after it. The stairwell was illuminated at each landing by a high-watt bulb in a wire cage. The stairs had been painted with gray deck paint; the walls and ceilings were white. A banister of two-inch pipe protected each flight.

There were a lot of stairs I never touched on my way down. I used the pipe rail, swinging like an ape, descending a half-dozen steps at a time, closing the distance between myself and the patter and swishing sounds, until I knew I was close behind whoever it was descending below me.

The bright drops of blood were evident now on the walls, spattering the left side. I could hear the sound of two men breathing, one more labored than the other.

I cranked it on. The floors were numbered in English and Chinese. I had reached six. The men below me were already on five, maybe four. My hands were sweating, and wanted to slip on the rail. The sandals Captain Rahman had provided for me had leather soles and gave me almost no traction at all.

I swung around the landing at five, then four, then three.

I caught up with one of my men at two.

He was Chinese, a slight, wiry, middle-aged man in a loose-fitting polo shirt and dark Chino pants. As I turned the corner, he sprang around, on a lower stair, to face me. His black hair was straight, razored back from his ears. Thin cult scars were visible at the corners of his mouth. He held the point of a dagger between the thumb and finger of his right hand.

We looked at each other for the space of a half second. Below us, I heard the street door open and close.

Then, he cocked his arm and threw the knife.

Chapter
SEVEN

There are times when liabilities turn into assets. This time it was the soles of my sandals. As I twisted reflexively away, trying to lunge for the shelter of the upper stairs, my feet went out from under me and I went down hard, crashing to the floor of the landing, half breaking my fall with my arm. The dagger clanged off the wall above me, just about chest high of the silhouette I had provided for the Chinese. The Chinese had wasted no time getting away. He must have been through the street door and gone while his weapon was still in the air.

I sat up slowly, rubbing my elbow. The dagger lay next to me. At first I thought it was nothing more than a run-of-the-mill dagger, the kind available in souvenir stores and barter shops throughout the Middle and Far East. Then I realized I had seen one like it before.

I started to pick it up, decided not to. Better, I thought, to leave it exactly where it had fallen. That way it could help corroborate my eventual account to the Singapore police of what had happened here.

The dagger was about eight inches overall length, with a slender, two-edged blade and jeweled handle. Aside from a now-broken point, the guard between blade and handle was its only distinctive feature. The guard was in the shape of a wide letter V that had been carefully hand-crafted out of gold. Four years ago, during my tour in Cambodia, I had seen a showcase full of these custom-made daggers at a shop called Villay-Phone's in Vientiane, Laos.

The moment of recognition passed quickly in the press of things at hand. I knew objects from Villay-Phone's could be found anywhere in the world. Open a middle drawer in my desk at the farm, and you'll find, along with some faded air medals and other mementos of those years, a heavy gold ID bracelet with a double elephant clasp—also crafted by Villay-Phone's.

I took the stairs back up to Graham Melbourne's apartment

two at a time. I found Terry in the library. She was sitting on the floor, cradling Graham's head in her lap, stroking his red hair. He was lying on his back. His suit coat was open. The butt end of a length of metal wire about the diameter of a coat hanger just showed at the upper left ribcage area, in the center of a growing stain on his vest. His face was pale, eyelids opening and closing in measured cadence. Something bloody was clutched in his right hand. He made a chuffing sound as I knelt beside him.

"Terry," I said, "did you call for an ambulance?"

She nodded.

"Police?"

She nodded again, unable to speak. Graham didn't seem to be suffering much pain; his body was already protecting itself by sliding into shock. I asked him if he could hear me. He made his chuffing sound again and I suddenly realized he was laughing— or, at least, was trying to—robbing his lungs of desperately needed air to let us know he had the situation under control.

"*Muh* . . . Matt . . ." he wheezed. "I got the bugger . . . I got the bugger, Matt. . . ." His lids closed on eyes that seemed to shrink back into his head. His lips were still moving. I had to bend closer to hear what he was trying to tell me. "It's the spur," he said. "It's something about the spur. . . ."

I took hold of his wrist. His pulse was erratic and feeble. "Graham," I said. "Listen to me. Is it about Toby?"

He shook his head, obviously having trouble making his circuits function, smiling weakly. "You sods bang a glass for me, will you?" he said. "I got the fucker right in my hand."

Just before he died, he slowly relaxed his clenched right fist. A bloody chunk of cartilage and skin lay in the palm: the upper two-thirds of a human ear.

Minutes later, the Singapore police arrived. Their preliminaries were swift and efficient. We gave our statements to Chief Inspector Kim Tan, whose staff of technicians quietly covered the apartment: dusting for prints, measuring distances, photographing the physical evidence from every conceivable angle. Terry got on the phone, called the solicitor who handled her and Graham's affairs, then their Lloyd's representative, several key executives of the company, two or three of Graham's local friends. She seemed businesslike and composed, reporting the basic facts of what had happened without embellishment. Certain things had to be taken care of. Life had to go on.

I tried to make myself useful by brewing up some coffee and

generally staying out of her way. Now and then she would ask me to get something for her, some trivial scrap of paper or item from her brother's desk, wanting, I think, to be sure I was still around, that I hadn't gone too far away.

After Inspector Kim had conferred with his medical man in the library, he joined us on the large balcony off the living room. He was a young-looking Chinese, probably older than he appeared: dark suit, high-gloss shoes, inconspicuous tie. The night was muggy. Ten stories below, traffic had begun to thin out. Mingled with its honk and rush, we could hear the discordant wail of a street opera.

Inspector Kim told Terry he would have to quarantine the apartment until his investigation was complete. He asked her if there was another place where she could stay. I told him I was staying at the Raffles, and would see to it that she had a room there. Terry, who hadn't replied to the inspector's question, was sitting erect and motionless in a white wrought-iron chair, gazing across the city lights, toward the harbor.

"If you need a sedative," the inspector said, "my medical man will be happy to give you one."

"I don't require a sedative," she said.

"If there's anything else we can do . . ."

"You can find the people who did this to Graham."

The inspector stood by the balcony rail, at a place where he could keep an eye on the work his people were doing inside the apartment.

"Colonel Eberhart's description of the one man was excellent," he said. "The other should be needing a hospital soon. We think the chances of finding them are quite good—though, of course, we can't be sure."

"You've seen this kind of thing before," I said. "Do you mind if I ask what it looks like to you?"

"Not at all," the inspector replied. "My initial impression is that two thieves were surprised while in the midst of burglarizing the apartment. A violent struggle ensued. It began near the front door and ended in the library."

"Then one of the bad guys went out in the hall and gummed up the lock?" I said.

"I would say so," the inspector replied.

"That doesn't make sense," I said. "Why not gum up the lock in the first place? If they'd done that, Graham's key wouldn't have worked. They'd have heard him futzing around with it and had their chance to get away, down the utility stairs."

The inspector nodded, sure enough of himself not to get touchy over the amateur speculation of a retired fighter jock.

"If you have a theory about that," he said, "I'd be pleased to hear it."

"Okay," I said. "Whoever these guys were, they didn't think anybody would return here until after they were through. When Graham came in unexpectedly, they got more careful. They sprayed the lock, then went back to their work. They must have done that just before Terry and I arrived. The only problem I have with this is that Terry says nothing of value is missing here—the wall safe is secure, silverware accounted for, cameras and radio equipment, color television sets . . ."

"There are two vases in the dining room worth more than a lot of that put together," Terry said. "Any smart thief would have known as much."

This led to a question the inspector had apparently been waiting to ask.

"There are a series of journals in the library," he said. "They're identified by year, and are written in code. Can you tell me what they are?"

"Yes," Terry said. "They're Graham's flight logs. He was a compulsive record keeper. He got used to writing in cipher when he was with the ASIS."

"These journals run consecutively through last year. Did he keep the current one somewhere else?"

Terry looked sharply at the inspector.

"No," she said. "He kept it in the library, on the same shelf with the others. He was very orderly, everything in a row."

The inspector took out his notebook and jotted a note.

"Are you saying it was Graham's flight logs these men were after?" Terry asked, incredulous.

"No," the inspector replied. "I am only saying that the flight log for the current year is not on the shelf with the others."

While Terry changed clothes and packed a bag, I told the inspector another one of my theories: that Graham Melbourne's Sabreliner had been rigged to explode, with its emergency transponder deliberately put out of commission. The inspector knew about the crash. He wrote down the rest with professional detachment. He said he would coordinate his investigation with the one that would be conducted by the civil aviation department. He asked me to remain in Singapore until further notification. I told him I would.

It was after three in the morning by the time Terry and I taxied back to the Raffles Hotel. To keep the media off her track as long as possible, I checked her in under my name to a room on the fourth floor, one floor below mine. The night manager was helpful and discreet. Once the porter was gone, we sat down on the edge of the bed, in the soft light of a single lamp, and she began to talk matter-of-factly about the arrangements she would have to make.

"There won't be a service," she said. "Graham would have hated that. I'll bury him here. . . ."

I took her hand. It felt clammy and cold.

"He really didn't have any ties in Australia," she said. "He seldom came back after the war; never once after our mother died. I have good friends in Sydney and go back for a visit whenever I can; but Gray never did. I'll bury him here, without any fuss. He'd have approved of that. I'll have to call the solicitor again in the morning. We'll have to sell the corporation. I wouldn't want to have to run it alone. . . ."

I put my arm around her.

"Terry," I started to say, but she interrupted me.

"No," she said, "you don't understand. There's so much to be done. . . ."

I reached over and switched off the bedside lamp, then pulled her closer to me, bringing her head slowly onto my shoulder, keeping my hand gently in place against her hair. We sat like that for almost an hour, gazing into the darkness. Finally it burst, everything she had been holding back.

"Oh, Graham, Graham," she sobbed into her hands. "Oh, Graham. . . ."

When I helped her lie down, she wouldn't let go of my hand. I stretched out on the bedspread next to her and held her through what was left of the night. By pink dawn she had exhausted herself, the last dry hiccoughing sobs coming from a reservoir of grief that had finally run dry.

When she was asleep, I slipped off her shoes and covered her with a light blanket from the closet shelf. I drew the window drapes above the air conditioner. I wrote a note by the bathroom light and left it on the dresser:

Terry,

I'm in 516. If you need me, give me a call. Don't worry about the time.

Love,

Matt

I stood in the darkness of the room for a moment, listening to her breathe.

Then, locking the door quietly behind me, I padded off to my room.

Chapter
EIGHT

Campbell arrived just before ten a.m. I woke to his loud knocking at my door. I had been dreaming something harsh and lonely, something that slipped away as I woke.

My body felt drained with fatigue. My arm was sore where I had fallen on it, head throbbing, muscles performing their functions under protest.

I pulled on a pair of slacks, checked through the peephole in the door, then let my father-in-law into the room. He strode past me without a greeting, his travel bag in one hand, a copy of the *Straits Times* in the other.

"Can you tell me what in hell happened here?" he snapped, slamming the paper down on the dresser. The news of Graham's murder had made the front page. There was a companion piece about the crash of the Sabreliner, accompanied by a file photo of Terry from her days as Miss Cosmos/World.

I scanned the story, then told Campbell what I knew, beginning with Graham's phone call to me at the farm, ending with my having tucked Terry into bed on the floor below just over four hours ago.

Campbell prowled the room while he listened. He has an uncanny resemblance to the picture of Abraham Lincoln on a five-dollar bill, except he is clean-shaven and has fuller, more closely cropped hair. His eyes are an intense blue. He is tall and long-boned, athletic, and—like Chief Inspector Kim—looks younger than his years. He was wearing an English terylene light wool vested suit, with a gold pocket watch and chain; wingtip shoes with a high gloss. He was not as well tanned as I was used to seeing him. There were dark circles under his eyes, and a gaunt, irascible aura about him, as though he had suffered some recent reversal, or was simply not feeling well. Campbell is a man I care about: part of my family, and a valued friend. Seeing him this way worried me. I was about to say so when there was another knock on the door. This time it was Terry.

She came in wearing a white jumpsuit, open at the throat, couple of big loop earrings, stack of bracelets on her wrist, leather bag draped from one shoulder—looking as if she had made a conscious decision not to play the role of sister in mourning. When she gave me a brief kiss on the cheek, I caught the scent of a fine perfume.

Terry and Campbell had never met. As I introduced them, they sized each other up. Campbell was formally courteous in that Boston Brahmin way of his, but I sensed he liked Terry from the start. She was cool toward him—so much so I felt uneasy when I excused myself after a couple of minutes and went into the bathroom to shower and shave. When I came out, she was just concluding her own unemotional account to Campbell of what had happened the day before.

"Does this business about 'the spur' mean anything to you?" she asked him. Her tone implied she assumed it would. Campbell shook his head.

"No," he said, "It doesn't."

"You were calling Graham a lot from Bangkok. . . ."

"That was about another matter."

"I think I have a right to know what that matter was," she said.

"I'm sorry," Campbell said. "It was confidential. I think it would be better to keep it that way."

"No, Mr. Cooke," Terry said firmly, "that won't do. I have a right to know. Graham was all the family I had. If the two of you were involved in something that got him killed, I want to

know what it was. I haven't mentioned those calls to the police; I
wanted to hear from you first what they were about. I know
you're with the CIA. . . ."

"All right, all right," Campbell said. "And please, for God's
sake don't call me Mr. Cooke. It makes me feel even older than
I am. I'll need some breakfast first; then we'll have to find a
place where it's safe to talk. *Dammit*," he said, picking up the
paper again, slamming it down. "Your brother was a good man.
He was a goddam good man, and I'll tell you something: If I had
the son of a bitch in front of me who was responsible for this, I'd
do a lot more to him than rip off his ear."

After breakfast, we taxied across town to the Tiger Balm
Gardens. Terry had put on a floppy-brimmed hat and designer
sunglasses with enormous frames. The gardens were located on
the side of a hill overlooking the sea. They displayed scenes
from Chinese mythology. There were grottoes and caves; giant
sculptures; small, garishly painted figurines depicting scenes of
what the artists thought life must be like in hell.

Campbell led us along the hard-surfaced paths until he found
an unoccupied bench apart from the nattering press of tourists.
Not far from where we sat, we could see a display featuring a
number of blood-soaked figurines being run over by a spiked
wheel.

"Nice place," I said. It annoyed me that Campbell had chosen it. To have done so seemed insensitive in light of Graham's
murder; and it was not like Campbell to be that way.

"Parents bring their children here," he said abruptly. "They
find a display such as that one with the wheel and say, 'This is
what will happen to you, short fry, if you don't behave yourself.' We should be able to talk freely here. I've gotten so I don't
trust hotel rooms. Or taxi cabs." Terry sat between us on the
bench, sunglasses perched on the tip of her nose, eyes still
slightly puffy from the crying she had done the night before.
Campbell looked at her, his expression softening as he did. "I'm
sorry," he said. "It was stupid of me to bring you here, wasn't
it. I never gave it a thought. I'm afraid I've gotten so accus-
tomed to violence . . ."

"You don't have to apologize," Terry said. "I'm not a frail
person."

"Good," Campbell said. "I've always been impatient with
people who were. Did Graham ever talk with you about the
Americans who were missing in action after the Vietnam War?"

"No. Graham hardly ever talked about the war at all. He would avoid the subject whenever he could."

"He was intensely interested in the problem of the MIAs," Campbell said. "He never believed all the prisoners of war held by the communist forces were returned."

"Most of us who were there don't believe that," I explained to Terry. "We know guys who got shot down and were still alive when they reached the ground. Some of them made contact using their survival radios—then were never heard of again."

"Isn't it likely they were killed by the enemy once they were on the ground?" Terry said.

"No," Campbell replied. "To the Asians, a prisoner of war is a chattel: something to be valued, held on to, bartered away when the time and price are right. There were no amputees or stretcher-borne among the men who were finally released. The odds for that occurring naturally are astronomical. It makes much more sense to assume the severely wounded were held back for political reasons—so there would be no possible implication that their condition had been caused by their captors. Since the release of the POWs by the NVA, hundreds of refugees have reported live sightings of Americans still being held in camps in Laos and Vietnam. Nobody knows how many. Over twenty-five hundred men were listed as missing in action. Their bodies have never been returned; they've never been accounted for. French soldiers kept turning up for years after the fall of Dienbienphu. It's all part of a familiar pattern."

"Then why doesn't your government do something about it?" Terry asked.

I shifted my weight on the bench.

"That's politics too," I said. "Once the released POWs were back, the tendency was to breathe a big sigh of relief and say, well, that puts an end to it. To push the POW question any further was going to get embarrassing for the USG. We never declared war in Laos, for example, so how were we going to explain what our pilots were doing getting shot down on bombing runs there? We signed a peace treaty with the North Vietnamese; they said all our POWs were out. The executive branch pretty much decided to settle for that. The work that's been done since has been done by a few dedicated people at enormous professional risk: Tuttle and Tighe over at Defense Intelligence; Campbell at CIA; a handful of others."

The cut on my forehead was stinging from sweat. A breeze showed in the rain trees and junipers along Pasir Panjang road, but all I could feel in this Year of the Horse was the probing heat of the sun. Warm-looking tourists shuffled along the garden paths not far from where we sat, a steady parade of slacks and blouses and short-sleeved shirts. Campbell had taken off his suit coat. He usually carried a small side arm these days. If he was carrying it now, I couldn't see it.

He went on to tell Terry about the National League of Families, the organization of parents and wives whose sons and husbands had been declared missing in action and who had never been accounted for.

"It must be nightmarish," Terry said. "To know there's a chance, even the slightest chance, that someone you love might be alive and held by an enemy against his will—to never be certain one way or the other."

"Your brother knew something of what it was like," Campbell said. "He had a close friend who was declared missing in action in Cambodia. He vowed never to stop searching, never to lose hope, until someone showed him his friend's bones in a body sack. Matt knows who it is I'm talking about."

"Yes," I said.

As he looked at me, the muscles along my father-in-law's jaw tightened with intensity. When he spoke, his voice was emotional.

"We know where Toby is," he said. "We know exactly where he is, and we think we can get him out."

Chapter
NINE

His full name was Tobias Godwin Porter III. He was born and raised in Asheville, North Carolina, the son of well-to-do parents, with a maternal bloodline that traced to Thomas Jefferson. His father was heir of a media dynasty that included important newspapers in a half-dozen southern cities and a politically powerful television station in the nation's capital.

A tall, slightly built, scholarly-looking man, Toby had an IQ in the high 160s, and the capacity of total recall. He did his undergraduate work at Princeton, where he knocked down a degree in economics in less than three years. After that it was graduate school at Harvard (international relations—master's degree), and Yale Law.

His father wanted him to represent the family interests. Toby, bored with that prospect, chose to go to work for the CIA instead. As he once put it to me, in his quiet drawl, "I wanted to add a bit of excitement to what, in truth, had been up to that point a rather dull life."

He became a Master of Karate, and held a Fifth Dan in judo. He explained he had finally gotten tired of being nonphysical. He never started a fight, but was delighted whenever the other guy would. He said he loved mixing it up, even if he finally lost. I don't think he lost very often. Bullies in bars tended to underestimate him. "My name is Tobias Porter," he would say, whenever one started to hassle him. "And I believe you're making an error in judgment."

His first duty tour for the Agency was in Saigon, where he was told by his station chief to keep an eye on some Vietnamese university students in the downtown district. The assignment seemed to have little purpose. Toby put up with it for about a week, then went back to the station chief and said, "Look here, I'm rather well-to-do, you know, and if you can't give me something more interesting than this, I'm going to go back to North Carolina."

From then on he was in the thick of things: Hue; Projects Delta and Omega; and finally undercover as a State Department officer in our embassy at Phnom Penh, Cambodia. It was there I first met him. We hit it off from the start: Toby, Graham Melbourne, Sir John Moore from the British embassy—all chumming around together, trying to win the unwinnable war, with the help of some outstanding Khmers.

My wife and son, Diana and Brian, had both adored Toby. That day in Phnom Penh when the bomb had exploded in my yard, Toby had been first on the scene after me. He had called in the ambulance, cleared the area, performed vital first aid for Brian, had sat up with me every night for over a week, pulling me through the worst of it, assuring me over and over that in the final analysis it was the quality of a person's life that mattered, and that the quality of Diana's life had been high.

Toby's job out of Phnom Penh had been to infiltrate enemy territory and recruit indigenous personnel to obtain vital military intelligence. He disappeared on an aerial reconnaissance mission with an Air America pilot in the Stoeng Trang region of north-

THE CHINESE SPUR 45

eastern Cambodia in the late fall of 1974. Officially listed as missing in action, he, like so many others, had never been accounted for in what was yet another undeclared war.

Sitting between Campbell and me on our bench in the Tiger Balm Gardens, Terry listened as we filled her in on Toby's background. I was on full charge now, eager to hear more detail from Campbell as to how he and Graham had finally managed to locate this brilliant colleague of ours who had been missing for so long.

"It began with some refugee reports from the Ban Vinai camp on the Thai border, west of Vientiane," Campbell said. "Several of them referred to a solitary Caucasian prisoner being held in the Quebec Bravo area of Laos. One man especially described Toby very well. He was a Hmong tribal chieftain who had served with the American Special Forces. He was captured by a group of dissident Pathet Lao who had been staging raids against villages along the Nam Yang River. Hoping eventually to barter him for weapons, they took him to a remote camp northwest of Vientiane. He managed to escape. Before doing so, he bumped shoulders there with a lone Caucasian. The Caucasian was kept in a separate hut, but was allowed to exercise in the compound. He was always accompanied by several guards. According to what the Hmong told our debriefers, the Caucasian kept repeating the word 'Toh-bas, Toh-bas.' The physical description he gave of Toby was close and accurate in all details."

"Was he able to pinpoint the location of the camp?"

"Yes. We showed him topographical sheets of the area, scaled to six-digit coordinates. He says the terrain is unmistakable. He put his finger right on the spot. Graham had been sneaking some flights over Laos out of Thailand. He started doing this after the first refugee reports indicated one of our MIAs might be in that region. His account of the general area tracked with what the Hmong was telling us. We were skeptical at first, of course; we naturally assumed if Toby was alive he'd turn up somewhere in Cambodia."

"Did your people run this Hmong tribesman through a lie-detector test? Put him on the box?"

"Yes. His name's Sisani. As a tribal chief, he's well respected by his people. He passed the test easily. He's volunteered to be part of the team we'll send in to bring Toby out."

"Have you got sanction?"

"No. The President won't touch it. The State Department is in the middle of some delicate negotiations with China. If anything should go wrong, the incident could be blown into an international crisis: U.S. military presence returns to Far East. You can write the rest. Our operation will be strictly private. I'm officially on leave. We'll have the backing of some powerful people in Thailand.''

"I want in," I said.

He smiled. It was a weary but genuine smile.

"I was sure you'd feel that way," he said. "We've been using the old-boy net at Langley. I'm glad you agreed to come to Singapore to visit Graham and Terry. The security on this was so tight, I couldn't risk calling you directly. We ran into some last-minute trouble with our Thai backer. He wanted the refugee reports backed up with an Argus satellite scan. I had to pull in a lot of markers at the Agency before I could get authorization.''

"That must have been what Gray was worried about," Terry said. She had been listening carefully to every word Campbell had spoken.

"It was," he replied. "If our Thai backer had withdrawn, we would have had to scrub the mission. He's putting up most of the money and providing key equipment and personnel.''

"What did you get when you ran the satellite scan?" I asked.

"A sharp, discernible shadow of a human figure taller than most Asians, right smack in the center of the Quebec Bravo camp.''

"That did it for your Thai?"

"Yes. The mission is on. That's what I came to Singapore to tell you and Graham.''

I shook a cigarette out of my pack and lit it up. The smoke drifted away on a light tropical breeze. The day continued clear and warm. Behind me, I could hear the buzz and click of cameras as the tourists filed by miniature renderings of a Chinese hell.

"What was Graham flying when he was poking around over Laos?" I asked.

"That Sabreliner you ditched in the Strait yesterday," Campbell replied. "Before he sold it, he'd been using it as his personal plane.''

"Then there is a connection," Terry said. "There has to be. The only thing those men took, after they killed Graham, was his flight log for the current year. There's no question it's missing. The police didn't find it in his car. I called the office this morning. His secretary assured me it wasn't there. That log would have a record of Gray's flights over Laos. Matt said the dagger the Chinaman threw had been made in Vientiane. Now you say Gray's friend Toby is being held prisoner in a camp north of that same city. Don't you see how it's all of a piece? When Gray flew over the camp, the men on the ground must have taken down the markings of the plane. They traced it back to Singapore, found out who the owner was, and decided to get rid of him before he could arrange any action against their camp. They wired an explosive device into the speed-brake well. As soon as they heard on the news that the plane had gone down, they went straight off to the apartment and began looking for the log. By making off with it, they'd remove any evidence of the flights Gray had been making. Then when he suddenly walked in on them . . .''

She had been talking rapidly in a strong voice, but now her voice broke. I put my hand on her shoulder.

"It's okay," I said.

"He flew where he shouldn't have," she said. "And they made him pay for it."

Campbell stood up. He looked haggard in the bright light of the sun.

"According to the refugee reports, we're talking about a small renegade camp," he said, "in the middle of a jungle, in a remote, undeveloped part of the country. We're talking about a small, primitive band of dissident Pathet Lao—not Chinese—who through some fluke have latched on to an important American prisoner of war. If the refugee reports are accurate—and we're ninety-nine point nine percent certain they are—the only person in the Quebec Bravo area intelligent enough to carry out a sophisticated act of sabotage is Toby Porter himself; and unless he's completely lost his grip during the last four years that's not bloody likely."

"Then you tell me what *is* likely," Terry said. "Somebody went to a hell of a lot of trouble to kill my brother and steal that log. If it doesn't have to do with this Toby of yours, what does it have to do with?"

"I wish I knew," Campbell said. "We've waited a long time for a chance to bring an American prisoner out of Laos. I suppose it's possible one of their Chinese military advisers got wind of what we were up to and decided to squash it. But killing Graham really wouldn't do that; and even if it would, why go to the trouble of making it look like an accident? Why not simply kill the man and be done with it?"

I could feel the tension in Terry as she listened to what

Campbell was saying. I wanted to take her away somewhere to a private place where I could hold her in my arms for a couple of weeks and help her cry some more; I sensed she needed to do that, that the reservoir was filling again and she was holding too much back.

But I knew, for a while at least, there wasn't going to be time for private places. I asked Campbell when the mission was scheduled to launch.

"Three days from now," he said. "We'll leave for Thailand tomorrow night. I'll take care of your reservation. Meanwhile, I'll need a room at the Raffles. I imagine you two will be busy with the authorities for the rest of today." He looked at Terry. "Needless to say," he continued, "everything we've talked about here is strictly confidential. No leaks, not a word."

"I'm going to Thailand with you," she said.

Before Campbell could reply, I told Terry I didn't think that was a good idea. I said if someone was out to sabotage the mission Campbell and Graham had organized to bring Toby out of Laos, things in Thailand could get nasty. I said Inspector Kim could give her around-the-clock protection here in Singapore. I said as soon as the mission was over, and assuming she wanted me to, I'd be back. She listened impatiently, sunlight glinting from the bracelets on her wrist. When I was through, she looked up at Campbell.

"I'm going to Thailand with you," she said.

Chapter
TEN

As we made our way to the taxi stand, we were stopped by a middle-aged Chinese man in a dark-blue tropical suit. He said his name was Lim Chee Wong, that he was a police detective working out of Inspector Kim's office on the Melbourne case. He said a body had turned up in Chinatown that matched the description I had given the inspector of the man who had thrown the dagger at me. He said several pages from what looked to be Graham Melbourne's flight log had been found at the scene. It was the inspector's wish, he said, that Terry and I accompany him and his partner to the Chinatown site. We had, of course, been under surveillance; it had been a simple matter for Detective Lim to find us. His partner, a young man in a similar suit, waited at the curb behind the wheel of an unmarked black Mercedes. The Mercedes had a radar scanning device on the dashboard and a trunk-mounted antenna. The license plate looked official.

As Terry started to move toward the car, I caught her arm.

"Before we go anywhere," I said to Lim, "we'll need to see your identification."

"Certainly," Lim said.

He removed a three-fold wallet from the left pocket of his suitcoat and showed me his badge and ID. He wore a shoulder holster on that side with what looked to be a .38 caliber short-barrel revolver. The badge and ID seemed okay.

"Have him get headquarters on his car radio," Campbell said. "Check him out there."

Detective Lim looked annoyed.

"There's no need for that," he said.

"I'm a personal friend of your prime minister's," Campbell said. "I have his private telephone number in the pocket of my vest. We're scheduled to have supper together this evening. We can either check you through your headquarters, or through him. I'm sure you know he can be very short on patience about a thing like this."

Lim grudgingly put the call through to his headquarters, then handed me the mobile mike. I asked the dispatcher to put me through to Inspector Kim. The dispatcher said the inspector had already left for Chinatown, that he would meet us there. Yes, the dispatcher said, Lim Chee Wong was one of the detectives working on the case.

"Somebody should replace the RF coil in your radio," I told Lim when I keyed off the mike. "You're getting all kinds of background clutter. Your dispatcher sounds like he's transmitting from a boiler factory." Lim did not reply. I looked at Campbell.

"Coming with us?" I asked.

He thought for a moment.

"No," he said finally. "I don't think so. I've got things to do back at the hotel."

"Can you meet us for a drink before you hook up with the PM for supper?"

"Yes," he said. "That sounds good. Let's make it the Long

Bar at the Raffles at six." He looked at Terry. "I think you're right about the situation we discussed," he said. "It will be nice to have you along."

She smiled. When Terry smiles, it's like one of the rarer gifts from heaven. Campbell received this gift with a courtly nod, and a very nice smile of his own. If I hadn't known him better, I would have guessed in that moment he had fallen for Terry. I knew from my own experience it was an easy thing to do.

Campbell hired a taxi, said a few words to the driver, and was whisked away. Terry and I climbed into the back seat of the Mercedes. Lim sat in the front seat, next to his partner. We took the coastal roads, heading east. Terry and I held hands. By the time we passed under the cable cars that ran from Mount Faber to Sentosa Island, she was snoozing, with her head resting on my shoulder.

We turned north off Keppel into South Bridge Road, drove into Chinatown, parked at the curb in front of a funeral shop on Sago Lane. Chinatown was all that was left of the old city: venerable two-story attached wood-and-tile houses with shops on the ground floor, rusting downspouts, tangles of frayed wires strung with bare bulbs, pitted walls, ceramic pots hanging from upper-floor windows, men in sleeveless undershirts and trance-like poses leaning on sills, No. 10 cans serving as window boxes with sprigs of green willow.

Remarkably clean streets crowded with trishaws, motorbikes, automobiles, pedestrians.

And noise. A belting, blasting cacophony of amped-up Western disco and rock blaring through triple-horn speakers in front of the black-market shops that did a thriving business in pirated tapes; car horns, gongs, bells; the continuous polyglot chatter of the crowd.

Detective Lim led the way into the funeral shop. We passed a group of workers who were building a replica Rolls-Royce out of a tissue-thin bright-red paper on a light bamboo frame. Once finished, the Rolls would be carried off to a Chinese funeral, where it would be burned with a number of other replicated luxury items. This would guarantee the departed a plush life in heaven. The idea had always seemed wacky to me, but no wackier, I guess, than some of my own.

We went through the funeral shop into a large back room. The room was poorly illuminated by thick red candles that dripped hot wax onto small porcelain plates. There were two

wicker chairs in the center of the room and a bench along the left
wall. The bench was cluttered with what looked to be artist's
paraphernalia: jars and pots and brushes. There was a two-way
radio with a police scanner and FM stereo receiver at one end.
The radio was playing a baroque concerto I didn't recognize,
with a lot of brass, at low volume. I could smell candle wax, and
the more pungent smell of a joss stick burning. At first I thought
there were only four of us in the room. Then I saw the body.

It lay on its back on the floor at the foot of the bench. It was
unclothed, hands folded over chest, dark eyes fixed and open.
Thin bamboo skewers had been run through the genitals and
mouth. Two-thirds of the right ear was missing. The wound was
a black mass of clotted blood.

As Terry gasped and backed away, Lim's young partner reached
up and took her by the hair. He jerked down hard, bringing her to
her knees with one hand, shoving a pistol against her throat with
the other.

"Matt!" she screamed.

I stood in stop time, the muzzle of Lim's revolver pressing the
base of my neck.

"You sit down," he said. *"Take one of the chairs."*

I sat down slowly where he told me to. His partner dragged
and wrenched Terry to the other chair. We were only a few feet
apart. The bench and body were to our left. Candlelight flickered
along the walls. A door opened at the far end of the room—
maybe fifteen feet away—then closed. I heard voices in the
shadows there, turned to look. Two figures had entered, one
larger than the other. The large figure was hooded and draped in
something that looked like a shroud. The smaller figure was the
Chinese who had thrown the dagger at me.

After the Chinese had finished his conversation with the hooded
figure, he came forward and stood just in front of Terry and me.
He had Graham Melbourne's flight log, opened to a particular
page. It and two other pages had been tagged with paper clips.
The hooded figure sat on a low stool near the door by which he
had entered the room. My eyes were still adjusting from the
sunlight on the street. Aside from the fact his posture was erect,
there was little I could make out about him. I looked at the
Chinese.

"You and I have a score to settle," I said. The man we knew
as Detective Lim probed the back of my neck with his gun,
reminding me he was there. Whoever he was, he was no cop.

The radio continued to play its baroque concerto. My Chinese friend ignored what I said and looked at Terry.

"Please read for us aloud all of what is written on the three marked pages," he said. His English was good. He held the book toward her. She took it from him, clutching it tightly, as if in a way he had handed Graham back.

"Bastard," she said. *"You killed my brother."*

"Please begin on the first of the three pages," he said. "Read every word."

She told him to fuck off. She said she didn't know the key to Graham's code, and wouldn't reveal it if she did: not to his murderers; not if her life depended on it. At this point, the hooded figure spoke a single sentence from his place on the stool. His voice was crisp and sharp. He spoke Chinese.

The man who had thrown the dagger at me nodded, and said something to Lim. Then he folded his hands in front of him and stood with his feet spread, eyes closed, mouth slightly ajar. He had changed clothes since yesterday, wore a blue denim shirt and pair of faded jeans. Gradually, the rhythm of his breathing began to deepen and slow.

Lim went to the bench and came back with a bamboo skewer. The skewer was over four feet long, sharp at both ends.

"This man is a spirit medium," he said. "He belongs to an ancient cult. He is in a trance now, and cannot feel pain."

To prove this was true, Lim slowly pushed the skewering rod through the man's cheeks, daubing away the blood with a small tissue as he did. When the rod was centered through the man's mouth, extending two feet through his face on either side, Lim stepped back. The man had not so much as winced.

"Except for the power of the trance, the pain would be excruciating," Lim said. He looked at Terry. "I urge you to cooperate with us," he said. "We only require that you translate the three marked pages of your brother's log. It may be what is written there is harmless. If this is so, and if we are convinced you have translated truthfully, we will let you go."

Blood was oozing from each corner of the medium's mouth, staining the rod. He continued to stand with his hands folded and eyes closed. I could see Terry trying to swallow back the rising horror she felt at the sight of him and of the mutilated body on the floor by the bench.

Lim reached down and touched her cheek with his hand.

"You are thought to be very beautiful," he said.

She recoiled from his touch, clasping Graham's flight log even more tightly to her chest.

"You will please begin to translate now," Lim said.

"Like hell," she said.

"You are a foolish woman. We were told to make an example of the man you see lying on the floor. He had been given a job to do, and he did not do it well. I advise you to look at him again. He did not have the power of the trance. When the first rod was inserted . . ."

Terry began to struggle. Lim's partner tightened his grip on her hair. I started to go for him. As I did, he thumbed the hammer back on his pistol, shoved the muzzle up hard against Terry's throat.

"Don't," I said.

He jerked his head toward my chair. Lim yanked me back onto it. The hooded figure had come forward. He was completely shrouded in the ritual sackcloth of a Chinese mourner. Through its rough weave, I could see the vague outline of his oriental features: thick face, pouchy around the eyes; salt-and-pepper hair, receding at the temples and closely cropped. He spoke curtly to Lim. Lim went to the spirit medium and slowly pulled the skewering rod through the man's cheeks. He cleaned it with tissue, and propped it against the wall. When the medium came out of his trance, he smiled. The scar tissue was thick at the corners of his mouth.

Lim's partner kept the pistol cocked at Terry's throat. Lim got some cord from the bench and tied my hands behind my back. There was nothing I could do. I tried to keep my wrists flexed as he secured the cord. The hooded figure looked on, his own hands clasped behind his back. He was the man in charge. If there was anyone to reach, it was going to have to be him.

"You're military," I said. "You've been in for a long while. It shows in the way you walk, sit, talk; you can't hide that under a few yards of sackcloth. Terry doesn't have the key to the code you want. Neither do I. The only person who did was Graham Melbourne, and your troops here killed him. If you torture either of us, all you're going to get is some noise, and that could be risky for you. There are people working in that funeral shop—"

"They are our people," he said.

I was so startled to hear him speak, I couldn't think of a quick reply. He nodded at the spirit medium, and the two of them left by the same rear door they had entered.

One of the candles guttered out as the door closed. Lim took

the time to replace it with another. While he did, he asked me to
help persuade Terry to cooperate. He said I was being kept alive
only for that purpose. He promised me a quick death if I helped
him get what he wanted; a slow one otherwise. Terry told him
again she did not have the key to her brother's code. The room
was warm. Lim took off his suit coat and hung it on a nail near
the bench. He had to step around the body of the man who had
been mutilated. After he hung up his coat, he turned up the
volume of the music on the radio. Then he picked up the
skewering rod from the place where he had rested it against the
wall and started to walk toward Terry.

He had a round, bland face, with too much chin over the knot
of his tie. To reach Terry, he was going to have to walk past me.
The torture routine was about to begin. He had wasted no time
running the rod through the face of the spirit medium. He would
probably start that way with Terry. Face first. Then the rest.
They wouldn't kill her. I was sure of that. Not until they were
convinced she really couldn't unlock the secret of the three key
pages in her brother's log. As for me, I believed Lim when he
said I was a dead man in any case.

I waited until he was almost in front of me, hesitated a
fraction of a second, then committed myself, lashing out hard
with my right foot. I angled the kick so the inside of my shoe
caught him just below the knee on the right side. He cried out
and staggered back, dropping the skewering rod, clutching his
leg. As he did, I rolled out of the chair, hitting him shin high
with my torso, sending him toppling backward to the floor. I
could hear his partner shouting to him in a frantic, high-pitched
voice; Terry shouting at me; words lost in the radio blare.

While Lim tried to get his revolver out of its holster, I got all
the leverage I could with my legs and rammed my skull up under
the point of his chin. I heard a sound like a pencil breaking, then
felt him go slack as a bag of rags.

I squirmed and kicked, backing into a position where I could
grab his gun, lying on my left side, snatching desperately behind
me with my bound right hand. Terry was grappling with the
other guy. He tried to club her away, but she stayed in his face
with her fists and elbows and nails.

When I finally got the gun in my hand, I rolled onto my knees
and struggled up. I knew I couldn't do much with it, knew I was
going to have to get close enough to pass it to Terry. Before I
took my first step toward her, the hooded figure reappeared at
the door.

He stood motionless, a short gun of his own poking through the sackcloth shroud, at his right side. The gun was fitted with a silencer. I didn't recognize him at first; then I did.

The light wool sleeve of his terylene suit gave him away, the fact he was taller than the man who had been here before, the familiar high gloss of his wingtip shoes.

It took the young Chinese two fatal seconds to realize he had been tricked.

Then, as the recognition dawned and he swung his pistol that way, Campbell shot him through the heart.

Chapter
ELEVEN

Terry ran to untie me. As she did, I told Campbell there were more bad guys in the front of the funeral shop. He went to that door and listened through one of its wood panels. He had already taken off the hood and shroud. No explanation as to how he had come by them. I was too relieved by his presence to ask.

"The police just arrived," he said.

Still standing by the door, he unscrewed the silencer from the muzzle of his pistol. He put the silencer into the breast pocket of his suit, where it joined a row of pens. The pistol was flat and small, about five inches overall length, .45 caliber. He slipped it into a clip holster at the back of his belt. Then he walked to the bench and turned the radio down.

"I'm licensed here to carry the gun," he said. "There might be a fuss over the silencer."

"I want to get out of this place," Terry said. Her voice was insistent. When I reached for her hand, she pulled it away.

"The police will be with us in a minute," Campbell said. "Is that Graham's log?"

She had picked it up and was holding it close to her as she had before.

"Yes," she said.

"Good," he said. There were three bodies in the room, but

they didn't seem to interest Campbell. He was looking with distaste at the burlap fibers that clung to his suit. "Maybe now," he said, "we'll learn what the mystery's all about."

Chief Inspector Kim Tan had checked Campbell's bona fides with the prime minister while Kim and his men were en route to the funeral shop. He greeted my father-in-law politely, apologizing for the time it had taken him to arrive. Apparently it had not taken long.

"The inspector runs a professional operation," Campbell explained to Terry and me. "His people are intelligent and courteous. Lim Chee Wong didn't fit the profile. Neither did the business about the police radio not working properly. I wasn't sure Lim was a phony, but I was uneasy enough to have my driver follow you when you left the Gardens."

Campbell went on to say he had followed us to Chinatown, where he had watched us go into the funeral shop. He said as soon as we were in, a man in laborer's clothes had come out of the shop and driven the Mercedes away. This had convinced Campbell something was wrong. There had been no other police presence in sight.

He found a pay telephone and called Inspector Kim. The inspector said he had never heard of Lim Chee Wong. He said he and his men would get to Chinatown as quickly as possible.

Campbell had suspected the funeral shop might be a blind. He began poking around the back alley, hoping to find a rear entrance. He said the alley was off the tourist track and he had felt very conspicuous there, walking along with a notebook and pen in hand, ready to identify himself—should anyone ask—as the prime minister's special consultant on urban renewal affairs.

Nobody asked.

He saw two men come out of the rear entrance to the funeral parlor, into a small courtyard off the alley. One of the men was draped in a mourner's shroud, which he proceeded to take off and hang on a low piece of latticework next to the door. The other man matched the description I had given of the Chinese who had thrown the dagger at me.

There had been a van waiting in the alley. Its plates had been made illegible. The two men got in the rear, and the van drove away. As soon as it was out of sight, Campbell had put on the shroud and taken his chances going through the door.

"Can you give us a description of the man whose shroud it was?" the inspector asked.

"I think I can do better than that," Campbell said. "I think I can tell you who he is. Let me check my sources first to be sure. We don't need a red herring on this."

He said in light of what had happened here we would be leaving for Thailand that night.

"The commercial airports will be watched," he said. "I'll line something up at Changi through the prime minister. Meanwhile, we'll need a safe house with a secure phone. Bill Leazar's chief of station here. His place should do."

"I'll order a car and driver," Kim said. "You'll have to leave through the back. The press will be here any minute."

"Matt and I have some things at the hotel," Terry said. She was standing a little away from me, eyes averted from the carnage in the room. Kim said he would arrange to have our things picked up. He said he would turn copies of Graham's flight log over to Australian Intelligence, that it was likely they would be able to break the code as quickly as anyone. Campbell agreed.

Within minutes, a drab unmarked Toyota sedan arrived outside the courtyard behind the shop. We rattled away, unobserved, a police driver in plain clothes at the wheel. Terry sat in the front passenger seat. Campbell and I rode, knees high, in the back.

Leazar's house was located in Highland Court, a small cul-de-sac near Singapore's cultural center. Leazar was away on business in Jakarta. Campbell had a key. He holed up in Leazar's library, working two phones at once through most of the rest of that day. Whenever there was a line free, Terry would use it to settle her own affairs in the city. She broke down once, sobs coming like a summer storm. I held her until it was over. Then she went back to her work. I made some sandwiches for all of us, uncorked some of Leazar's Tiger beer, tried to be useful when I could and stay out of the way the rest of the time. Finally, I fell asleep in one of the the back bedrooms. I hadn't been asleep very long when Campbell woke up me and asked if I knew how to fly a C-130. I told him no. He looked disappointed and went away. Later, he woke me again.

"How about the U-10?" he said. "You can handle one of those, can't you?"

"Yes," I said.

"Piper Chieftain?"

"Should be okay," I said.

"Any preference?"

"The Piper is a twin," I said. "It's got more space and a faster cruise speed. Terry can help me get it off the ground."

"Good," he said. "They'll have one waiting for us. It was confiscated two months ago by Kim's people. It belonged to a narcotics dealer. High-level type."

"Swell," I said.

He smiled, delighted to be doing one of the things he did best: greasing the skids, making things work.

"Go back to sleep," he said. "I'll wake you up when we're ready to leave."

We left Leazar's house without incident at 0100 hours, driving east on Tampines Road toward Singapore's military airport at Changi. The night was hot and muggy; Kim's man drove with the windows up and the air conditioner on. Terry sat next to him, gazing into the lights of the oncoming traffic. From my place on the back seat, I could see her profile in flare and shadow, strikingly beautiful, but etched sharply now with a sense of her loss. She had left instructions that her brother's remains were to be cremated, the ashes scattered on an outgoing tide.

"Gray never had any use for cemeteries," she told me. "For ceremony, or monuments, or any of it. I think he would have approved of this. I hope he would."

I told her I thought she had done the right thing. Campbell and I had arranged to have Diana buried in Arlington National. We thought that had been the right thing too. Maybe it had for Campbell, but I had long since stopped visiting the site. The marker only reminded me, in a way that was painful, of the irrevocability of her death. She lived in a private part of my memory; she always would. In that special sense, no one would ever take her place.

The prime minister had alerted his air force, clearing our arrival at Changi. As we approached the west gate, I could see two armored vehicles and a squad of military police in position flanking the red-and-white barrier pole. Floodlights over the military police guard shack were sweeping the road and shoulder abutments. Kim's driver gave a short burst on the concealed siren in the Toyota, the barrier pole shot up, and—joined by a motorcycle escort—we sped onto the base.

The Piper Chieftain Campbell had arranged for us to use was parked on the transient ramp. It was long and sleek, propeller-driven, with tricycle landing gear. The large windows and stubby wingtips gave it away as Piper-built. It looked as if it might hold eight or ten people. All its markings had been painted over with the same shade of red used for the swirling roundel of the Singapore Air Force. The Chieftain's engines were running. It was guarded by military police.

Kim's driver braked sharply next to the officer in charge. They conducted a rapid-fire exchange in Chinese. When they were through, we said our goodbyes and entered the plane's cabin through a small door on the left side. The ship was rigged with the executive-group configuration: six reclining seats, two folding tables, small galley, and private head. Our luggage was on board. Campbell selected a seat and strapped himself in. Terry and I went to the cockpit to get a quick briefing from the young SAF flight lieutenant who sat at the controls.

He had already serviced the aircraft, preflighted, and run the engine checks. He gave Terry the route cards and maps, apologized to me for not having the proper pilot's handbook, asked if I'd ever flown a twin Piper. I said no, but I did have time in twin-prop C-47s and a variety of light single-engine planes. We agreed that experience should serve pretty well.

In a matter of seconds, the flight lieutenant showed me the things you need to know when you are about to fly a particular plane you've never flown before: engine start and shutdown procedures, fuel-tank switching, location and operation of the gear and flap levers, where the trim and autopilot controls were. It was the fastest aircraft checkout I'd ever had. He showed me the parking-brake release lever, gave me the takeoff and landing speeds, and was out of the cabin and on the ramp before I could say thanks.

I released the brakes and taxied toward the runways. It was just after two in the morning. Our tower frequency was dialed in. Terry sat next to me, microphone in hand.

"What call sign do you want to use?" she asked.

"Papa Wolf," I said.

"Changi Tower," she transmitted, "this is Papa Wolf. . . ."

She got clearance on and off the active runway, the altimeter setting, surface winds, transponder code, and a frequency to contact Departure Control once we were airborne. I turned onto the runway and eased both throttles forward. As the engine noise roared through the airframe, Terry told Changi we were rolling.

Chapter
TWELVE

I held us between the dual ribbon of runway lights, watched the speed build to 100 knots, then brought the control column back just enough to raise the nose wheel. At 110, I felt the light twin lift off smoothly.

"Gear up," I said as soon as we were clear.

Terry found the lever and raised the gear. I reduced prop pitch and manifold pressure to what I guessed was appropriate power, climbing out north from Singapore. For a few minutes, the city lights reflected through an atmospheric haze, giving us the sense of flying through softly illuminated clouds. Then, just north of the Singapore River where Malaysia lies, we traded city lights for jungle dark: the transition sudden and complete. I leveled at 10,500 feet, trimmed the ship, stuck it on autopilot, and began to go through the route cards and maps with Terry. Campbell, in shirtsleeves, came forward to stand hunched behind us while we checked the flight plan he had arranged.

"Destination Khon Kaen?" I said.

"Correct," he said. "That's our mission staging area. It's fifty-five miles south of Udorn. The code name there is Miami Base."

"What's our time in the air?" Terry asked. She looked very tired.

"Just over four and a half hours," I said, checking the route card. "Go on back and get some sleep. I'll take the first leg."

She went aft without complaint. Campbell took her seat. The light in the cockpit was dim, the thrum of the engines smooth and in synch. I found the heater controls. You lose two degrees Celsius or about three and a half Fahrenheit for every thousand feet of altitude you climb. At 10,500, our outside air temperature was fifty degrees Fahrenheit. I adjusted the cockpit to cool, the cabin slightly warmer. Campbell sat moodily, chin in hand.

"My instincts tell me we've slipped the hounds in Singapore," he said. "At least for a while."

"Thanks to your connection with the PM."

"We go back a long way."

"Is he current on our situation?"

"Yes. I had to tell him about Toby. He's completely in favor of the mission."

"Were you able to ID the guy in the shroud?"

"Yes. He's who I thought he was: Major General Hua Hailing, People's Republic of China. Name ring a bell?"

"Vaguely. I think I've heard it before. Nothing specific."

"He's something of a renegade—brilliant and ruthless. He earned his reputation, as a young officer, by putting down the revolt in Tibet in '59, carrying out a policy of mass execution and forced labor against the Tibetan people. According to Defense Intelligence, he's supposed to have fallen out of favor with the current regime for having been too dedicated a Maoist. CIA thinks he's retired now in the province of Liaoning, northeast of Peking. They were surprised to learn he was in Singapore."

"How does this guy fit with Graham and Toby Porter?" I asked.

"I wish I could tell you," Campbell replied. "At this point, I don't have a clue."

"Did you run it by Terry?"

"Yes. She's never heard of Hua; can't make any connection between him and her brother. The prime minister thinks Hua could turn out to be the leader of Singapore's communist underground. He asked me if Graham's overflights of Laos put him anywhere near the Golden Triangle."

"Did they?"

"I said I wasn't sure, but I thought there was a possibility they had. He said if this turned out to be true, Hua might also be tied to the opium trade in that area. He admitted it was only the start of a theory, that there wasn't enough data to advance it very far."

Campbell volunteered no further information regarding the impending mission to free Toby Porter from his jungle prison in Laos. I had a hatful of questions I wanted to ask, but I knew my father-in-law well enough not to ask any of them now. When the time was right, he would lay things out in his crisp, logical way.

The Singapore Air Force had filed a military flight route for us with Malaysian and Thai aviation authorities. It was understood we would maintain radio silence throughout the trip. We were heading northwesterly on a track of 348 degrees and had just swung the beacon at Kuantan. That put us thirty-seven minutes into the flight, with just about four hours to go.

I puttered in the cockpit, rechecking engine RPM and manifold settings. When I was through, Campbell turned our conversation to family matters and my son, Brian.

His history had been extraordinary. At age thirteen, living with me as a military dependent in war-torn Cambodia, he had been critically injured in the same bomb blast that had killed his mother. He had spent eighteen months in a deep coma at Walter Reed Hospital until, with help from the U.S. business tycoon J. Robert Coyle, we were able to transfer him to the Franki Clinic in the Swiss Alps above Bergheim.

There, subject to experimental treatments with lasers and enzyme injections, he had come out of his coma and had begun the long, painful process of cognitive retraining and physical therapy. This program had taken over three years. Last month, on his eighteenth birthday, Brian had been released from the clinic. His prognosis for eventual full recovery was favorable.

I had flown to Switzerland to be on hand for the event. Brian's benefactor J. R. Coyle and Coyle's Parisian consort Dominique Fabray had been there as well. So had Campbell's wife, Midge. Campbell himself had been unable to come.

"I've been feeling a lot of guilt about that," he said. "I was up in the Ban Vinai refugee camp when one of Bob Coyle's people tracked me down to tell me the news about Brian. Sisani, the Hmong tribal chief I told you about, had just then escaped from Laos. He was giving us incredibly detailed information about his live sighting of Toby. I wanted terribly to be on hand when Brian came out of that clinic, but . . ."

Campbell did not continue. It was clear he thought there was nothing more to say.

"We can trade off some guilt there," I said. "I've been feeling bad I wasn't in Thailand with you and Graham on this thing from the start. Toby was a friend of mine. He hung it out for me a couple of times. When I picked up the farm and settled into it, I felt I was finally putting the war behind me. The MIA thing went with it. I never forgot, but it was way on the back burner somewhere."

"No matter," Campbell said. "It's on the front burner now."

"Bob Coyle's not mixed up in this, is he?" I said.

Campbell laughed. He has a splendid laugh, and it was nice to hear it again.

"No," he said. "He's not."

"By the way," I said. "Midge looks very handsome these days: sharp wardrobe, weight down, hair in a new style."

I had meant to please Campbell with this remark about his wife, but he ignored it, asking me instead how I felt about the fact Brian had chosen to live in Paris with Coyle's friend Dominique rather than return to the States. The subject was a sore one.

"I'd rather have Brian with me at Cedar Run," I said. "It was a dream of mine all those years that he'd get well someday and come home."

"But you didn't insist."

I shrugged.

"He's eighteen now," I said. "I joined the Air Force when I was that age. He's got a right to make his own decisions."

"I agree," Campbell said. "Furthermore, I think Paris will be good for him. He used to speak French. He should be able to pick it up again once he's a little further along. Have you had any recent word from Jillion Leggett?"

"She got married," I said.

He looked surprised.

"To that Aussie chargé?" he said.

"Yes. He's got ambassador rank now."

"Should I say I'm sorry to hear the news?"

"I got drunk for four days when I heard it."

"I knew you and Jillion had fallen in love for a while after Diana was gone. I guess I thought it was over."

"It is," I said. "We tried to keep the friendship going after she got married, but there was no way."

"She was stationed in Singapore, wasn't she? Bureau chief for API?"

"Yes. That's where she and the ambassador hooked up again."

We were silent for a moment. Two miles over Malaysia the sky was clear, and pricked by stars. The engines throbbed. I felt the close sense of shelter I always do in the cockpit of a plane at altitude at night.

"Midge and I have had some trouble," Campbell said after the pause.

I glanced at him. He looked gaunt and irascible again, the way he had when he had first come into my room at the Raffles Hotel. He and Midge had been married to each other for over thirty-five years. They had always struck me as perfectly suited.

"Trouble?" I said.

"She's had an affair."

"Midge?"

"By God," he said impatiently, "didn't you just get through telling me how fine she looks? Yes! Midge! With a man bloody near half her age."

"Jesus," I said. "I'm sorry to hear it."

"Oh rubbish," he said. "It's my fault. I've been away so much on this MIA business. Her arthritis started kicking up. I told her she'd get no sympathy from me until she lost some weight and started to exercise. . . ."

"Which she obviously did."

"Yes. She took up tennis, took lessons at the club, had an affair with the pro." Campbell threw up his hands. "The pro at the club!" he said. "It's more than an affair, it's a bloody cliché!"

"Is it over?" I said.

"I don't know," Campbell said. "I've never had to deal with anything like this before. I thought about shooting the son of a bitch, but that would have put Midge in a twist."

He fell silent and soon began to doze. I swung Kota Bahru and maintained heading for the beacon at U-Tapao. The leg was long, 410 miles, all of it over water. To keep from falling asleep, I took the Chieftain off autopilot and flew manually, listening to the airline chatter, in accented English, from the big commercial jets high above me.

Midge, I thought.

And the tennis pro.

An hour short of U-Tapao, Terry came to the cockpit. She said she was ready to take over the controls for a while. She seemed short-tempered, as though her nap hadn't done her much good. I put the ship back on autopilot and creaked out of my seat. As she took my place, I told her where I thought we were, when U-Tapao was due, where we stood on fuel transfer. Campbell was still dozing. I intended to get some sleep myself in the aft cabin.

"Call if you need me for anything," I said.

"I'll be fine," she said, sounding annoyed, as if I had implied she might not be capable of doing the job on her own. I hadn't meant to imply that, or anything like it. I wanted to say so, but didn't. I wanted to kiss her on my way out of the cockpit. I didn't do that either. We were two people who had clicked from the minute we had met, drawn like a couple of magnets. But the fact was we didn't know each other very well, and as I walked aft from the cockpit I began to realize how fragile our relationship was, how easily the magnetic fields could reverse.

Let it ride, I thought. If it's good for either of us it'll come back.

I fiddled around with opposing seats until I could stretch out. We were due to land at Khon Kaen at 0630. That gave me nearly two hours to sleep; but I was restless. I tossed and rearranged. From where I lay, I could see the Southeast Asian heavens. They seemed to have a million stars per mile. I had a lot of time logged under those stars, on the ground and in the air: Bien Hoa, Ubon, Phnom Penh; a hundred runways and strips in between.

And always the men. The ones that had never been accounted for. The ones who had been killed in action. Aircrews and Special Forces. Good Viets, Thais, Cambodes, and Lao.

I fell asleep, into a dream. The dream was a celebration where all the lost men were assembled. They wore flight suits, tiger suits, jungle fatigues, all filthy with red mud and sweat. They were laughing and shouting and singing. I wanted to be part of them. In a way I was. In a way I was not.

Then suddenly striding toward me out of their midst, immaculate in white slacks and dress shirt, came Toby Porter. I felt a surge of emotion at the sight of him, a flooding over me of joy that he looked so well. But as he came closer, I could see he wasn't immaculate after all.

He was wan and thin and bloodied.

And he looked at me through the sunken eyes of the betrayed.

Chapter
THIRTEEN

I woke to the sound of the engines being throttled back and the whine and clunk of the gear going down. Bright sun was flooding the cabin. I blinked and struggled up in time to see the flaps extend, surprised to discover we were on final to Khon Kaen.

I should have been up front helping Terry, I thought.

But Terry hadn't asked for any help, was doing just fine on her own, bringing the airplane in toward an asphalt runway I could see over her right shoulder and through the windscreen. Campbell, his craggy face shadowed with whisker, grinned back at me.

"We've got a surprise waiting for you down there!" he called, stabbing his finger toward the ground.

I fished my back-up pair of sunglasses out of my pocket, put them on, peered out my window. The view was familiar: newly planted rice paddies, emerald-green; oxcart trails starting to bake rock-solid after the monsoons; a small thatch village off to the south; then a high concertina fence that we topped at about a hundred feet as Terry throttled back slightly on her descent.

The early-morning air was clear and smooth. Inside the fence, I could see a dirt road that formed the perimeter of the Khon Kaen base. Once nothing more than a small dirt strip used by the Thais, the facility had been expanded by the Americans during the war to include a 5,000-foot asphalt runway and a training compound used by the 46th Special Forces Company. There were a number of buildings in poor repair, several dilapidated one-story barracks fronting an athletic field. As we came in, I caught a glimpse of a dozen men holding an exercise formation in front of an instructor's platform. They were lithe brown men in tiger-suit pants and olive-drab T-shirts, doing vigorous jumping jacks under the direction of a somewhat taller man who led the exercise from the platform.

The scene passed in a flash as Terry greased the ship onto the runway, the main gear making little squeaks as we touched down. She lowered the nosewheel, braked lightly at first, then heavier to make the turnoff at the center of the runway. As we taxied toward an operations shack, I could see the drill instructor had assembled his men and was double-timing them toward the ramp.

Terry's landing had been splendid. Now, with a flourish of light brake and engine, she turned onto the ramp, built up a little speed, chopped both throttles and mixtures, then coasted neatly toward a smiling Asian ground crewman who stood waiting for us, holding a pair of wheel chocks.

By this time, the drill instructor had lined his men up in two rows parallel to the left side of the approaching plane. The men stood at attention, chins in, chests out. The instructor stood in front of them, one man positioned between him and the two ranks. As we coasted to a stop, he spoke a command that was repeated by the man behind him. Then, smartly and as one, the entire troop rendered and held a salute. It was a fine display of military courtesy, and I was impressed enough by it to take a closer look at the leader of these men. As soon as I did, I let out a whoop of recognition.

He was Cambodian, taller than the average by half a foot, broader at the shoulders, with high cheekbones and skin the color of caramel. Black hair. Even blacker eyes. A striking mixture of Khmer, White Russian, and Harbin Chinese. I had known him since 1972. We had fought side by side many times, on the ground, in the air, as officers of our respective countries, as mercenaries and friends. I thought of him as my blood brother from the East. His name was Kam Trak.

I unbuckled from my seat and bolted for the cabin door. As I fumbled it open, I heard Campbell chuckling up front, obviously pleased with his surprise.

Kam, who must have assumed it was me piloting the plane, blinked when Terry slid the cockpit window open and gave him and his troops a breezy wave. He held his salute a moment longer, then barked a command at which his men dropped their hands to their sides, remaining at attention.

I jumped out and made my way toward him. He stood straight and proud—not like the half-strung puppet he usually resembles when he's off the battlefield—eyes front and center, features composed with the discipline of a person who has spent long years in the military. I knew I had to stifle my own exuberance as I approached, that in this environment, in front of his men, Kam was going to go by the numbers.

He barked his command again and they all saluted, holding the salute until I returned it. When I reached him, we shook hands.

"*Chum rip seur*, my brother," I said.

For a fleeting half second, he smiled.

"*Chum rip seur, Lōk*," he said.

I wanted to embrace him; I think he felt the same. But this wasn't the time or place. He turned to introduce me to the man who stood behind him in the formation, pausing a moment until he had his English sorted out.

"My brother Colonel Eberhart," he said finally, with great formality, "I present you Major Sisani."

Sisani was a short, sharp-featured man, whom I guessed to be in his early thirties. He did not have Kam's pronounced definition of muscle, but there was an aura of quiet strength about him. Though I was a good foot taller than he, and must have outweighed him by seventy-five pounds, there was nothing at all to indicate he was intimidated by these facts. He saluted me indifferently, ignored my offered handshake, fastened on me a clear expression of distrust. I did what I could to break the ice.

"I understand you're of the Hmong tribe, with the rank of chieftain," I said. "Do you speak English?"

"I, Sisani, speak small English," he replied. "Also some more French." He pronounced it "Franch" in the guttural way of the Hmong.

"Your tribe is the best," I said. "I have good friends who served with your people in Laos. They say the Hmong are great soldiers."

His face darkened. When he finally spoke, his voice was harsh.

"I led my people many times against bad mens to help your country," he said. "Your country never come back when we needed. Some your mens good. The Beret mens good. But your country no help us even now we die from bad men's yellow rain."

I held his gaze, but did not reply. The Hmong were a fiercely independent people who inhabited the mountainous country in the north of Laos. Hired by the CIA in the '60s, they were among the best fighters in all Southeast Asia. Since the United States had folded the war, their culture had been devastated by a policy of gas warfare and genocide carried out by the communist Vietnamese and Pathet Lao. Their population in Laos had fallen from over half a million to under seventy thousand. Many thousands more were living in refugee camps in Thailand. Sisani and the other men assembled here had been among these.

I knew Sisani's bitterness was not directed at me in particular, but at the United States in general, a country whose botched and fumbling foreign policy during the Vietnam War had, almost in passing, resulted in the destruction of his culture. Kam, sensitive as always to the nuances of a situation, did his best to smooth things between us.

"My brother the colonel is also very brave and has saved the lives of many good Khmer," he said. "He is not of the Berets, but he is like them. Sisani also too is very brave. He has known much combat in the Plaine des Jarres, and twice was given medals of valor by his general, Vang Pao. You *Lōk* and Sisani will soon know each other and be friends, I do believe."

Kam immediately followed this speech—which was a long one for him—by asking if I would like to inspect the troops. I said yes I'd consider it a privilege. We walked down the ranks.

The men held rigid positions of attention, thumbs along the seams of their pants, feet, some bare, some clad in canvas Bata boots, at exactly forty-five degrees. Their faces were blank, dark-brown eyes gazing straight ahead. They had been trained by the CIA and Special Forces, and they showed it. Most of them appeared to be in their late thirties or early forties, making the usual allowance for the fact they almost certainly looked younger than they were. Many showed the scars of battle. My overall impression was that this team of Hmong tribesmen Kam and my father-in-law had assembled to bring Toby Porter out of Laos was sharp, smart, and combat-savvy. Only one ran counter to the form.

He was the last man in the second rank. As I came toward him, he broke suddenly into a broad grin. He was shorter than the others, less than five feet, had the face of a baby, and jet-black bangs. I stopped in front of him, felt a touch of the colonel rising in me.

"Votre nom?" I asked soberly.

His dark eyes flashed, bubbled almost, in an effort to keep a straight face. He was apparently delighted I had singled him out.

"Oh, sir," he said in a high, clear voice, "I speak English. You are Air Force I am told. I worked Air Force long, long time. I worked with the Ravens, sir, for Colonel Pratt and Major Blake."

I ignored this, reminding him I had asked for his name. He did not look at all chagrined.

"I am Shit Hot's cousin, sir," he said. "My name is Little Pea."

I heard Kam chuckling behind me and, though I tried, I couldn't help smiling. "Shit Hot" had been the nickname of a Lao T-28 pilot who had flown an extraordinary number of missions for us during the war before he finally got skragged. His favorite expression in English had been "shit hot," which was USAF slang for "terrific." "Pea" (spelled *Pi* in Lao) meant "spirit." Keying off his knowledge of English and his verbal energy, I asked him if he had ever done any radio work.

"Oh sir, oh yes," he said. "Many, many times. Oh-one Fox Mike and Prick-25. You bet I call airstrike, kill many, many bad mens. They all know Little Pea. Now I tell you how one time—"

Kam cut him off here. I think if he hadn't, Little Pea might have gone on talking through what was left of the Year of the Horse.

Chapter
FOURTEEN

At two o'clock that afternoon, Terry and I were summoned by Campbell to a mission brief in the base radio shack. The shack, which doubled as a command post, was a small rectangular wood-frame building with a thatched roof. There was a jeep parked in front with a trailer-borne generator. A lead-in ran from the top of the shack to a long-wire antenna strung between twenty-foot poles. The sun was high now, the day hot and humid. There were single windows in the walls of the building, each with a shutter raised to the outside. The shutters were flaky with green paint.

Terry and I had swapped our civilian clothes for "Asian Large" tiger suits out of the base storeroom. The garb was familiar to me, but not to Terry. She looked uncomfortable in it at first, rolling the sleeves up, then down, fussing with the waist, glancing over her shoulder into the cracked bathroom mirror of the old AID bungalow where, in separate rooms, the two of us had slept away the morning. Over a late lunch, sitting alone in a barracks mess hall, she had not wanted to talk. She had avoided my gaze, seemed preoccupied, given me the impression I had done something to offend her. No hint as to what it might be. After several attempts to pry it out of her, I had lapsed into a dour silence of my own, convinced more than ever that Campbell had made a mistake by dealing Terry into the mission. I knew I had to move now into the combat mode. While I was doing that, I didn't want to have to think about Terry, our relationship, what had gone wrong, whether or not we had a future. I liked her enough to care. I liked her enough to be distracted by her presence and troubled by her silences; and I knew that kind of distraction could prove fatal on a mission into Laos. Earlier, Terry had asked Campbell what her brother's role was to have been. Campbell had put her off. Now, I suspected, we were about to find out.

The shack consisted of a single room. There were maps

pinned neatly to the wall at one end; an MK-28 radio pallet rested on a rough wood table at the other. Little Pea sat at the radio. He had a headset clamped over his ears and beamed happily when Terry and I walked in. Kam slouched against the far wall, arms akimbo. Except when he is on the battlefield, where he has the grace of a jungle cat, he tends to look like a collection of spare parts: extra hips and elbows, knees that work both ways, a head that seems capable of swiveling 180 degrees on his shoulders. When I had introduced him to Terry I thought I had sensed through his implacable courtesy reservations similar to my own about Campbell's apparent willingness to include her as a member of the team. This had nothing to do with our respect for Terry—Kam had seen and remarked on her fine landing of the plane—but rather with an ingrained belief, right or wrong, that the physical rigors and hazards of combat were more naturally confronted by men.

Campbell, wearing dark slacks and a dress shirt with the sleeves rolled back, stood by the wall maps, a bamboo pointer in his hand. He looked refreshed as he greeted us, was cleanly shaved, had lost some of the gaunt look now the countdown was about to begin.

"Another member of the team will be joining us shortly," he said. "He's already familiar with the mission detail, so there's no reason we can't get started without him. I want to remind you that our operation here has not been officially sanctioned by either the Thai government or the USG. We have the financial backing of a prominent Thai businessman and we'll be directly though not officially aided by ISOC, Thai Internal Security Operations. We also have friends in Defense Intelligence and the CIA.

"Frankly, if I had my way, the United States Government would be running this show. We've given them the tapes in which Major Sisani recounts his live sightings of Toby Porter at the camp in Laos. We've also given them the results of Sisani's lie-detector test, and of the Argus satellite scan. And we've given them Graham's confirmation of the camp terrain. They're impressed, but not convinced. They've put everything we've given them into a priority file, and have made it clear they'd like more. The trouble with that is that Toby Porter's a perishable commodity. He's already been a prisoner for four years. By the time we get more evidence, he might be dead. I guess the sum of what I'm saying is that we've done all we can to go through official channels and right now those channels are blocked. If we trip on our knickers in Laos, no one's going to pull us out."

Campbell used his pointer to indicate a position on one of the maps.

"The camp where Toby is being held is located at Quebec Bravo 292723," he said, "nine kilometers north of the Thai border, seventeen south of Muang Mongsa. It's run by dissident Pathet Lao. There are no North Vietnamese advisers or cadre there. The camp lies on the south side of the Nam Yang River, at a site between that river and a mountain, here, of seven hundred meters. Several huts are scattered through a grove of palms. According to Sisani, Toby is being kept in the hut nearest the mountain, at the base of which are a number of caves. These caves were used as shelter from air strikes during the war. Sisani says they're now used exclusively for storage, but that the PL could withdraw to them if attacked, and once there could hold out for a long period of time. Hence we need to be very damn certain the PL don't get to the caves.

"The insertion will be by a single helicopter. The assault team, numbering fourteen men, will be set down, here, at Landing Zone Alpha at 0530 tomorrow morning. From there they'll march through most of the day to the south side of the mountain. Four men will go over the mountain and descend to a point just above the caves. Five more will go around the mountain to the north, five to the south. The three squads should be in position by dusk. Once they are, they'll have the PL caught between them on three sides and the river on the fourth. Sisani says the camp population runs to about thirty. The actual attack will take place at sunrise the next morning."

Campbell went on to give us the details of how the three squads would operate during the attack, how Toby would be freed, how he and the men would withdraw from the camp to a helicopter evacuation site where they would be picked up and flown to the Thai air force base at Udorn.

As my father-in-law concluded his briefing, I became aware of the buzz of the generator through the open window, and the gentle hiss of the radios manned by Little Pea. Kam caught a fly in his fist, opened his fist slowly and let the fly go. Terry stood tall in her tiger suit, so attentive to what Campbell had been saying she seemed caught in suspended animation, wisps of auburn hair lying damp along the deeply tanned contours of her cheek and brow.

Out of an old habit, I popped a cigarette and lit up. Campbell looked at me disapprovingly.

"I'd like you to go in with the assault team," he said. "Toby should recognize you, even at fairly long range. That's an advantage we want to have. Otherwise he's liable to think it's Vietnamese attacking the camp, and we're not sure what he might do in a case like that. We also want to maintain credibility with the Hmongs. They know you've been trained as a fighter pilot and that we wouldn't risk losing you in a meaningless cause. Sorry to have to put it that way. The mission's voluntary, of course. Graham and I simply assumed from the start you'd want to be part of it.''

"I'd have paid my own way to get here," I said. "Have you picked your team leader?''

"Yes. Sisani. He's the only one who's been to the camp and has firsthand knowledge of the terrain. He's seen a lot of combat, has a battlefield commission. I wanted to put Kam in as number one, but Kam himself thinks Sisani's the logical choice.''

Kam flashed me his shy smile. He had removed the knife he carried in his boot and was using it to clean a speck of dirt from under his nail.

"I be number two," he said. "I keep eye on you, *Lōk*. You fall out, I kick you up again, chop-chop.''

"Just stay away from the seat of my pants with that number-eight blade of yours," I said. He laughed. He had cut it out once to keep me from leaving a safe room in Bangkok. Terry, impatient with our banter, looked at Campbell.

"Gray had a role in the mission," she said. "I'd like to know what it was.''

"He was going to handle the radio work from the helicopter, and assist the pilot during the pickup and drop," Campbell replied.

"Then I want to take his place," Terry said.

"That chopper could come under fire," I said.

"Yes. I know.''

"And I know how you feel about having lost Graham," I said, "and how right now you want to be part of something he was part of. But if he was here, I don't think—''

"Matt, if he was here," she interrupted, "he'd expect me to do exactly what I am doing: volunteer for a job that needs getting done. I'm good friends with the man who runs the helicopter service at Seletar. Thanks to him, I've got over a dozen hours in choppers—Graham didn't have any. And I'm bloody good on a radio.''

"Matt's right when he says you could come under fire," Campbell warned. "The ground troops almost certainly will.''

"I understand that," Terry said with conviction. "I'm willing to risk it. I want the place Graham would have had."

I had a feeling Campbell had already made up his mind.

"There are good reasons why that makes sense," he said. "You are better qualified, and more important I know we can trust you. It's late in the day to bring in somebody we don't know."

"Then it's settled," she said.

Campbell nodded in the affirmative, glanced to the far end of the room.

"Any trouble with that, Little Pea?" he said. The baby-faced Hmong, headset surreptitiously slipped back from his ears, had been listening wide-eyed to everything we said.

"Oh no, oh sir, no problem here," he cried. "I be RTO on ground, Miss Terry in the air. You let men roast pig tonight. We get strong that way and satisfy the Nongven spirit. Then we go get Toh-bas from bad mens and bring him back."

Campbell smiled, then cocked his head toward the *whap-whap-whap* of an approaching helicopter. I glanced through the open window in time to see the chopper land on a pad that been hacked out of the vines and ground creeper not far from the radio shack itself. Moments later, a tall figure wearing a black flight suit and white neck scarf strode into the room. He was a Thai, skin tone darker than most, mid-thirties, teeth white and even in a generous mouth. His black hair was combed rakishly back, spirited eyes alert and energized by everything they saw. Dash, flair, charisma—whatever label you want to use, this man, whoever he was, had it in abundance.

Campbell greeted him with exceptional warmth, then introduced him to Terry and me as Lieutenant Colonel Sakoon Panapong, commanding officer of the 13th Fighter Wing, Royal Thai Air Force. Blank Velcro on his shoulder and left chest indicated where his unit insignia and name tag had been affixed before he had removed them for security reasons. He shook my hand vigorously, with a powerful grip.

"It's a pleasure to meet you, Colonel," he said. "I went through the Fighter School at Nellis in '65. They remember you there."

"Probably for something I did during beer call," I said.

He laughed appreciatively at this, then turned his attention to Terry. He said she was even more beautiful than the photos he had seen in news magazines and Sunday supplements. He said he had known her brother well, that Graham had always spoken of her with great fondness, that his loss was immeasurable. He said that he, Sakoon, would, with her permission, consider her from this moment forward as a special friend. When he had finished speaking, he locked his gaze on hers, took her hand, held it for a moment, then let it go. By the time he did I could have sworn Terry—who had once known the acclaim of kings—was blushing through her tan.

"Well, Sakoon," Campbell said with relish, not missing any of this, "you've just held hands with your new copilot. She'll fill you in on her background." Then, with a merry look, my father-in-law turned to me. "Sakoon will be piloting the chopper tomorrow," he said. "We couldn't ask for a better man."

He was, Campbell went on to explain, the nephew of our Thai backer: a man I had once had occasion to meet, whose name was Mr. Adune.

Chapter
FIFTEEN

Before we concluded the briefing, Little Pea copied a radio message from the Australian Secret Intelligence Service. They said had had cracked Graham's code and expected to be able to transmit the clear text of the three key pages within the hour. It was now just after five in the afternoon. Barring any problems, the mission would launch from Miami Base at two the next morning.

Campbell remained in the radio shack with Panapong and Little Pea, waiting for the decoded copy. Kam went off to see how things were going with Sisani and the men, while Terry and I went back to the AID bungalow.

The bungalow was ramshackle: sagging roof, screens rusted through on the front porch, floorboards that creaked under our weight. There were three small bedrooms and a kitchen, all opening onto a large living room, sparsely furnished with inexpensive rattan furniture. Terry plopped down on one end of a three-cushion sofa; I plopped down on the other. My focus was narrowing more and more toward the mission. As it did, I could feel myself getting edgy. Terry watched me for a while, then got up and began to pace.

"Who was she?" she said suddenly.

"Who was who?" I asked, annoyed at the interruption of my thoughts.

"Jillion Leggett."

I glanced up, surprised Terry knew the name.

"A friend," I said.

"A woman friend, you mean."

"That's right."

"An Australian journalist once based in Singapore?"

"Yes."

"And you were in love with her?"

I stood up. I could feel an irrational anger flooding through me at the question.

"Goddammit," I said, "what if I was? How do you know about Jillion? Have you been talking to Campbell?"

"No, I haven't," she said. "I overheard you talking to him on the plane flying up. And dammit, don't swear at me."

"Sorry!" I snapped, blood rising to a fine boil. Terry paced back and forth, fists clenched at the sides of her tiger suit, amber eyes throwing sparks.

"We had a lovely time, didn't we?" she said. "Doing our Singapore fling? Wining and dining in all the best places? Picnics at the lagoon? Having it off in Graham's plane at forty thousand feet?"

"It was fine for a week and a day," I said. "Maybe we'd better leave it at that."

"So! I was just another Aussie bird, is that it?"

"That's nonsense and you know it."

"I *knew* you must have had your own reasons for coming half way around the world."

"Dammit, Jillion!" I said, the mistake blurting out before I could stop it.

"*Jillion!*" she shouted. "Now you're calling me by her name!"

"All right! You do remind me of her! You've got the same stubborn temper!"

"Well, then, maybe you should dress me like her too! Put a key in my back so you could wind me up and I could be your pretty life-sized Jilly doll!"

At that I walked out of the house, slamming the screen door behind me. It was a ridiculous fight, as most fights between lovers are; but Jillion Leggett had been the only woman after

Diana's death who I felt I could have lived with the rest of my life, and I didn't need to be reminded of her, not by Terry or Campbell or anyone else.

I took a long walk around the perimeter road. The base was surrounded by terraced rice paddies and fields of groundnut and corn. The compound itself had a few palm trees and was otherwise heavily overgrown with vines that had been cut back in the essential areas. The sun, setting through an atmosphere of haze and high cirrus, lay a spectrum of pastel color over the varied terrain.

I whistled a melancholy tune while I walked, exchanged nods and smiles with the Hmong guards, tried not to think about Terry. At dusk I was back at the mess hall, where I had some fried rice, steak, and bottled water. Afterward, I sat with Kam on the front steps of his barracks, listening to the jungle chirps and clicks as they came on louder and louder with the increasing dark.

"I've never seen you look better," I said to my Cambodian friend. He smiled.

"My job is good," he said. "I am now foreman for Mr. Adune."

Adune ran the largest beef ranch in Thailand, nearly 60,000 acres of prime land, 150 miles southeast of Bangkok. He had once fought heroically under Wingate against the Japanese and was now revered by his countrymen for his wealth and religious devotion. There were some who said Adune was more powerful than the Thai prime minister. He had been a friend of Campbell's for years and, finally persuaded by the satellite scan that Toby was indeed where Sisani said he was, had put up the money for the mission to rescue him. Kam and I had met Adune during a mercenary operation that had brought us to Thailand in the mid-'70s. Adune's previous ranch foreman, a brave man named Chai, had been killed during that mission. It pleased me to know Kam had been given Chai's job at the ranch.

"At first I am not accepted by the men," he said. "They are Thai and I Khmer. I fall many times off horse. They laugh at me. I try again at night when they all asleep. I keep falling off. Then one night I get on and stay for many miles."

"Good," I said. "Did the men accept you after that?"

"No. I try everything, but they are Thai and I am still Khmer. Then one day I dig big pit in front of bunkhouse. I tell men to come into pit and try to throw me out. They all come, one by one; but I am like Bull Simon. I throw them out instead. They accept me after that."

We laughed. The night was closing around us with its chorus of jungle sounds. Fifty yards from where we sat, a bonfire burned in front of the mess hall, where the Hmongs had gathered to sacrifice a pig. I asked Kam how he felt about tomorrow. His eyes gleamed in the soft light.

"This you know, I do think," he said. "That I will go back anywhere or anyplace to kill them, just as they have killed my family, my children and my wife."

"It was Khmer Rouge who did that," I said. "This will be Pathet Lao."

"They are all the same."

"Yes," I said. "I think they are."

It was a simplification that rested finally on the difference between societies that valued the life and freedom of the individual, and those that did not. That distinction was, for me at least, ground zero for everything else.

Kam and I caught up on our own lives since we had last met. He seemed especially pleased to hear about Brian's progress, was silent when I told him the news about Jillion's marriage. I filled him in on everything that had happened to Terry and me in Singapore. We went over the mission detail again, speculated on what Campbell would learn when he got the page translations from Graham's log. A kerosene lantern burned in the AID bungalow now. I could see Terry puttering alone in the kitchen there.

"She's a good woman," I said. "You knew Graham. She's just what you'd expect his sister to be."

Kam nodded gravely.

"She'll work out," I said. "Campbell's probably got that right."

"You will not stay with this woman, *Lōk*," Kam said. "You will wait for the other."

"Even though she's married?"

"She will not be married long. She will live with the ambassador and think of you. This I do believe."

"I don't agree," I said. "It took Jillion a long time to make up her mind. She's committed now. She won't look back."

Kam stood up and stretched, assuring me I was wrong.

"I go eat pig now," he said. "Dig pit, maybe, and throw out Hmongs."

*   *   *

I went back to the bungalow. Terry was sitting on the porch.

"I'm sorry," she said, as I came up.

"So am I."

"I feel foolish, acting the way I did, mad as a meat ax just because you fell for an Aussie once."

"You Aussies," I said. I placed myself behind her and began to massage her neck. She sighed, muscles relaxing, tension going out. "That feels good," she said. I kept it up. After a few minutes had passed, she twisted around and caught my hand. "Let's make it up," she said. "Let's make love."

We went into one of the bedrooms, and we tried. I know I did, and so did Terry. It just didn't work. She would start to respond, then be distracted by some innocuous sound outside the bungalow. I'd lose the command of her presence in visions of Graham's last hour, of a Laotian dagger thrown by a scarred Chinese, of a communist major general draped in sackcloth who had first honed his cruelty in Tibet.

So we tried, the two of us, laboring toward love in an ambience of moonglow that gave the room and us discernible form and shape.

After the passing of an awkward time, Terry finally sat up.

"Well, that's it," she said. "We can't even do this anymore. Stupid of us to try, I guess."

"Wrong time," I said. "We're both on edge. We'll do better."

"When," she said, her voice like wrinkling tinfoil.

It wasn't a question. Just a way of saying she was disappointed. I was disappointed too.

I went out for another one of my patented walks, stopping by the radio shack, where I found Campbell sitting alone at the rough wood table, lantern hanging from a hook overhead.

"Take a look at this," he said.

He handed me the transcribed copy of everything that had been contained on the three critical pages of Graham's flight log. I read the material quickly, then again slowly. According to the decoded text, Graham had flown several search patterns in the region of the Quebec Bravo camp. Most of the log entries had to do with his detailed description of the terrain. At one point, he had jotted a reminder to himself to "check Pak Beng," a small Laotian village north of the camp where Toby was being held. Otherwise, I could see nothing in the text of interest or value. When I told Campbell as much, he banged his fist on the table top.

"Hua was willing to torture and kill for this information," he said. "And there's not a scrap of it you couldn't pick up from an eighth-grade geography book. *Why?*"

"He must have thought there was more."

"Of course he did. He thought Graham had stumbled onto something. Not some penny-ante camp run by a ragtag bunch of Pathet Lao. Something big. What in blazes was it?"

We read the text again. We studied the maps, Nothing jumped out. As we worked under a cloud of insects that had gathered around the lantern globe, I kept hearing Graham's words just before he died:

It's the spur, he had said. *It has to do with the spur.*

Two hours later, Lieutenant Colonel Sakoon Panapong fired up his UH-lH chopper and flew Campbell to the American consulate at Udorn. Campbell would monitor the mission from there, forestall international repercussions if things went wrong, inform the President if things went right.

Panapong would return to Miami Base in time to refuel before the launch.

I started back to the bungalow, detoured to the barracks, found a spare bunk, and went to sleep.

Chapter
SIXTEEN

Kam shook me awake at twelve forty-five a.m.

"Time, *Lōk*, time," he said, turning the lanterns up. It took me a half second to come around. Except for the two of us, the barracks was empty. The rest of the troops had already left, so quietly I hadn't heard them go.

I pulled on my tiger suit and jungle boots, feeling the same tugs of apprehension I always used to feel before flying missions in the war, niggles of doubt I knew had to be shunted aside in the carrying out of small tasks.

I used the wash bucket, then ate the cold rice Kam had brought for me, chasing it with tea. He had assembled my gear at the foot of my bunk. It was not as familiar to me as combat flight gear, but familiar enough. I began putting it on, starting from the inside, working out.

I tied the cord of a metal signal mirror to my blouse, putting the mirror itself into an adjacent pocket. To other pockets, I added a lensatic compass, field bandages, Ace bandages, two bandannas, and a crushproof box of morphine syrettes.

Once these items were in place, I picked up my equipment harness. Kam had already taped a serum albumin container to the left strap, and to the right a K-bar knife, handle down, and a strobe light, pointing up. Smoke and fragmentation grenades, several canteen covers serving as ammunition pouches, a medical kit, survival kit, and rice rations hung from the various carrying rings. I checked the grenade cotter pins to be sure they were secure and not corroded. A rolled poncho with ground sheet, mosquito netting, and extra socks was slung on the back of the harness. Below that a claymore mine was secured.

I put the harness on, including its web belt with additional ammunition pouches. I would carry two canteens, with a vial of water-purification tablets taped to each. Maps of the landing zones and target area went under my blouse. I estimated the total weight of my gear minus weapon at about twenty-seven pounds.

I used both ends of a camouflage stick on my face and hands, striping them dark green and loam. When I was ready to go, Kam gave me the automatic rifle I would carry. It was an AK-47, clean, slightly oily, with a full magazine and a modified sling. Green duct tape had been wound around portions of the stock and muzzle to alter the outline of the piece.

Kam, already kitted up, looked me over, nodded approvingly. He had been a teacher before the war, then had served in the Cambodian army as a forward air controller with the rank of captain. More than once in that theater he had saved my life. If I had to come under fire again, there was no one I would rather have at my side.

The air outside the barracks was slightly cool and clammy-damp. The insects chirped and clicked. I followed Kam to the flight ramp where Sisani and his men squatted in a loose formation near Panapong's big Huey chopper. Two battery lamps illuminated the scene. The men looked confident and eager. Last night they had placated their lowland spirit by eating a pig. Today they would return to the mountains of Laos that had once been their beloved home. For luck and protection, their shaman had tied a series of strings around the left wrist of each man.

Sisani, still distant toward me, took Kam aside and began to talk.

I found Terry standing alone, apart from the rest of the group. She wore her tiger suit, combat boots, and a tan scarf around her head. She looked tired in the diffuse light from the lamps. A holstered revolver hung from a web belt that circled her narrow waist.

"Sakoon wants me to carry it," she said. "In case we crash."

"Does it bother you to carry it?" I asked.

"Yes. In a way. I don't know much about guns," she said. "Graham tried to teach me to shoot once, but I wasn't very good."

"There's still time to back out of this," I said. "No one would blame you if you did."

She shook her head.

"I'll be all right once we're up," she said. "It's the standing around I don't like."

"Were you able to get some sleep?"

"Some. When you left the bungalow, you didn't say you wouldn't be coming back. I waited up for you."

"I'm sorry," I said. "Campbell and I got sidetracked going over the transcript of Graham's log."

"There wasn't much to go over, was there?"

"No."

"They went to all that trouble and wound up killing Gray for nothing."

"Maybe not. It could be the answer's there, staring us in the face, and we're not seeing it. Campbell says Adune has a network in Laos. He's tapping it to see if he can come up with anything on Hua. Assuming he does, he'll let Campbell know."

Terry didn't look convinced.

"Sakoon stopped by the bungalow when he got back from dropping Campbell at the consulate," she said. "He saw my light burning."

I thought there was a hint of confession in the way she told me this. I couldn't think of a good reply. We stood silent.

"You look awfully fierce with that greasepaint on your face," she said after a while. "Please come back safely after we let you off."

"I will," I repied. "We'll all be back."

It was what you said, even when you knew the odds against it were very long.

*   *   *

We lifted off at exactly two a.m., leveling at 6,000 feet, flying without navigation lights over dark, sparsely inhabited terrain. The air at this altitude was cool. During the first leg of our flight the sliding doors on each side of the chopper's wide cabin would be closed. The men sat on the cabin floor, huddled together for warmth, gear and weapons stacked around them. Kam, Sisani, and I sat on folding seats aft. Panapong flew the chopper from the right-hand seat, Terry carried out her duties as copilot from the left; the crew placement for helicopters is the reverse of that for fixed-wing aircraft.

An hour later, we landed and refueled from a tanker truck under portable floodlights at Muang Ngop, eight miles from the Laotian border. The refueling was done by a special cadre of Thai border police wearing civilian clothes.

During the refueling procedure and at Panapong's request, Kam and I rolled the rope ladders out from each side of the chopper, checked their tie-downs and climb ropes, then rolled them back into the ship. Kam had already explained to me that using a rope ladder differed from using a conventional ladder. To provide rigidity, the rope ladder required the user to ascend and descend from the side, rather than face on. Sisani warmed all of us up with a series of light exercises, then each member of the ground assault team drank heavily from a field water tank before filing back into the chopper in split-descent order. The team call sign would be Miami Tiger, that of the chopper Miami Wing. Campbell would be referred to, if and when necessary, as Delta One.

At twenty minutes after four, Panapong restarted the Huey's big jet engine and we lifted off again for the final ten-minute flight across the Laotian border to Landing Zone Alpha. Panapong continued to maintain strict radio silence, but both he and Terry had their headsets on. Our cruising speed on this brief final leg was a hundred miles per hour at minimum altitude to avoid radar detection.

I sat near the open left cargo door. We were skimming over karst country now: a jagged limestone terrain full of gray bulging knobs, sharp spires, deep ravines, and dark jungle green. According to the briefing Campbell had given us, Landing Zone Alpha was a small clearing on a hillside, just below a prominent pinnacle of karst. In what seemed no time at all, we were there.

Panapong worked his pitch and collector, causing us to start down in a fast swooping descent. First light was just breaking. As we got lower and the dawn brightened I could see more clearly the upper level of the triple canopy: an emerald explosion of treetops reaching for the sun, rising as much as a hundred feet above the ground. Some fifty feet below that would be the secondary cover of bushes and vines, then the funk and rot of the lower zone where there was not enough sunlight to nourish growth.

Sakoon leveled at twenty feet over the steeply slanted clearing, his rotor blades dangerously close to the surrounding trees. The clearing wasn't much bigger than the roof of a barn. I threw out the rope ladder on my side; Sisani threw out the one on his. They tumbled down into the scattered growth of the LZ. As soon as they were in place, the first of Sisani's men scrambled down in their prearranged order. They would set up a defense perimeter. Those who would be last to descend the ladders squatted in the doorways, their weapons pointed out and down. The noise of the chopper was shattering in the still morning air.

When it was my turn, I slid backward out of the door, face down on the chopper deck, hands holding the ladder tie-downs, automatic rifle slung over my shoulder. Terry had turned in her seat to watch me go. Her face looked pinched and white. When Panapong spoke to her through the intercom, she turned away. I had to grope with my feet for the first rope rung. When I found it, I started down the swinging ladder, buffeted by downwash from the whirling blades. Kam was coming down the ladder opposite me. He held his pace to mine, watching me and the surrounding jungle at the same time. The secondary growth in the clearing was thicker than it had looked from the air. My rifle caught in it once as I came through. I shrugged it free; then Kam and I were on the ground, standing under a light canopy of vegetation.

When the last of the men were down, Little Pea used his radio to tell Panapong we were clear. Scarcely visible above us, Terry pulled the ladders up. Then the *whap-whap-whap* of the chopper faded away as Panapong headed northeast, back toward the refueling base at Muang Ngop where he and Terry would wait out the mission and our eventual arrival at the evacuation site.

I was still looking skyward when Kam tugged at my sleeve.

"We go now, *Lōk*," he said. "We go get Toby Porter and bring him home."

Chapter
SEVENTEEN

Sisani had already brought in the perimeter guards and had formed the men into their route order. There were fourteen of us in all: twelve Hmongs, Kam, and I. We were well equipped and well armed. Our point man carried a cut-down M-60 machine gun with two extra belts of ammunition slung around his neck. Next came our compass man, carrying an AK-47. He was followed by Sisani, carrying an AK and a squad radio. Little Pea was directly behind him with the more sophisticated PRC-77 radio strapped to his back, telephone receiver hooked to his left front harness. His weapon was a sawed-off Rossi 12-gauge side-by-side with external hammers and a Greener crossbolt, a gift, he had told me, from Colonel Pratt and Major Blake for his service to the Ravens.

I followed Little Pea; eight of the Hmongs followed me. Kam, as assistant team leader, would bring up the rear as our defensive tail-end Charlie. He would also erase any trail we might leave. The Hmongs who were between Kam and me carried a variety of weapons: AKs, M-60 machine guns, and RPG-7 rocket-propelled grenade launchers. We moved out heading north through the jungle toward our first objective, the mountain that lay between us and the POW camp.

Our movement was slow, cautious, and quiet. We had good intelligence as to the size and location of the camp where Toby was being held, but we didn't know what enemy hazards might lie between that camp and our present position. When you trek a patrol in the jungle, you've got to maintain visual contact with the man in front of you. I had a hard time. My large frame wouldn't fit through the tiny jungle passageways that suited the Hmong. I made a lot of noise, though I tried not to make any. In an hour I was uncomfortable. In two hours, when Sisani finally signaled a break, I was sweat-soaked and thirsty.

We rested for fifteen minutes, squatting with our gear on and weapons pointing off-trail. I took several sips from my canteen,

swishing the water around in my mouth before swallowing.
Water had never tasted that good. No one spoke; no one smoked.
There were no shafts of sun, just an overall suffusion of light.
The tree trunks, mostly teak and palm, were thickly wrapped by
creeper and festooned with cable vines. There were bushes with
thorns that could have sliced through canvas; mushroomy plants
and giant ferns. We could hear the chatter of monkeys, and the
occasional shriek of a bird. The odor around us was like that of
an old death.

When Sisani tapped his rifle, we moved on. Each hour after
our first break we'd take ten minutes. After the fourth break, I
found it harder and harder to get to my feet. I was sweating
profusely; my back and thighs felt as if they had been beaten
with a club.

We climbed hills, bent under low vines, crossed streams with
steep banks. I tried to concentrate on placing my steps effective-
ly, and counting each step I took. At noon I was allowing myself
a swig of water every hundred; by two o'clock every fifty; by
three every twenty. I had already emptied one canteen, refilling
it with stream water, adding two of the purifier pills.

We wore floppy jungle hats. Mine was snatched off so many
times as we crept along I finally stuffed it in a pocket and tied
one of my Ace bandages around my head to keep the sweat out
of my eyes. I used a bandanna to mop my face. I had to wring it
out every thirty steps. Time did not seem to pass, just steps:
three more to a swig; five more to a mop. I had done hard
physical labor at Cedar Run throughout the summer and into the
fall and was in as good shape as I had been in since flight
school. But I realized very soon I wasn't in shape for this.

By four that afternoon, when Sisani called a rest, I knew I
would have been useless in a fire fight. I was dizzy, staggering,
could only do ten paces without taking a drink. I sprawled on my
side. The ground was a beautiful bed; my body sweat-soaked
mush. My ears were roaring. I closed my eyes against a sea of
red flecks. For a moment I was dimly aware of Sisani posting
perimeter guards. Then I was out. Seconds later, or so it seemed,
someone squatted next to me. I opened my eyes tiredly and saw
Kam. He looked worried.

"I have to kick you up now, *Lōk*," he said. "It's not too far
to go. Sisani say we are almost at the mountain now. We split
into three teams. Dark will be over us soon."

I said okay. The roaring in my ears had dropped to a decent
level. Both my canteens were empty. Kam gave me water from

his. I struggled to my feet. Sisani watched me, annoyed. He had divided us into three squads. He, his point man, and three other Hmong would go north around the mountain. Four others would go over the mountain. Kam, Little Pea, the remaining Hmong, and I would skirt the mountain to the south. We were to be in position by nightfall, hit the Pathet Lao on a radio signal from Sisani at sunrise. If things turned bad, we had a rallying point on the riverbank, six klicks above the camp.

The tribesman took the point for our squad, Little Pea took compass, then me, then Kam. I checked my watch as we set out. Sisani had let me sleep for twenty minutes. I felt stronger, but not much.

We reached our position just after six o'clock that evening, with barely thirty minutes left before dark. Under a triple-canopy jungle, there is no gradual fading of light as the sun goes down. It's sudden; takes two, maybe three minutes. Lights on, lights out. Our position was 1,000 meters south of the enemy camp.

We gobbled some rice, spread our ground sheets in a star pattern. Kam and Little Pea placed claymore mines, with phosphorus grenades taped to their fronts, about forty feet out in each direction. Little Pea took a message from Sisani saying the other two teams were already in their night bivouacs. I rubbed insect repellent on my face and hands. Then, as the others would, I lay down head to the center of the star, feet pointing out. I lay on my back, crossed my ankles, and propped the muzzle of the AK between my feet, stock resting on my gut. I pulled the mosquito netting over me and placed my hand near the trigger. Through the mesh, I heard Kam arrange the order of the night watch with the others. When he finished, he came over to me.

"Thanks," I said, "for leaving me out."

"You feel better in morning," he said. "We only wake you if trouble comes."

"How's Little Pea holding up?"

"He quiet now, all business. Very strong."

"Like Toby," I said. "He doesn't look tough, but he is."

We talked for a while, then Kam was gone and it was dark. Pitch-black dark with no moonlight, though I knew the moon was up there above the canopy—surrounded by a million Asian stars. I gave myself a minute to think about Brian, another to think about Terry. They were good thoughts.

Then, with the jungle noises coming up loud around me, I fell into a deep, oblivious sleep.

* * *

"Time, *Lōk,* time," Kam said.

It was still dark. I could barely see him through the netting. I peeled the Velcro flap back from the phosphorescent dial of my watch. Quarter to five. Less than an hour before sunrise. I got up, my pains, aches, rippling cramps all reduced by a rising adrenaline surge. We broke camp quickly, gobbling rice, taking in the claymores, rolling up the wires. I used my camouflage stick again. At first light, we moved out on our final approach.

We walked the first 500 meters, crawled the last. I went second behind Kam, who had the lead. He looked like a shadowy supplicant kneeling in front of a statue of Buddha: hands and arms slowly rising and falling, one at a time, from over his head to the jungle floor and back as he inched forward, feeling for trip wires. We followed him on our hands and knees, in single file, ten feet apart. The air was damp from the river, and cool. Tall grass grew where the bank had been cleared. We bellied through the grass, following Kam. The ground here smelled like sulphur and had the texture of snails. There were rat tunnels that came up from the river through the grass. We breathed insects, crushing them in our nostrils and ears.

The camp was as Sisani had described it: a dozen thatched huts scattered through a grove of palms. From our position just inside the grass, we could see the river to our right and the steep mountainside to our left with its series of caves. The distance between the mountain and the river was about 1,000 feet. There was a low mist on the river. We could have tossed a stone and hit the nearest hut.

The camp was quiet. There were no sentries. The perimeter had not been mined. I looked at Kam. He shook his head. When Sisani radioed the signal to attack, we sprang up and crouch-ran into the camp, weapons on full automatic, safeties off. There was no alarm. We checked the hootches on the south side; Sisani and his men checked the ones on the north. The men who had come over the mountain checked the caves. No Pathet Lao. No Toby. The camp was deserted. Bits of crockery and items of clothing were scattered about as if the people who had once been here had left in a hurry.

Fearing an ambush, Sisani set up a defense perimeter and sent out scouts. Then he showed me the hut where five months earlier he said he had seen the American he referred to as "Toh-bas." I went in. There was a bamboo cage about five feet square resting on the dirt floor. Inside the cage there was a pallet of dried grass and a couple of clay pots. Nothing to indicate Toby might have been there. Nothing.

I sat down, resting my back against the bars of the cage, trying to feel and absorb the presence of Toby. I wanted the earth or the grass pallet or something to tell me where he was and what had happened.

The hut was quiet. I got no returns. Deep within me a rage was building. I wanted to scream and crash around and kill. I wanted to find the men who had captured Toby, tortured POWs, lied about MIAs, and make them pay. Our government had abandoned too many of them and I felt guilty as hell. When I get this close, this involved, and I fail, my personal beast wants out of its cage and wants to kill. I had to swallow hard to keep down the bile in my throat. I was still sitting there, at the edge of exploding, when Little Pea came in.

He said two of the men had found a fresh grave near one of the caves. I asked him if they had opened it. He said yes. He looked uncomfortable. He said the body was that of an American.

Chapter
EIGHTEEN

As a fighter pilot, you rarely have to look at the bodies of friends killed in action. They simply disappear. They take direct hits and go up in a fireball of black and orange, or fly into the karst at night, or eject into a fire zone, or auger into the sea. Sometimes they limp back to base in a crippled fighter, leaking fuel, and blow up on the runway. Even then there's not much left, maybe a charred piece of bone and some teeth. This wasn't going to be like that.

I felt a sense of dread as I followed Little Pea to the burial site, I could barely walk. My legs were rubber and reluctant. He seemed to understand, shaking his head as if he wished there were something he could do to change this unhappy outcome of the mission. He said the American had been dead for three or four days. He said I might want to use a bandanna. He was right.

The men had removed the body from the grave. It lay on its

back on a poncho. They had examined it and said there were no
wounds indicating the man had been killed in combat. The body,
stripped of clothing, was emaciated except for the belly, which
had begun to bloat. There were deep leg-iron scars around the
ankles. The hands were broken-knuckled, thickly callused, ingrained with dirt. On his right forearm was a castle tattoo
superimposed over a pair of paratrooper wings and below that
the words *De Oppresso Liber*. The phrase meant "To Free the
Oppressed," and was the motto of the Special Forces. The castle
indicated Army Corps of Engineers. He was about Toby's height,
had the same color hair, but different color eyes.

"Did you find his dog tags?" I said.

"Oh, sir, no," Little Pea said softly. "I tell men dig deeper.
They rake earth with hands. Not find."

He asked me if the body belonged to Toh-bas. With a sense of
relief marred by what I had seen, I told him no.

Whoever the man was, he had served in the United States
Army as a Green Beret engineer, and, as the American presence
here, I wanted to bring him home. I told Sisani this when he and
Kam joined us at the grave. I said we had a body sack in our
gear, that we could fashion a litter out of a poncho and a couple
of bamboo poles. I said we had planned to carry Toby out that
way if Toby wasn't able to walk. I said I'd do my share of the
carrying, that yesterday had been hard for me but I'd gotten my
second wind. Sisani listened impassively, shook his head no
when I was through.

"You come to find live friend, not dead," he replied. "Bad
mens will be at this camp again, soon soon; we will better go
now fast; no slow."

"I won't leave him not buried," I said.

"You have left many of our people not buried," he said.
"You and your country. You have left us to die under yellow
rain. We go this mission, maybe no come back. We no go
because of you or your friend. We go because last chance to kill
those who kill us. Is better this than squat like beggars in refugee
camp. We are the People. We die fighting, not begging." He
held an AK-47 by the stock, jabbing the muzzle toward me while
he talked. His men had formed a semicircle around him, all
except the scouts, who were out, and Kam and Little Pea, who
stood next to me.

"Sir," Little Pea said quietly. "We must follow the orders of our number one. He has much disappointment that this camp was empty."

"I share his disappointment," I said. "But I won't leave this man unburied."

"Bury him," Sisani snapped. "Put him in earth by the river where ground is high. Bury him quick. We no wait long for you."

Kam was carrying a green field message book. I borrowed it from him and noted the description and condition of the body, sketched its features, drew a replica of the tattoo. Using my camouflage stick, I took partial palm and fingertips. Then Kam and Little Pea and I found a site away from the camp and buried the body there, wrapped in the poncho, under a bamboo cross. When we were through, Kam sprinkled river water on the mound and chanted *Arahan, Arahan* to help the American soldier continue the wheel of life. I was gritting my teeth. In the US there were officials who had referred to the man we were burying and the other MIAs as "acceptable losses."

"No," I thought, "not acceptable! Not to me, not to the people who loved him, not to his comrades."

Twenty minutes later, we moved out from the camp, heading southeast along the river toward a point where we would turn due west to skirt the mountain again. Our destination was Landing Zone Bravo, a jungle clearing ten kilometers away. We were scheduled to rendezvous there with Panapong and Terry at two o'clock. It was now seven-thirty. If we missed the first rendezvous, they would return in the chopper every two hours throughout the day—or until we made radio contact with them from the ground.

The men were sullen as they marched. They had been ginned up for a fight. They had been promised rewards by Campbell if they brought Toby out alive. Now they were returning empty-handed. I knew how they felt. I slogged along, paying little attention to the man in front of me. By the time we made our turn to skirt the mountain on the right, I had stopped worrying much about the Pathet Lao. It was here we walked into their ambush.

They opened fire from our left and front. Slugs cracked and zing-hummed through the air. An instant after the fusillade began I was flat on my belly, with no memory of having flopped down. I saw nothing around me but jungle. I steadied the AK and touched off three and four-round bursts in the direction the fire was coming from. Uptrail, I could hear the continuous roar of an M-60. AKs were going off all around me. During the brief intervals when there was no fire, I could hear cries and moans of men who'd been hit.

There were no visible targets to shoot at. I wanted silhouettes in front of me and all I had were trees. I kept firing the AK. The answering fire was close. One of the Hmongs who had been on my backtrail wriggled up next to me. He had an RPG and was using it. Between rounds, he tapped one of the grenades on my harness and made a throwing motion. I'd forgotten all about the grenades. I got them off fast, all four, crouching in the trail, lobbing them as accurately as I could in the direction of the ambush. As soon as the fourth was in the air, I hit the ground again. The Hmong smiled, motioning me back off the trail. I inched my way toward him, eating dirt. I had almost reached him when his head exploded in a rain of soft tissue and blood.

"Kam!" I shouted. *"Where are you?"*

He didn't answer. Neither did anyone else. I felt a clutch of panic, dug out another magazine for the AK, fumbled it in place. A claymore went off uptrail in a terrific roaring blast. The concussion flattened my ears. I heard more screams and shouts. White phosphorous smoke was drifting heavily up into the jungle canopy. The fire on each side of me became more intense, then seemed to advance in the direction of the ambush. Return fire began to slacken. Another grenade went off, this one so close fragments slashed through the foliage over my head.

I got up and began to move in the regular pattern, shooting and moving, shooting and moving, with no visible targets until a PL in black pajamas popped up thirty feet away. We squared off and fired at each other. I could see the muzzle flash of his gun, but all I could hear was the sound of my own. I hosed off a whole magazine before he finally dropped. There were Hmongs to my left and right. I saw them slip like shadows through the trees, firing shots, throwing grenades. Then suddenly it was quiet. No shooting or explosions. No bird song. Just a crashing silence broken only by the sound of my own hard breathing and gulping for air.

I loaded the AK again. My hands were so slippery it was hard to grip the magazine. I figured my pulse rate at 120.

"Kam!" I shouted.

The sound of my voice was still in the air when I saw him appear at the curve of the trail. *"Lōk!"* he said. "You come quick!" I hurried toward him. There was a streak of blood on his face. "Little Pea take four prisoners," he said. "They come from camp same as Toby. Sisani shoot them now."

We ran together up the trail. I heard the dull flat crack of a sidearm, once and then again. The Hmongs who had survived the ambush had reassembled. Sisani had lined the prisoners up in front of them. They were thin, barefooted men in faded black pajamas. Now two of them lay dead, sprawled on the ground. Sisani held the muzzle of an automatic pistol behind the ear of a third.

"*Don't do it*," I said. I had leveled my AK at him, safety off. I was so full of rage the barrel was trembling. He looked at me with contempt, the two of us standing ten feet apart.

"*I* team chief," he said. "Not you."

"You kill one more prisoner and I'll cut you in half," I said.

Kam stepped between us. He spoke to Sisani in Lao. Sisani snapped something in reply. They talked back and forth. Little Pea looked on anxiously, his shotgun draped in the crook of his arm. Finally, Kam turned to me.

"Be all right now," he said quietly. "Sisani has four dead from ambush, three more wounded, two okay, one very bad. Wants to make these PL pay. I tell him you need PL to talk, maybe they help you find Toh-bas. I tell him Toh-bas is like your brother. He say all right then, let these PL live, short time only."

Little Pea said something to the prisoners. One of them snarled something back. Sisani heard it and issued a series of rapid commands. In a flurry of activity the surviving members of the team fashioned a stretcher for the wounded man, tied a rope around the neck of the two PL, had them pick up the stretcher, and we were back on the march. We moved out so quickly the Hmongs didn't have time to bury their dead. I'd been luckier with mine. Kam was just ahead of me in line, point and compass men ahead of him.

"What the hell's going on?" I said.

"PL say they are advance party," he replied. "More PL follow behind. They hear fire fight, catch up soon."

I glanced behind me, saw Little Pea, then the stretcher, followed by three of the surviving Hmongs.

Sisani, our new tail-end Charlie, was out of sight. He had taken an M-60 with him.

Chapter
NINETEEN

We skirted the mountain. Kam carried the squad radio and maintained contact with our rear guard. We were still an hour from LZ Bravo, running late, when Sisani radioed that the PL were closing fast on our backtrail. I slung my AK, pulled the map out of my blouse. Little Pea was on the PRC-77 trying to reach Terry and the chopper. When he finally did, he handed me the receiver. I did my talking as we moved along.

"Miami Wing, this is Tiger, do you copy?"

Terry's reply sang in my ear.

"Loud and clear, Tiger. We're orbiting south of Bravo. Can you give us your ETA? Over."

"Negative," I said. "Disregard Bravo. We need an alternate. We're still six klicks west, and we've got a tail."

"Do you have new coordinates?"

On the map, I had located what looked like a reasonable evacuation site, close, clear, on top of a hill. I gave her the new numbers as indirectly as I could.

"Roger that," I said. "Take the Bravo cords in sequence. Add two to the second, four to the third, one to the fifth. All the rest same-same. You copy?"

"We have good copy, Tiger. The pilot wants to know if you got your package."

"Negative," I said.

She was silent for a moment. Up to this point her voice had been as brisk and concise as a tower controller's. Now, it became more gentle.

"We'll be waiting for you," she said. "Keep us current. We have one hour loiter fuel."

I rogered that. Kam went uptrail to give the new coordinates to our compass man. Hmongs were notoriously bad at reading maps. Our guy was good. The line of march had paused in sight of me and Little Pea during my conversation with Terry. The two PL had set the stretcher down. One of the Hmongs was

giving the wounded man a shot of morphine. I had just racked
the receiver when I heard Sisani open up behind us with his
M-60. The new attack was on.

"*Move out! Move out!*" I shouted, telling the Hmong to help
me carry the stretcher. Little Pea goosed the prisoners along with
his double-barreled gun. We crashed through the jungle like
elephants gone berserk. Kam stayed up front with our point and
compass men, breaking trail toward the new evac site. The M-60
continued to chatter behind us. There was answering fire, but
nothing reached us through the trees. I heard the roar of a
claymore going up. Then the M-60 again.

We thrashed our way to the base of the hill I had picked from
the map: eight of us in all, counting the prisoners and the
wounded man. The chopper was orbiting slightly south to avoid
giving the evac site away. We turned at the edge of the jungle,
perimeter guards out, reinforcing Sisani, firing at an enemy who
fired back relentlessly. We couldn't climb the hill without being
exposed, and we were trapped against it if we stayed where we
were. The slope was a thick green tangle of vegetation with one
passable clearing. Kam and Little Pea crouched next to me. They
had tied up the two prisoners, separately, arms and legs. They
said the man on the stretcher had died. Kam jerked his thumb
toward the clearing.

"We go out from there, *Lōk*," he said. "No way we can
reach top of hill."

I grabbed the Prick-77 phone. Little Pea cleared the wire. His
face was doll-like under his hat. "Oh, sir," he said. "We need
one big air strike now."

"Yeah, I know," I said. I punched the transmit button.
"Wing," I yelled, "this is Tiger, do you copy?"

"We copy," Terry replied, voice shaky. "Can you give us
your situation?"

"We're taking fire. We're pinned against the south base of our
alternate. We've got a clearing down here. You'll have to use
the ladders."

"The pilot wants to know if we'll take fire coming in."

"That's affirmative. Small arms—so far, nothing big."

Kam was talking on the squad radio. He said Sisani had lost
two men. He and the remaining man were retreating toward the
hill. They would hold off the PL as long as they could. We were
to call in the chopper and get out now. Kam was to be in charge
of the evacuation.

"He say leave gear for him in this place," Kam relayed.

"Weapons and ammunition. He say we take prisoners and go."

I didn't like Sisani much, but he was in trouble and I wanted to help him and I knew I wasn't worth shit on the ground. I grabbed the 77 phone and shouted angrily into it.

"Miami Wing, I'm popping smoke! Put your ladders in the middle of it. Move! Move! Move!" I pulled the pin on an M-18 green can and tossed it into the clearing. It went up like a blown stack. *"Got the green?"* I yelled into the phone. God I was pissed. If I could just do what I do best: get in here with an airplane loaded with nape, CBU, and 20-mike-mike. Good close-in stuff.

"Roger, we're coming down!" Terry yelled.

During the next few minutes the world was nothing but flash-bangs, whopping chopper blades, screams, crashes, ripping tears of full auto, and twin booms from Little Pea's 12-gauge.

Kam drew in the perimeter, shouting orders. The Hmong who had been our compass scooped up the smaller of the two bound prisoners, threw him over his shoulder, and headed for the clearing.

"*Lōk*, you take other man," Kam said. "You go quick now. We follow."

I junked my gear, threw the other PL over my shoulder, and started for the clearing. The man was limp as a rag doll, bone-thin, and I was scarcely aware of his weight; if I'd had to, under this impetus, I could have carried him to Bangkok.

Panapong was holding the chopper fifteen feet above the ground. I ran toward it, grabbing one of the wildly swinging ladders. I got one boot on a rung, then another. I pulled and stomped my way up. Terry was braced in the doorway to help me, hair pulled tight under her scarf, tiger suit whipped by the downrush. Bullets were crack-zinging in the air around us. Something tugged at my trouser cuff. On the opposing ladder, I saw our compass man stiffen and fall back, taking his prisoner with him.

Terry reached down from the chopper, grabbed my guy by the shirt, and wrenched him in. I bellied in after him. Kam was on my ladder now, coming up. Little Pea was on the other, shotgun slung over his shoulder. I lay on the chopper deck, fighting for air, watching, helpless, as they came. I knew they were scrambling, but they seemed to move in slow motion, as if they were on ladders that lengthened a foot with each foot they climbed. I shouted to them, voice hoarse, words lost in the rotor din. Then I saw Sisani.

He and our point man had backed into the clearing from the jungle and had reached the base of the ladders. Our point man emptied his AK, turned then, and started up. Sisani sat on the ground below us, the M-60 on his lap, firing steadily, waving us away with a hand he only pulled off the gun for an instant.

Little Pea was in the chopper now. Terry had helped him in. I reached through my door and helped Kam. "What about Sisani?" I shouted. Kam didn't even look at me. He jerked a thumb at Panapong, who nodded and pulled the chopper straight up then, tail-high and accelerating. Our point man was still on the ladder. Terry and the others helped him in. I lay flat on the deck, gut churning, eyes riveted on Sisani. He continued to fire steadily, smoke drifting around him. He never looked up. No one else appeared in the clearing.

My last image of him, one I knew I'd carry the rest of my life, was of his body being flung sideways like a wet red towel, from the close impact of an enemy grenade.

Chapter **TWENTY**

I lay sprawled flat on the chopper floor, cheek pressed to the cool metal, feeling the deck's vibration. For several minutes I couldn't move, not to help Kam and Little Pea pull in the ladders, not to help our point man tie the prisoner into a seat. In my head I kept hearing the rattle-bang of combat. Behind my eyes, the film clip of Sisani's death ran over and over. Vaguely, I heard Panapong radio the bad news to the Thai Internal Security people who were helping us—and to Delta One. Terry sat next to me on the deck, sensitive enough to know this was not a time to talk. We had failed to get Toby; we had lost ten men. There was nothing more to say.

We refueled at Muang Ngop, then flew on to the Royal Thai Air Force Base at Udorn. En route, Kam and Little Pea interrogated our prisoner. He had little to say at first, then a great deal, none of it comprehensible to me. He was still talking when we set down at a remote corner of the base. Campbell, with two

Thai military police, met us on the pad. He looked as if he hadn't slept in a while. His suit was wrinkled, eyes rimmed red. He was visibly shaken by what had happened, even more so than I had expected. I climbed out of the chopper, dog-tired and drained.

"The base commander has given us a room where we can debrief," he said. "Is Kam getting anything out of your prisoner?"

Kam popped his head out the chopper door.

"Need time," he said. "Man talks more than Little Pea."

"Turn him over to the security police when you're finished," Campbell said. "They'll tell you where we are."

The debriefing room was a classroom in a building near the Thai provost marshal's office. There were maps and a blackboard, chairs and a desk, grease pencils and a tape recorder. By the time we got there it was five-thirty in the afternoon. The room had an air conditioner and was blessedly cool. We still hadn't cleaned up. My face, streaked black, was crusty with dried sweat. There were bloodstains on my tiger suit, salt rings under the arms; a bullet had grazed one boot and put a hole in my pant leg. The Hmong who had been our point man on the final march looked worse. He had been wounded in the first ambush and was starting to feel feverish. Panapong arranged to have him taken to the base hospital. Then, with Panapong and Terry listening, I filled Campbell in on what had happened during the ill-fated mission.

"We'll run the description of the body you found through JCRC and DIA," he said when I had finished. "There's a good chance they'll be able to come up with a name. Was there any evidence at all that Toby had actually been in the camp?"

"No," I said. "Just the cage and a grass pallet and a couple of pots."

"That could have been where they kept the Green Beret before he died," Campbell said.

"But why would Sisani have referred to the Green Beret as 'Toh-bas'?" Terry asked. The answer was quick to come. A moment later, Kam entered the room, followed by Little Pea. Campbell, who had been taping our session, identified them for the record. Then Kam told us what he had learned.

According to the man we had captured, he and the other members of his camp had once belonged to a Pathet Lao battalion. This battalion had taken many prisoners during the war. Most of these were U.S. fliers and navigators. One was the sole survivor of an Air America crash in the Laotian jungle north of Khong Island. The men in the battalion always referred to this man as "Toh-bas."

"Good. Fine," Campbell said. "Go on."

Kam smiled. He was working hard on his English. Little Pea stood with his hands folded in front of him, moving from one foot to the other, as if it was all he could do to keep from breaking in. He still wore his floppy jungle hat, and his dark eyes danced very close under the brim.

After the war, Kam continued, the PL battalion fell on hard times. There were not enough supplies. Most of the American prisoners had died. The troops were going hungry. The officers in charge made many bad decisions. Eight months ago, forty men split from the battalion and fled into the jungle. As a chattel to trade eventually for weapons, they had taken Toh-bas with them.

They had trekked steadily north and west, establishing themselves finally in the Quebec Bravo camp, sustaining themselves by raids and forays on the farms and small villages along the Nam Yang River.

Two weeks ago, an American, emaciated and near death, stumbles into the camp. The PL deserters throw him into the small cage with Toh-bas. Toh-bas nurses him without success. Nine days later, he dies. That same morning a large, well-armed Pathet Lao patrol with two Chinese advisers surrounds the camp and takes it without firing a shot.

"How sure was he about the Chinese?" Campbell said.

"I ask him this many times," Kam replied. "I tell him advisers more likely Vietnamese. He say no, they are Chinese. He is very sure."

Campbell glanced at Panapong.

"What do you think, Sakoon?" he said.

Panapong shrugged. He looked good in his flight suit and scarf.

"The Chinese vie with the Vietnamese for influence in western Laos," he said. "It's quite possible."

The PL patrol says it's been searching for an American prisoner who, they say, escaped from a compound near one of the villages north of the camp. When they discover the American is dead, they become interested in Toh-bas. He talks to the Chinese through a Lao interpreter. He tells them who he is, that his father is an important man in the United States, that he owns a television station in the nation's capital, that he can influence opinion there. The Chinese radio this information to their headquarters. Word comes back they are to take Toh-bas to a village thirty kilometers southeast of the Quebec Bravo camp. A helicopter will meet them there and take Toh-bas to Vientiane.

Campbell, whose brows had risen steadily during this part of the narration, asked how sure the prisoner was about Vientiane.

"Very sure," Kam said. "He hears Chinese tell this to Toh-bas through interpreter."

"All right. Go on."

The PL patrol is short of food. They have been on the march for sixteen days. They rifle the Quebec Bravo camp, taking most of what is there. They leave pamphlets urging the camp population to join with them and the Chinese against the Viets. They say they already control everything northwest on a line from Pak Beng to Moung Sai.

Once they are gone, the deserters leave the camp to stage more raids along the river and replenish their own supplies. On their return, their advance party catches wind of the Miami team and set up an ambush. They hope to acquire many new weapons and much ammunition by doing this.

The rest, Kam concluded, we knew.

"Did the prisoner have any more details about Toby?" Campbell asked when Kam was finished.

"Oh yes, oh sir," Little Pea said, who simply couldn't contain himself any longer. "He say Toh-bas in fair-good shape. Learned himself to speak Lao. Taught men to speak English, same words many times. Not make sense."

"What words?" Campbell asked.

Little Pea looked at Kam. Kam nodded that he should go ahead. The tiny Hmong took a deep breath, then recited the words in his clear high voice.

"Will have no man in boat," he said, "who is not afraid of whales."

It wasn't a time to laugh, but Campbell laughed in spite of himself.

"The quotation's from Melville's *Moby-Dick*," he said. "It was one of Toby's identifier codes."

"Then he bloody well was in that camp," I said.

"No question."

"And now he's in Vientiane."

"Hold on," Campbell said. "We're a long way from having any solid proof of that."

"How much proof do we need?" Terry said. "The prisoner seems to know what he's talking about."

"There are parts of his story I don't like," Campbell said.

"Like what?" I said.

"Like the implication he makes that Toby, after four years in captivity, has decided to cooperate with the other side."

"If he's doing that, he's got his reasons," I said.

"Maybe. Maybe not. Four years is a long time. . . ."

"Come on, Campbell," I said. "You knew Toby. He was one of the best people CIA ever fielded over here."

"Then what in hell is he doing passing information about his father to the PL? Or to the Chinese, for that matter. Maybe it's too easy to say, but Toby was trained to go by the book: stick to his cover as a foreign service officer; reveal nothing that could be of value to the enemy."

There was a sudden tension in the room. I felt the blood pounding in my neck. I didn't like what Campbell was saying. He was usually tough, but he was also usually fair. I didn't think he was being fair to Toby. I thought he was jumping to conclusions, and I told him so. He was about to reply when there was a knock on the door. Panapong opened it. In the corridor, I could see a young Thai in civilian clothes. He spoke quietly to Panapong. Panapong listened, said a few words back, then closed the door again.

"A message has come from my Uncle Adune," he said. "He wishes for us to assemble at a villa he owns on the outskirts of the city. He has information regarding Major General Hua."

Panapong smiled his box-office smile.

He said his uncle also had information regarding an American who had recently been brought to Vientiane and was being held prisoner there.

Chapter
TWENTY-ONE

Terry and I cleaned up in a private suite at the BOQ, near the Officers' Club. The water in the shower was hot. When it was my turn, I stood under it so long, Terry finally had to reach in and pull me out. Our luggage had been sent up from Miami

Base. I lathered up and shaved, brushed my teeth, brushed them again, got into a pair of slacks and a safari shirt.

"God, do you look better," she said.

"You look pretty nice yourself," I said. She had on the white jumpsuit again, the earrings and bracelets. Her hair was blow-dried and clean.

"It's like stepping out of one world into another," she said. "What happened today doesn't just seem a long time ago; it seems more as if it didn't happen at all."

"It happened," I said.

"But it's schizo, isn't it?" she said. "You can't really think about it, because if you do start thinking about it, dwelling on it, I mean . . ."

"No," I said. "You don't do that. The people who do that wind up with their circuits burned out—or dead if they take it with them when they go into combat again. When I ran the Wolf Fac's I got so I could pick those people out. You can see it in their eyes. It's like a mote that's gotten between them and the job they're supposed to do."

"I was doing all right until Sakoon said he saw gunsmoke coming up through the canopy; and then you radioed you were under fire. God, did I get shaky then."

I told her she'd done fine. I told her I'd had some shaky moments of my own. She asked me why Sisani hadn't tried to get away. She said the ladders had still been down, that no one else had been in the clearing. I said my guess was that the clearing was about to be overrun. I said Sisani must have known if he laid off his M-60, the chopper would have come under close enough fire to bring it down. I said Kam must have known that too.

"Sisani sacrificed himself for us?" Terry said.

"Yes."

"Was there more to it than that?"

"He wanted to die fighting his enemies."

We talked about this, and some of the other things that had happened since my arrival in Singapore two weeks ago. While we talked, I packed up my kit. She watched me.

"I'll bet you wish you'd never left your farm," she said.

"Things get slow there in the fall," I said. "I needed something to do."

She looked at me skeptically.

"Besides," I said. "If I hadn't left the farm, I wouldn't have met you."

"Oh balls," she said.

We ate supper at the Officers' Club. Shortly after eight o'clock, Panapong drove us to his uncle's villa, in a blue passenger van. The van was unmarked and had civilian plates. Campbell sat in front, Terry and I climbed into the middle, Kam and Little Pea sat in back. They had cleaned up too, had exchanged their tiger suits for slacks and short-sleeved shirts. They seemed pleased that Adune's invitation had specifically included them.

Udorn is a city in northeast Thailand of about thirty thousand people, thirty miles south of the Mekong River. The Thais spell it Udon; Americans tend to add the *r*. The area around the city is flat. We drove in light traffic past the Chaiporn Hotel—where I had once stayed with Jillion—turned off Kahpoor Road finally, through the iron gates of a private drive. The drive was of white crushed stone and wound for nearly a mile through an irrigated stand of rubber trees. Just before we reached the villa, we went through a second gate, this one guarded by two armed men in safari suits. The men recognized Panapong and waved us on. We drove past a four-stall garage, parked at the end of a circular drive.

The villa was a graceful wood-frame structure, two stories high, built around a large central courtyard. Cluster lamps in tinted globes bathed its contours in soft, almost mystical light. The roofs were rounded, with a texture like cork. The exterior walls, ventilated with many recessed windows, had the lustrous sheen of polished teak. There was a goldfish pond in the courtyard, with a statue of Buddha at one end, sitting in meditation under a bo tree.

"When my uncle was a young man," Panapong said, "he took impermanent monastic vows. He is deeply religious."

"This place is beautiful," Terry said. Her eyes shone as she took it in. Panapong looked pleased.

"It is one of many owned by my uncle," he said. "But also one of his favorites. He is waiting for us in the second living room. We can reach it most easily by going through here."

We followed him, the five of us, across the courtyard, through an open door, down a corridor with teak walls. The second living room was at the end of the corridor. It was hung with tapestries depicting the enlightenment of the Gautama. Below the tapestries were rows of glass-covered book shelves. Flickering candles atop ornate stands provided subdued light. There was a partner's desk with a high-intensity lamp at one corner. Leather club chairs and semicircular sofas had been arranged in a conversational grouping out from the desk. The room was cool, and smelled pleasantly of incense.

Adune had not changed in the three years since I had seen him: a man in his seventies who looked much younger, shaven skull and brows, contemplative face, light-gray vested suit. He knew all of us except Terry and Little Pea who "wyed" very deeply when introduced by Panapong. The "wye" is an Asian greeting made by making a steeple of the fingers and bowing the head. The more elevated in status one greets, the higher the steeple, the lower the head. Adune casually returned it. He then turned to Terry saying he knew of her by reputation.

"It is my pleasure to welcome you to this house," he said in his serene, cultivated voice. "My nephew has spoken of you with admiration."

Terry fielded the compliment nicely, glancing at Panapong, who flashed his smile. We took our seats. Adune opened the discussion. He expressed deep regret over the failure of the mission. He said his nephew had related to him the story told by the man we had captured. He said judging by that and by what he had learned from his own sources in Vientiane, Toby was now a prisoner in that city, that he was being held there by Major General Hua.

Campbell interrupted to ask Adune if he knew what Hua's motives might be, if in fact he was holding Toby. Adune said sadly he did not. He said on the positive side if we were prepared to act quickly he thought there was a chance, albeit a risky one, that we might still be able to get Toby out of Laos. At this I moved up on my seat.

"What are the details?" I said.

Adune smiled.

"Are you familiar with the Triumphal Arch in the center of Vientiane?" he asked.

"Sure," I said. "We used to call it 'the vertical runway.' Old King Vatthana built it with the cement we gave him to enlarge the air strip at Wattay. He said his soothsayer told him the Arch was necessary to protect the king's life on earth. It's on Lane Xang Avenue at the traffic circle, looks like an Asian version of the Arc de Triomphe."

"That's correct," Adune replied. "Six months ago, Major General Hua negotiated with the ruling Pathet Lao to use the Arch. He paid them a large sum for the privilege. Since then, he's been having the Arch renovated, cleaning the exterior walls, converting the old bonze cells on top into private offices for him and his officers. The structure is the most conspicuous in the city. By possessing it, Hua has impressed many of the superstitious that the People's Republic of China holds the way to the future."

"Where's he keeping Toby?" I said.

"In one of the cells at the top of the Arch."

"You said you thought we could grab him. How do we do it?"

"It will be difficult. Vientiane is overrun with Pathet Lao. They are of the Lao Teung tribe and are detested by the populace of the city. They carry rifles and fire at the slightest provocation. They have machine-gunned many innocent refugees who have tried to escape to Thailand by swimming across the river. They watch the ferry from Nong Khai, and all small boat traffic—"

"Oh sir, excuse me, sir," Little Pea broke in. "I know one captain from Nong Khai who can pass the river close to either shore. He has the old Tom Dooley boat, with many midgets in a musical band. He bribes the checkpoint guards, takes people up and down for parties. Bad mens not shoot at him. He is called Captain Kong, and was one of Shit Hot's friends."

Adune touched the tips of his fingers together and closed his eyes. Panapong broke out laughing. Little Pea glanced nervously back and forth between the two men, as if wondering from which to take his cue. Kam, Terry and I, began laughing with Panapong. It was one of those nice moments, the laughter getting louder as it went. Soon Adune himself joined in. When he did, Little Pea looked very relieved.

"It's not such a bad idea, Little Pea," Panapong finally managed to say. "But this captain you speak of has become unreliable. He drinks too much, and has trouble controlling his midgets. He runs the boat into sandbars. The only people in Thailand who will go out on the party boat now are young men from the academies who wager on their chances of getting back."

"Sir, this is true," Little Pea said. "I only thought . . ."

"Your captain has strayed from the eightfold path," Adune said.

"And we have strayed from the purpose of our meeting," Panapong said. "The safest way to make an illicit crossing of the Mekong is to use diving equipment and go underwater at night."

"Has anyone tried it?" I asked.

"Yes. Last year a journalist crossed the river in that way to bring his Lao lady friend out of Vientiane into Thailand."

"Did they make it?"

"Indeed they did, with the help of some special equipment."

"Who provided the gear?"

"A loyal friend of this family," Adune said. "He will arrive here in the morning."

Chapter
TWENTY-TWO

There was a portfolio of maps and photographs on the desk in the corner of the room. Panapong switched on the high-intensity lamp and began to pull out the ones we would need. Adune said we were all welcome to spend the night, should we wish to do so. He said his servant, a man named Pushpinder, would take care of our needs. He excused himself and went off to bed. The rest of us gathered around the desk.

For the next three hours, we brainstormed a plan. In rough outline it was simple enough. Two divers in scuba gear would cross the Mekong two nights hence, surfacing at a prearranged site. There they would rendezvous with certain people who lived in Vientiane and were trusted by Adune. These people would transport them to the Arch, where, under cover of darkness, they would climb to the top of the monument by means of the scaffolding that had been erected for the renovation of the exterior walls. Once the team reached the top, they would subdue any guards, locate Toby, reverse their tracks, and bring him back across the river. Kam and I volunteered to make the actual raid. Terry would handle the radio on this side. Panapong and Little Pea would take care of contingencies. The more we brainstormed the idea, the more enthusiastic we got. All of us, that is, except Campbell.

"No," he said finally. "I don't like it."

"Much, of course, remains to be done," Panapong replied. "Matt and Kam will have to be dive-trained. They will have to be provided with weapons. Our people in Vientiane will have to be contacted—"

"We dotted every *i* and crossed every *t* on the Quebec Bravo raid," Campbell said. "And we still got our tails burned. I'm already catching flak from Langley and DIA. Some good people went to the well for us there and they want to know why we didn't produce."

"We didn't produce because, like Son Tay, by the time we got to the camp, Toby was gone," I said.

"All right. What if he's gone when you get to the Arch? Do we know how long Hua plans to hold him there? Do we have any guarantee he'll be in his cell when you and Kam arrive—assuming, that is, that everything goes well? Do we even know for a hard fact that Toby's there right now?"

"He was brought to the Arch two days ago," Panapong said. "My uncle's people have kept the monument under surveillance since that time. If he is taken away, they will notify us at once."

"Then why this rush on the mission?" Campbell said.

"Well, of course," Panapong replied, "he could be taken away any time."

We argued it back and forth. Campbell wouldn't budge. He said he wanted more information, more time; he said one fiasco was enough, he wanted no part of another. We walked out together, through the courtyard to the van where Little Pea waited to drive him back to town.

"I think the plan's a good one," I said.

He didn't respond to that. He held his hands at arm's length in front of him, fingers extended. They were trembling. Badly.

"I'm burned out on this thing," he said. "You'll be better off without me."

"No one who knows you would believe that."

"How well do you know me, Matt?" he said. "How well does anybody know anybody? I thought I knew Midge, but I was wrong. Maybe I'm getting old. Maybe there are ten good Hmongs dead tonight because I'm getting old."

"That's nonsense," I said. "You and Midge will put things back together, and be the better for it. The Quebec Bravo raid was well planned. We ran out of luck is all. Now we've got another chance. Panapong's one sharp cookie. So's Adune. We've got one hell of a good team assembled here. Nobody's going off half cocked."

"I've told you what I think," he said. "You'll have to deal me out."

He got into the van, indicated to Little Pea he was ready to leave. I asked him what his plans were once he got to town. He looked at me through red-rimmed eyes under a dark tangle of brow.

"I'm going to do what you did when Jillion got married," he said. "I'm going to buy myself some whiskey and get drunk."

By the time I got back to the second living room, Kam had gone off with Adune's man Pushpinder to turn in for the night. Terry and Sakoon were still sitting at the desk. A portable bar had been wheeled into the room. They were drinking vodka and tonic. I made myself a stiff scotch rocks. There were cigarettes in a small silver hamper on the bar. I asked Sakoon if it was all right to smoke. He said fine, he would join me. The two of us lit up. Terry was studying one of the larger maps. It included Laos and Thailand. She was tracing a line, with her finger, north along the Mekong. Her bracelets shone in the tight circle of light from the lamp.

"Where's Pak Beng?" she asked.

"Northwest of the Quebec Bravo camp," Sakoon replied. "Right on the Mekong, sixteen miles north of our border. Why do you ask?"

She found the place and studied it for a moment.

"Gray mentioned it in his log," she said. "He wrote 'Check Pak Beng.' It doesn't look all that big. Is it important?"

"Not really," Sakoon replied. "It's a small village. We worried about it some during the war. The Chinese were building a road network then in northern Laos." He showed us on the map. "They started in the early '60s. They came south from Yunnan Province to Muong Sai, here, then east toward Dien Bien Phu and southwest toward Pak Beng. They intended, by building the road, to strengthen their influence with the Pathet Lao who controlled the northern provinces, and to help supply communist guerrillas in northeast Thailand."

"I flew over that road once," I said. "It looked to me like a strategic nightmare for you."

"In those years it was," Sakoon replied. "We had good intelligence of a planned invasion. But since the United States has withdrawn from Southeast Asia, our own relations with the Red Chinese have necessarily improved. We keep an eye on the road, but it is abandoned now, and overgrown with brush."

"The Pathet Lao who took Toby from the Quebec Bravo camp said the Chinese controlled everything northwest on a line from Pak Beng to Muong Sai," I said. "That would include the road."

"It's a common point of reference," Sakoon replied.

"There's got to be more to it than that," Terry said. "Look. Most of what Gray wrote in his log on those three days had to do with the Quebec Bravo area. He was focused on that because he thought Toby might be there. But let's suppose on those same three days he also overflew Pak Beng—either going to or from Quebec Bravo, or both. It's not impossible, is it?"

"Not at all," Sakoon said. "Your brother's journal entries seem deliberately vague regarding takeoff and landing points. His flights were, after all, surreptitious."

"All right," Terry said. "Let's put Gray over Pak Beng at least once on each of those three days. The notation he made was on the last day: 'Check Pak Beng.' Something must have caught his eye. We have no idea what it was. All we know is he didn't get back to it. He returned to Singapore. . . ."

"I see what you're getting at," I said. "According to what the prisoner said, we've got a pretty direct link between Hua's people and the Pak Beng area."

"Exactly. And it was Hua's people who killed Gray."

"But for what possible motive?" Sakoon asked.

"Because he saw something they didn't want him to see—or at least they thought he did."

"But what? An invasion force? That would be impossible. They would have to field an expedition of half a million troops. The supply lines would stretch all the way to Yunnan Province. There would be no way to keep such maneuvers a secret from our intelligence people. And as I have said, our relations with China are now quite cordial."

Terry sighed.

"I'm so tired my eyes are blurring," she said. "I want to think straight, but I can't."

"Roger that," I said. "Let's put it away until tomorrow."

Sakoon, who seemed as sharp as ever, showed us to our rooms on the second floor of one wing of the villa. The rooms faced each other across a spacious hall. Pushpinder had seen to it our luggage was in place and beds turned down. Sakoon bade us a breezy goodnight and walked jauntily away. Terry watched him go.

"The old expression was 'A penny for your thoughts,' " I said.

"Wouldn't get you much these days, would it?" she said.

"I might go as high as two bits."

"You Yanks," she said.

We kissed each other, stifling yawns, then disappeared behind our separate doors. I got out of my clothes and into the shower. Then I got out of the shower and into bed. I slept hard, waking only to involuntary twitches and jerks, then going right out again. No dreams of combat, just a lot of red and a lot of bangs.

Some time in the early morning, with a lemony first light showing through the recessed windows of the room, and a chatter of bird song outside, Terry came in, closing the door softly behind her. She had on a very sheer something-or-other, short at the sleeve and hip.

"You awake?" she whispered.

"Since the birds started," I said.

"Want company?"

"Depends a lot on who," I said.

"Let me give you a clue," she said, sliding under the sheet. "It isn't Captain Kong."

Chapter
TWENTY-THREE

The scuba gear arrived at ten o'clock that morning. It arrived in a Land Rover driven by Rajah Banerjee. Banerjee backed the Land Rover into the courtyard and offloaded the gear next to the goldfish pond. Kam and I helped. So did Sakoon, who had made the introductions.

"Rajah is a masterful engineer," he said. "You're in excellent hands."

Adune had left the villa in a chauffeur-driven limousine before Terry and I had gotten down for breakfast—off, Sakoon explained, to attend to pressing business elsewhere. Little Pea had spent the night at the air base in Udorn. He was waiting there now for Sakoon to drive in and pick him up. The two of them would confirm timetables and pickup points via coded radio with Adune's people in Vientiane, and would fill our shopping list for weapons, clothing, and other essential items. They would return to the villa the next afternoon. Barring hitches, the new mission would launch from a fisherman's shack owned by Banerjee on the river's edge below Vientiane at eleven-thirty p.m. the next night. Campbell, meanwhile, had disappeared.

"When they got into town, he took over driving the van," Sakoon explained. "He dropped Little Pea at the base. Little Pea wanted to ask him where he planned to go at such a late hour, but didn't quite have the nerve. The van should be easy enough to trace. I can put someone on it, if you like."

"Thanks," I said. "Maybe what Campbell needs is to be left alone for a while. He's taking the failure of the Quebec Bravo raid pretty hard."

"This is understandable," Sakoon replied. "He worked tire-lessly in preparation for many months. There were obstacles that appeared insurmountable. He always refused to yield."

Terry and I walked Sakoon to the garage, where his personal car was parked in one of the four stalls. The car was a Jaguar roadster, white with red leather upholstery. The top was down. I could smell the leather in the heat of the morning as he climbed in and started the engine. The exhaust sounded like the exhaust of an expensive inboard boat.

"Gray used to have one of these," Terry said, caressing the boot. "It was when I was young. He'd take me for rides around Sydney, and I'd feel very swank."

"Come with me," Sakoon offered. "We can fit Little Pea in the trunk when the time comes."

"Along with the rifles and radios," Terry said. "Thanks, but I'll stay here. If it's all right, I'd like to go through some of the books and periodicals in the room where we did our planning last night; I'd like to see if I can find anything about Pak Beng or that Chinese road you told us about."

"Consider the room yours," Sakoon said. "Much of what's there is in English. If you need something translated, ask Pushpinder. He's fluent in many languages."

The handsome pilot switched on the car radio and dialed in some traveling music. There was a speaker in each door; the sound was terrific. *"Au 'voir,"* he said, and sped away.

Terry went off to her self-imposed appointment in the second living room. I rejoined Kam and Rajah Banerjee by the goldfish pond. Banerjee was a stocky, florid-faced man in his mid-fifties, with a drill sergeant's mustache, close-set eyes, and an aggres-sive, sun-inflamed nose. He wore khaki Bermuda shorts and shirt, Argyle knee socks, canvas shoes, and a white safari hat.

The waxed points of his mustache leaped and twirled as he talked.

"Let's have it again, then, Colonel," he said. "You're the diver?"

"I did some once off the coast of Libya with Simon Coddrington, near Tripoli," I said. "Just for recreation. And that was a long time ago."

"It'll come back," he said. "Like riding a bike. Strip to the briefs now, boys. Let's get on with it."

The dive tanks, or aqualungs as Banerjee called them, were single-cylinder rigs with carrying harnesses and pressure gauges. Each aluminum cylinder held eighty cubic feet of compressed air. The regulator unit consisted of a single mouthpiece attached to a flexible hose. We would use standard face masks, covering eyes and nose, full-shoe fins, buoyancy vests, and weight belts with quick-release buckles.

The goldfish pond was about eight feet deep, ten feet wide, and thirty feet long. We entered the pond opposite the end where the sculpted Buddha sat under his bo tree. The water was warm. There were lily pads on the surface, and algae along the sides. The fish swam away from us as we went in.

Kam readily understood the physics of breathing the compressed air, through the regulator mouthpiece, from the tank strapped to his back. At first, he had trouble clearing his mask underwater; he surfaced twice, coughing and spitting, before getting it right. After an hour, we could both put on our equipment underwater without getting the straps tangled. Banerjee worked us hard. No break for lunch. Into the pond, out of the pond: practice with the weight belts, hand signals, buddy-breathing off a single regulator, forward rolls, backward rolls, locating and retrieving coins tossed by Banerjee into the murkier recesses of the pond.

"All right, boys," he said finally. "Let me show you the rest of it."

He had designed two pieces of equipment for the journalist who had crossed the Mekong to retrieve his lady friend from Laos. One was a six-foot aluminum canister, torpedo-shaped, and painted black. The canister was watertight, Banerjee explained, and had its own air and buoyancy-control systems. The other was an aerodynamically shaped fiberglass flutter board with a hooded compass, depth gauge, carpenter's level, and clock—all with illuminated dials. A snaplink was fixed through an eyelet at the center of the trailing edge.

"You'll be swimming underwater at night, cross-current," Banerjee said. "Instruments for navigation; one diver on each side of the board; divers kicking in tandem. Line attaches from board to canister. You put your weapons in going over, friend in coming back."

Kam looked for a while at the gear, and then at the pond.

"How dark is water in river at night?" he said.

Banerjee's mustache twitched nervously.

"Dark as a buffalo's arse," he said.

At six o'clock, Pushpinder wheeled the bar cart out by the pond and set up some chairs. He wore white ducks and a Nehru jacket, had an aristocratic bearing, iron-gray hair, skin the color of tea. Kam and I had been in the water so long we looked like a couple of prunes. Pushpinder brought robes for us, and big soft towels with lots of nap.

"Best time of day, here at last," Terry said. She had come out to join us.

"How did it go?" I said.

"I found out everything there is to know about Laos except why," she said.

"Nothing on the road?"

"Not a scrap. At least not yet. I'm afraid I've left the room in a mess."

"Sakoon said it was yours. What would you like to drink?"

"Vodka tonic."

"Cigarette too?"

"Certainly not," she said. "What a corrupting influence you are."

"Old fighter pilot," I said. "Can't help it."

"Keep smoking those blasted things and you'll wind up with a lung strapped to your back twenty-four hours a day," Banerjee said.

"Want one?" I said.

"Thenk you," he said. "Don't mind if I do."

We drank for a while and then we ate. There was chicken satay, Siam noodles, curried beef, and a fine abalone in oyster sauce. We ate by the pond, Pushpinder wheeling the carts on and off. By the time we had finished, the wind chimes in the courtyard were sounding under the lilt of an evening breeze.

"Now," said Banerjee, who had consumed as much food and drink as the rest of us combined. "Your contact in Vientiane will be Pamela Banks. She's the widow of Monte Banks, the

Englishman who ran the old Purple Porpoise tavern. Pamela is Chinese—Monte gave her the name. She walks a delicate line between the Pathet Lao who occupy the city, their Vietnamese advisers, and the indigenous Laotians. She's resourceful and trustworty. Her husband was a mystic, clever with cards, good at telling fortunes. Did you happen to know him, Colonel?''

"Yes," I said. "I liked him. He kept a big Papa-san chair in the bar, reserved for the return of Earthquake McGoon. I thought that showed a lot of class." McGoon was the pseudonym of an outsized U.S. pilot who was shot down in a C-119 over Dien Bien Phu, helping the French in the mid '50s.

"And has McGoon returned?" Terry wanted to know.

"Not yet," I said. "But no one's giving up."

We chatted away. I asked Banerjee what his connection was to Adune. He said they had fought together with Wingate's Raiders against the Japanese in the Burma campaign of '43. Adune had been one of Wingate's special advisers.

"Beautiful man," Banerjee said. "Preached the Sermon of the Turning of the Wheel of the Law, and knocked off the Nips like flies. He's a realist first, Buddhist second—though he'd have me shot for saying it."

Pushpinder set up a couple of torches on portable standards near the pond. The torches smelled of citronella and kept the mosquitoes off. Banerjee, into the brandy now, began telling stories from the Wingate years. Terry listened for a while, then tuned to some private frequency of her own. I put my hand over hers, sipped my drink. Kam, who had begun to look sleepy, excused himself quietly after a while and started to walk away.

"Trak!" Banerjee called after him. "Where in blazes are you going?" He was the only person I had ever heard call Kam by that end of his name.

"Must relieve self," Kam said very politely. "Then go to bed."

"No, no," Banerjee said, getting up. "No, no. You boys have more to do. You've got to practice using the board in the dark. Pushpinder! Get rid of these torches! No, no," he said. "We're on a time schedule here. You can pee in the bloody pond."

It was late when I finally padded down the corridor to my room. A slice of light showed under Terry's door. I knocked softly, telling her it was me. She said to come in. I was barefooted, wearing the robe Pushpinder had provided. She was still dressed, sitting in a chair by the window.

"Long day," I said.

"Is everything going to be all right?"

"Yes. I think so. How are things with you?"

"I went back to my reading. I found an article that described the gassing of the Hmongs. There were photographs. They were hideous."

I pulled up a chair and sat next to her. A tear had formed at the corner of her eye. She brushed it away impatiently.

"The gas usually doesn't kill them right off," she said. "They pass blood, lose their ability to hold food, waste away. Men, women, children. Sometimes it takes weeks. When the Pathet Lao find them that way, they say they have medicine that will help. Then they inject the Hmongs with poison to finish the job."

I was silent. She tried to smile.

"Your hands are wrinkly," she said.

"Too much time in the pond."

"I wanted to be one of the ones who would cross the river," she said. "I would have said so if I hadn't been afraid. I don't like myself very much for being afraid."

"I was ready to hit the ceiling if you volunteered," I said.

"No place for a woman?"

"That's right."

"You said I did fine in the chopper."

"That's right too, but I'd have been a lot happier if you hadn't been there."

"You know you're awfully old-fashioned?" she said.

"Guilty as charged."

"Do you think you and Kam will be able to get Toby out?"

"Yes."

"Even after what happened yesterday?"

"The wrong numbers came up yesterday. We'll do better this time."

"I don't see how you can be so optimistic."

"Remember," I said, "I'm the guy whose son was in a coma for almost two years. The doctors told me he'd never come out. Now he's in an apartment in Paris, clumping around on his crutches, relearning French."

"Brian," she said.

"Right."

"I'd like to meet him some day."

"I'd like that too."

"Sakoon asked me last night what the nature of our relationship was," she said. "Yours and mine, that is."

"Naughty boy, that Sakoon."

"I told him I really wasn't sure."

"Well, let's see," I said. "We started off by liking each other, I think, and having fun."

"And then a bomb went off in the plane."

"Yes."

She clenched her fist slowly until the knuckles were white.

"I want those bastards to pay who killed Graham," she said. "I want them to pay with their lives for what they did. It won't be enough to get Toby back—though I hope to God you do. It won't be enough for me until Hua and his men are obliterated from the face of the earth."

"They keep coming, Terry," I said. "Men like Hua. They're always there."

"I never thought I'd hear myself say this," she said, "but if Hua were here right now in this room and I had that gun Sakoon made me wear, I'd kill him without a thought."

I covered her hand with mine. She sat very erect in her chair.

"I understand Sisani now," she said. "Having read the article about the Hmongs. I understand who he was and why he did what he did. He was full of rage. So am I."

Chapter
TWENTY-FOUR

Kam and I spent the next morning with Rajah Banerjee, working out with the scuba gear twenty miles southeast of Udorn at Han Kumphawapi Lake. This time we wore the black body stockings, and wet-suit boots we would use during the actual raid. The lake water was as silty as the Mekong, visibility poor even under full sun. We practiced navigating via the instruments on the flutter board, weighted the canister and towed it between designated points.

"Miss fish in pond," Kam said when the session was over.

"There when I look out through glass, they look in. Here, not see anything but mud."

"You won't see that much in the Mekong at night," Banerjee reminded us. Dark as a buffalo's arse.

We grabbed a quick lunch in the city, then Banerjee dropped us at the villa, where I caught up with Terry again in the second living room. She was sitting on the floor, in green slacks and matching blouse, surrounded by piles of books and periodicals. She was so engrossed in her reading I don't think she heard me come in.

"Banerjee's authorized a nap," I said. "You look as if you could stand one too."

"I found it," she said, without looking up.

"Found what?"

"What Gray was trying to tell us. Here, have a look."

She handed me a bound volume of the *Far Eastern Economic Review,* covering the year 1970. She had inserted a marker at page 32 of the November 14 issue. The title of the article, authored by Kim Woodward, was, "At Thailand's Back Door." The blurb read:

> "Bangkok officials are increasingly concerned about
> a Chinese-built road edging its way across northern
> Laos in the direction of Thailand's troubled north-
> east border areas."

"I don't get it," I said. "Sakoon already told us about the road. The story might have been news in 1970, but that was eight years ago."

"Go on," Terry said. "Read the first paragraph."

I did, reading aloud. " *'How close can they come?'* Thailand's government officials are asking themselves this question about continuing Chinese construction work on the Muong Sai–Pak Beng road spur. . . ."

I stopped reading, the last phrase triggering an image of Graham Melbourne's death, the *chuff-chuff* of his desperate laughter alive again in my ears, his whispered words: *It's the spur. It's something about the spur.*

"Simple, wasn't it?" Terry said.

"Another piece in the puzzle," I said. "Nice going."

"We still don't have the why."

"No," I said. "But we're going to get it."

"From Hua?"

"I don't think so," I said. "I think we're going to get it from Toby Porter."

I tried to nap, but couldn't sleep. I was ginned up now and ready to go. In recent years I'd gotten particular about how far and for whom and what I was willing to risk my life. For years I'd done it out of a sense of patriotism and duty, helping carry out official policy. During my last days in Phnom Penh, after Diana's death and before the city fell, I wasn't fighting for the politicians anymore, but for the smaller nation of the people I knew: Kam and the good Khmers, Jillion Leggett, Graham Melbourne, Toby Porter, and the rest. Since then on two occasions I had risked my life for money when I had needed the money to help my son. Otherwise, I was a retired fighter pilot who ran a small horse farm in Virginia with the help of an ex-jockey and trainer named Dawson Jones.

So why was I here at a villa in Thailand, ready to risk my life again? I wanted the answer to be clear before night fell and Kam and I slipped into the river. I wanted to know that what we were doing made sense and was worthwhile. There was no money involved. There was no patriotism, except perhaps of an old kind that said you didn't turn your back on men who had fought for you, who had been declared missing in action and were still unaccounted for.

What there was was Toby Porter. He had been the answer when I had joined the Quebec Bravo raid, and I knew he was the answer now. I had seen the cage where they had kept him prisoner. I had sat down and leaned my back against it and wondered if I could have endured what he must have endured, if I could have disciplined myself to stand the physical privations and emotional abuse, to learn the language of my captors and teach them fragments of my own, to sustain a belief—*truly sustain it*—that my countrymen would never rest until they found me, and freed me, and brought me home.

Had Toby finally broken under the stress of four long years in captivity? Had he cut some kind of deal with Hua, or tried to? Was he really a prisoner now in a bonze cell on top of the Arch? Or was he using his incredibly high IQ and blue-ribbon pedigree to help Hua and the Pathet Lao? Campbell had raised the possibility.

No, I thought. I don't buy it.

I had seen our POWs who had been released by the North Vietnamese in '73, how they had survived, some of them for as long as eight years, how in the face of torture and deprivation they had held on to their pride and self-esteem. Toby would be like that. I had seen him under fire, had seen how he had taken over the day Diana had been killed. He was tough and professional. He wasn't one of the ropers and dopers who cut deals with the other side. He was one of us, and he needed and deserved our help. If I'd thought otherwise, I'd have packed up my kit and gone home.

Sakoon and Little Pea returned to the villa at four-thirty p.m. Kam and I met them out by the garage. Their shopping trip had been a success. Little Pea was very excited. He had on a clean tiger suit and floppy jungle hat. There were two leather carrying cases in the trunk of the Jaguar, each about the size of a case designed to carry a slide trombone. Little Pea opened one of them up. There, nestled in molded Styrofoam, was the lightest, most lethal-looking automatic rifle I had ever seen. Little Pea identified it as the AR-180. Sakoon said he had procured these two weapons through his connections in ISOC, the Thai Internal Security Operations Command. On each stock was a "happy face" decal, with the initials DH.

"Your father-in-law helped ISOC acquire the AR-180," he said. "By lending these to us, they have acknowledged their indebtedness. Are you familiar with the piece?"

"No," I said.

"Then come with me," he said.

We followed him through the rubber trees to a place where the red earth had been quarried to make the laterite brick used to surface the villa's courtyard. Along the rim of the excavation, mature palms rose fifty and sixty feet against a backdrop of clear sky and westering sun. The AR-180, Sakoon explained, fired .22 caliber long rifle bullets at a rate of 36 rounds per second from a 177-round magazine. The gun came with laser sights, a silencer, and several drums of match-grade subsonic ammunition.

Little Pea assembled the weapon, settled the butt against his shoulder, aimed up toward the rim of the excavation. When Sakoon gave the command, the tiny Hmong ticked off a two-second burst that sawed a palm tree in half. The sound of the rifle was no more than that of a sewing machine. The sound of the palm tree falling was loud.

Kam smiled happily.

"Wait long time for weapon like this," he said. "Not make noise." With Sakoon's permission, he borrowed the rifle from

Little Pea. He switched on the laser sight, settled the red target dot on a cinder block at the far end of the quarry, ticked off another short burst. The cinder block disintegrated in a puff of dust, the rifle making its soft tearing noise.

Kam went through the rest of that magazine; I went through another. By the end of a half hour we could both have qualified as experts in handling the AR-180, a beautifully engineered, very specialized piece.

"Oh sir," Little Pea said. "Now I wish it was I instead of this Khmer who will cross the river with you to get Toh-bas; for with this weapon you will be able to kill many bad mens."

"We're not going over there to kill bad mens," I reminded him.

"Oh sir, I know," he said. "But if you must, it will be a happy thing to do so with such a gun; and so I wish I too could cross."

"When it was time to volunteer," Kam said, "why did you not raise your hand?"

Little Pea looked crestfallen.

"I tell you this truly," he said. "I cannot swim."

As we walked back to the villa, I told Sakoon about the additional link Terry had established between those who had killed Graham, Major General Hua, and the Pak Beng spur.

"I was skeptical when she brought this matter up the other night," Sakoon said. "Frankly, I still am. ISOC assures me there has been no recent activity on the road."

"You said the Chinese had once planned to use it as an invasion route?"

"Yes. According to our intelligence reports at the time, their intention was to occupy northern Thailand. Once they controlled that much of our country, they would supply an army of insurgents to invade the south. There were longer-range plans to take over Laos, Burma, Malaysia, and Singapore."

"Leaving Vietnam and Cambodia to the Russians?"

"Only if necessary."

"So," I said, "the United States pulled out of Southeast Asia, political realities changed, the Chinese dropped their invasion plan in favor of diplomacy."

"Yes."

"Who was the architect of the original plan, do you know?"

Sakoon looked at me, amused.

"No," he said, "but I could probably find out. Are you suggesting Major General Hua?"

"Yes," I said. "I am."

I admitted I didn't have much to go on. I said most of what I did have was instinctual, based on my first impression of Hua, formed even before I had known who he was—a hooded figure in the back room of a funeral shop in Singapore, standing with his hands clasped behind his back, looking on while his lieutenants prepared to torture an innocent woman. I recalled what I had said to Hua that day in my futile attempt to change his mind: *You're military. You've been in for a long time. It shows in the way you walk, sit, talk; you can't hide that under a few yards of sackcloth.*

I said suppose the original invasion plan had in fact been Hua's baby. Suppose he had masterminded it, hung his career and reputation on it, and then just before it was ready to go, the boys in Peking had pulled the rug out from under him. Suppose a power struggle had ensued, he had lost finally and been exiled to the provinces—as DIA and CIA had thought. What would a man like Hua do in a case like that? Raise his own army? Carry out his original plan in spite of the boys in Peking?

"You mean an army of Pathet Lao?" Sakoon asked.

"Probably. Say Pathet Lao and maybe some renegade Chinese."

"Forgive me, Colonel," Sakoon said. "I realize we are not the most powerful of nations; but neither are we without resources. Should any such band of mercenaries as you describe decide to cross our borders, we would easily eliminate them."

I really couldn't argue with that.

"You're right," I said.

He smiled.

"I will monitor your mission from the air base," he said. "Terry has given me the frequencies. Everything is arranged on the Vientiane side. I gather you never met Pamela Banks. You don't have to worry; she's completely reliable. Is there anything else I can do?"

"Yes," I said. "You can find Campbell for me. He should have been in touch by now."

Chapter
TWENTY-FIVE

The old Dooley boat was moored at the bank of the river, above Nong Khai. It was a houseboat, forty feet long, painted a garish black and yellow. A bunch of helium balloons had been tied to the stern. Smoke coiled from a rusty stovepipe jutting through the roof. We passed the boat, near sunset, as we headed up the 211 tertiary road in Rajah Banerjee's Land Rover. Banerjee was doing the driving. Terry and I sat in front; Kam and Little Pea sat in back with the diving gear. Little Pea had his Rossi shotgun. As we went by the old Dooley boat, he heaved a sigh.

"I remember Graham telling me about Tom Dooley," Terry said. "He was an American doctor who helped take care of refugees after the Viet Minh defeated the French at Dien Bien Phu, am I right? That would have been mid '50s. I was probably nine or ten at the time."

"Quite right," Banerjee said. "Dooley kicked off a few years later. Another Yank doctor established the Dooley Foundation and picked up the work."

"The other doctor's name was Vern Chaney," I said. "He's a friend of Campbell's. During the war, Chaney ran that houseboat down the Mekong from Vientiane to Khong Island. He used it as a hospital ship."

"It was taken by the Pathet Lao in '75," Banerjee said, "after the fall of Laos. A PL general sold it, later, for personal gain."

I leaned around in my seat and smiled at Little Pea.

"And now it's the home of Captain Kong and the midgets," I said.

"Oh sir," he said.

The road grew rutty, narrowing between stands of bamboo that scraped the Land Rover as we jounced along. Fork-tailed swallows swooped and whisked in the gathering dusk. There was a depressed sense of a dying day, an apprehension of what was to come. We rode in silence, Banerjee looming over the wheel, using his strength to keep the vehicle from sheering into the deeper ruts.

When we finally came out of the bamboo, the riverbank was close and fairly steep to our right. We swung left into a grove of old palms, where we pulled up in front of a small fishing shack. The shack had bleached board siding and a corrugated-metal roof. The steps leading up to the rusted screen door were soft with rot and had been recently reinforced with quarter-inch steel cables stretched across them and bolted to the frame.

"Scraps from another project," Banerjee explained. "I barter my services as an engineer, get paid off in everything from yams to rubies. I picked up this shack that way. Come on, let's get the hardware inside."

We did this quickly. Banerjee got a couple of kerosene lanterns going, then began double-checking the diving equipment. He had refilled the scuba dive tanks that afternoon. Now he unsealed the entry hatch on top of the canister and began fine-tuning the systems there that would keep Toby Porter alive on our underwater return from Vientiane.

"Three things to remember," he said. "Air in, air out, and buoyancy. The first two are automatic. Your chap will have a sixty-minute supply from the time he seals himself in and switches the systems on. Tell him to relax. If he hyperventilates, the allowable time goes down. There are audible and visual warning mechanisms that will activate when the air supply in the canister is within three minutes of depletion. The buoyancy regulator is here. I've got it set for eight feet, rifles, extra drums of ammunition, and radio included. Your chap will have to adjust for his own weight. Best to let the canister ride slightly higher than the divers to keep it clear of obstacles. Except for the air reservoir, the rig is thin-skinned; you don't want a puncture. Arrange a set of signals: two raps on the canister to increase buoyancy; one rap to decrease. Each time the signals are exchanged, your chap should toggle this dial one calibration up or down as indicated."

"If something goes wrong, will Toby be able to open the hatch from inside?" I asked.

"Yes. He goes in on his back, feet first, arms folded under his chin. The seal bolts and instrument panel will be directly in front of him, awkward, but accessible. The panel gauges are luminous."

Kam and I field-stripped the AR-180s, made sure they were clean, reassembled them with silencers, laser sights, and full magazines in place, then slid them muzzles first into the canister along with four extra drums of ammunition and carrying vests.

Banerjee had attached spring clips to the inside walls, two on each side for each of the guns. Terry and Little Pea rigged a long-wire antenna for the PRC-77 radio and set the transceiver up on a workbench by the door of the shack. We agreed to use a simple code: *One* meant Kam and I had crossed the river; *Two* we had rendezvoused with Pamela Banks; *Three* we were at the Arch; *Four* we had Toby; *Five* we were back at the river, launching for return. I'd carry the squad radio and use the call sign Papa Wolf. Terry would be Sierra Echo. Sakoon, monitoring our frequency from the air base at Udorn, would answer to Campbell's call sign Delta One.

"We'll keep radio traffic to a minimum," I said. "There are a lot of ears in Vientiane. We don't want some clown in one of the embassies tuning us in and getting curious."

"I hope to God Toby's where we think he is," Terry said.

"If Pamela Banks says he's on top of the Arch," Banerjee said, "you can bloody well be sure he's there."

"Prisoner also say Chinese bring Toby to Vientiane," Kam put in. "He is there, I do believe."

"How did you get that rag-tailed PL to talk?" Banerjee wanted to know.

"Sir," Little Pea said, looking at Kam. "This Khmer carries with him the long thin blade of a saw. He showed this blade to the prisoner and said its teeth could cut through steel. He said if the prisoner did not tell us all we wished to know, he would proceed to saw off his head. In this way, he said, the prisoner would not continue in the wheel of life."

At eleven-thirty p.m., we had our gear laid out on a narrow stone beach below the riverbank just across the road from Banerjee's shack. Kam and I had the black body stockings on and the wet-suit boots. We each carried a long knife in a leg sheath; I had used a camouflage stick on my face. We attached the regulators to the tanks, turned on the air valves, tested the masks. Our squad radio, the AR-180s, and the ammo were sealed up in the canister. The mosquitoes were terrible. We rubbed on repellent, working quietly in the dim light of a waxing moon.

The Mekong flows down through Laos from its headwaters in the highlands of Tibet. At Vientiane, the river makes a sharp east-to-south meander. The distance between banks at the widest part of the meander is about half a mile. Along the outside sweep of the turn, an eight-foot levee protects the city from floods during the monsoons. For over a mile in front of this levee on the Laotian side, a sandbar follows the curve of the river. The sandbar is barren except for a swamp of reeds and cattails at the southern end. We planned to surface at the edge of this swamp, conceal our equipment there, then wade across a shallow backwater to the levee wall.

"There are sampan patrols on the river, foot patrols along the levee," Banerjee said quietly. "No predictable schedule. Pamela will have a radio; she'll warn you off if necessary."

We stood silent for a moment, Terry and I, Banerjee, Kam and Little Pea—all of us a little in awe, I think, of what we were about to do. Under the moonlight, the river looked like an asphalt road, broad and black, gurgling softly where it swirled and sucked around the shore. On the other side, most of the city's lights were already out. We could see a few isolated yellow glows, the occasional wink of a vehicle moving through the empty streets.

"All right, boys," Banerjee said. "Let's bring one home for the Gipper."

Chapter
TWENTY-SIX

Kam and I put on the dive gear and fins, pulled our masks down loosely around our necks, attached the canister tow line to the flutter board, then shuffled backward into the water. No further words were spoken by any of us; there were no goodbyes. I could see Terry hesitate for a moment, then turn and climb the embankment, heading back toward the shack. Little Pea followed her, shotgun over his shoulder, held by the barrels.

The water felt cool at first, then warm. The current tugged at my legs. When we had sufficient depth, we flushed our masks, dunked our heads, then pulled masks and mouthpieces in place and rolled over. Kam put his wrist through the left strap of the flutter board, I put mine through the right. We grabbed the handholds and pushed off. Behind us, Banerjee launched the canister. The tow rope was fifteen feet long. As soon as it felt taut, we submerged.

There was absolutely no light as the water closed over us. Kam and I instinctively pulled ourselves closer to the instrument grouping on the flutter board, until our heads were almost touching and the green-lit gauges were only inches from our eyes. During our practice at the lake, we had loaded our weight belts to give us neutral buoyancy at a depth of ten feet. The canister would ride at eight. To counter the effect of the current, we would be swimming upriver as well as across. The tow line ran on a diagonal up off my side of the board. There was a lot of drag until the canister was true with the flow of the river, then not so much. Banerjee had estimated our time in the water at about thirty minutes.

We kept our depth easily, but wandered on heading several degrees to either side until we synchronized our kicking. I found I had to stare at the gauges, to see some light in order to keep my sanity in an environment where I had no sense of up or down. Without the carpenter's level and compass, it seemed to me Kam and I could be slowly revolving around each other and never know it.

Follow your exhaust bubbles to locate the surface, Banerjee had said. That was fine, except I couldn't see my exhaust bubbles. All I could do was hear them. They had a close-in, erupting sound. I was already feeling claustrophobic. When my knee brushed something hard, my heartbeat tripped, breathing speeded up. I felt a strong sense of vertigo, an overwhelming need to surface.

Slow down, I told myself. Concentrate on the gauges.

I deliberately paused between breaths. The dizziness caused by my hyperventilating quickly passed. My knee had only brushed some harmless submerged object, a stump or rock.

I reached through the water, squeezed Kam's wrist in the "Are you okay?" signal. His answering squeezes were like shots from a bolt cutter, as if he was hanging on all right, though sure we had been swallowed by the black worm of Dharva.

We kicked along at a depth of ten feet, keeping the compass true to our heading. At thirty-eight minutes by the clock, I felt the silt and bottom muck under my fins, saw in the green glow of the panel light Kam's hand gesturing we should go up.

We surfaced slowly in five feet of water. Our navigation had been good. We were just offshore from the reed swamp. I slipped off my mask, looked directly across the river. The shore there was dark, Banerjee's shack hidden behind the bank. Downriver, a few tiny lights showed at Tha Bo. I was about to congratulate Kam on our successful crossing when he suddenly grabbed my arm and pulled me toward the swamp.

We lumbered in without a word, catching our fins on the bottom, twisting through the first row of cattails, bringing the flutter board with us. There was a racket of frog sound in the swamp that diminished as we came in and then got big again. We shucked our weight belts, tanks, and fins. Kam slipped his knife out of its leg sheath.

"What's wrong?" I whispered.

"Hear boat," he said. "Come this way up river."

"Christ," I said, "the canister's still out there."

The line from the canister was black. It ran out from the reeds and into the river. The canister was downstream from us, the length of the line and still underwater. I started to pull it in. Kam shook his head. As he did, I saw the boat coming into view.

It was a sampan with a long dark silhouette, high at the prow, lower at the stern, powered by one man standing there working a scull. Two other men stood in the bow. They wore uniforms and carried rifles; and they were going to pass no more than ten yards off the place where we were.

I slipped my own knife out of the sheath; nothing else to do. We hunkered down. The sampan made its slow way against the current. The men in the bow were watching the shore. I heard them talking to each other. The line to the canister looked like a snake where it angled out from the reeds. As the sampan drew alongside, the frog noise quieted again. I could hear the slap of water against the hull. One of the men seemed to be looking directly at me. He was young and slight, with a flat broad face and the green uniform of the Pathet Lao. He said something to the other man. The other man bent down and came up with a battery-operated spotlight. He switched it on. The bright beam slashed through the cattails just over our heads where the reeds had been separated by our going into the swamp. He started to say something. I felt Kam gather himself at my side, as if to spring. There was a half moment of silence. Then, a rattle of gunfire from somewhere upriver shattered the night. The man in the bow extinguished his light, spoke an order to the man in the stern. I heard the man in the stern grunt as he leaned hard into the scull. The sampan pulled away. As it did, Kam and I gripped hands in the dark.

We waited ten minutes, then pulled the canister in. It slid

noiselessly out of the water, looking like a giant slug. We opened the seal locks, took out the squad radio, the AR-180s, ammo drums, and vests. I would carry the radio on a web belt. The ARs had shoulder slings; the extra ammo drums fit into pouches on the vests. Kam looked very pleased to have his rifle in hand. We dragged all the gear farther into the swamp, concealing it there as well as we could. Then I switched on the radio and pressed the transmit button.

"One," I said quietly.

Terry's voice came back at once, echoing the number. Then Pamela Banks broke in. Her voice was cultured and assured.

"Papa Wolf," she said, "this is Mama-san. The margin is clear now."

"Okay, Mama," I said. "We're on our way."

We left the shelter of the reeds, waded across the backwater, climbed the levee wall. Pamela met us in the shadow of a stand of sandalwood trees. She was a trim Chinese woman in her sixties, with black, closely cropped hair, a lined, intelligent face, dark slacks and long-sleeved shirt. I radioed "Two" to Terry, who gave the number back. Pamela spoke no greeting, simply motioned for us to follow her.

At the shoulder of a gravel road beyond the trees, an ancient truck was parked, engine off and lights out. I could see the bulky figure of a woman at the wheel. A built-up cargo platform extended from the roof of the box out over the cab. Several barrels were strapped to the front of the platform. The area around the truck smelled like a latrine. When Pamela opened the rear doors, the stench became overpowering.

"*Aiie*," Kam muttered, wrinkling his nose as we climbed in. Pamela climbed in after us. She pulled the doors shut, then banged on the wall between us and the cab. The driver started the engine and we lurched off.

"Liu is one of my closest friends," Pamela said. "She is not a good driver, but she is loyal, and quite brave."

Kam spoke to Pamela at some length in Chinese. She answered quickly and I heard them laugh as she switched on a flashlight. My eyes were tearing.

"Your gracious Cambodian friend has said my voice is more restful than a thousand brooks and if he could but gaze once again upon my face, he would be forever blinded to other women." She laughed again, good-naturedly. "I think what he meant was, 'For the love of God, turn on a light so we can identify the cargo!' '' She put the beam on a large open vat strapped by the rear door. It was filled with excrement.

"Liu's papers give her clearance to go out after curfew and collect honey buckets from clientele throughout the city," she explained. "As Rajah must have told you, Vientiane swarms with Pathet Lao of the Teung tribe. They are uncouth, trigger-happy wretches, who fire their rifles at the slightest provocation. Most Laotians native to the city detest them and try to thwart them whenever possible. The gunfire you heard upriver that drew the sampan patrol away is one example: a trusted friend, with an illegal weapon, who agreed if necessary to fire it as a diversion on a radio signal from me. Many others stand ready tonight—''

Pamela stopped. There had been a sudden, sharp rap from the cab. She made a chopping motion with her hand for us to be silent, then abruptly extinguished her light. In the dark, I thumbed the safety off the AR-180, heard Kam do the same.

Liu braked the truck to a slow, drum-squealing halt. There was a rattle of Laotian dialect, Liu's voice singsong, a man's, guttural and peremptory at first, then an exchange of laughter and the sound of a wood barrier being dragged away. The truck lurched forward and promptly stalled. Liu ground away on the starter. Men's voices called to her. She answered, pleasantly, grinding away. The body stocking I wore, still wet and now much too warm, clung like a cobweb to my skin. Gas fumes had started to permeate the putrid atmosphere of the pitch-black box. My face was pouring sweat. I was ready to smash through the rear doors and hit the ground firing when the truck finally started and we pulled away, banging hard against something as we did.

"Jesus," I croaked.

"She's really an awful driver," Pamela said.

"How many more of these do we have to go through?"

"That's the only one. We're inside the city proper now. There could be a random search, but it's not likely. Liu bribes the checkpoint guards with exhorbitant cumshaw and contraband. She's well known throughout Vientiane. Her cargo is also well known. The Teung usually have no desire to open the doors."

"What's our first stop?" I said.

"The fair grounds at That Luang Temple. They're deserted now and provide an excellent view of the Arch. We have a pair of night binoculars."

"Fine," I said.

"Honey buckets offend nose," Kam said. "Will be glad to reach destination."

Chapter
TWENTY-SEVEN

Fifteen minutes later, we stood in the shadow of a tumbled-down vendor's stall in the empty, heavily treed park. I had last visited the That Luang fairgrounds in the spring of '72, and had watched the annual rites the Laotians used to hold here to ensure rain for their rice crops. The new regime had forbidden these rites, and since they had, there had been drought.

The Arch was visible, 300 yards up one of the road forks leading into the circle at Lane Xang Avenue. There was an eerie feeling to the city now that a curfew was being imposed: no cars, no people about. At the Lane Xang intersection, a single light changed monotonously from red to green to red. The night was so quiet we could hear the clicking of the solenoids. Pamela explained it was the only light in town. Since the Pathet Lao had taken over two years ago, gas had been heavily rationed. There was little vehicular traffic, even during the day.

The Arch bulked up against the sky. It had been built of gray cement, but the light amplification of the binoculars gave it a greenish caste. Tiered bamboo scaffolding, rising a hundred and twenty feet from ground level to upper cornice, had been erected around the exterior walls. The cornice overhung the wall, and was crenellated like a medieval fort. The roof of the Arch was flat; there was a bonze cell at each corner. The bonze cells looked like small temples. A much larger templelike structure, with yellow lights visible through its window slits, rose forty feet from the center of the roof.

"The Chinese officers stay up there in the place where you see the lights," Pamela said. "It was the first of their renovations. Four inside staircases lead to the top of the arch, but each of these is well guarded. You must climb the scaffolding."

"Which one of the bonze cells is the one we want?" I said.

"I wish I could tell you, but I can't. Liu knows one of the guards. He's easily bribed, but his information is usually incomplete. She was afraid to press him too far. The reconstructed doors of the cells are of steel, and can be bolted from the outside."

"All right," I said. "How do you want us to make the approach?"

"The Arch is one of Liu's regular stops. She will park close to the scaffolding on the east side. You should be able to gain the scaffolding from the roof of the truck. The barrels will provide concealment."

"Do we exit the same way?"

"Yes. Signal by radio when you are ready. Liu will bring the truck back. She will say she forgot to drop off a wristwatch she has obtained for one of the guards. We believe this will be the most dangerous part. The guards could easily become suspicious. You must be prepared to shoot if an alarm is raised."

"We'll be prepared," I said. "Is Liu willing to run this one alone?"

"She's willing," Pamela said, "but I've promised to stay in the truck until you are all safely back at the river. I'm afraid without my presence to settle her, her driving would become impossible."

"There might not be time for a thank-you when this is over," I said. "I knew your husband, and liked him. He married a hell of a lady."

"Monte liked the Americans and believed in them," she said. "I am only doing what he would have done."

I radioed the number three to Terry. Her voice sounded tight when she gave the number back. Kam and I climbed up on the truck's platform and crouched behind the barrels there. The barrels were the size of oil drums. We crouched with our rifles in hand, each covering one side of the truck. When Pamela had climbed back into the box and closed the doors, Liu started the engine up and we lurched our way toward the Arch.

The night was warm. A breeze had freshened and was stirring the branches of the palms and sandalwood trees along the way. The traffic light blinked red. Liu ignored it, lumbering through in the truck's lowest gear, at a pace no faster than a man could walk.

The waxing moon was in the west; the east side of the Arch was in shadow. As we approached, I could just make out its upper reaches, the primitive scaffolding, the crenellated roofline, the bonze cells at the near corners, the higher structure behind them with its slits of yellow light.

Be there this time, Toh-bas, I thought. *Be there.*

Liu braked to a halt when the nose of the truck was just inside the open archway. She had done her best to get us close to the scaffolding, but she hadn't done too well. We were still a good eight feet away. Kam pointed to the ground, indicating we should jump down from the truck and take our chances there. Before we could do that, or anything else, Liu got out of the cab and walked around to look the situation over. She shook her head, got back in, reversed the truck out from under the Arch and took another pass. As she did, Kam looked at me in disbelief, a lot showing of the whites of his eyes.

Now someone was shouting from under the Arch. Liu must have gotten excited about that because she began to blow the horn. As the truck finally ground once again to a halt, Kam slung his rifle and dove for the second tier of the scaffolding. I slung my rifle and followed him. The scaffolding was rickety under my weight, the working space narrow. I had to duck my head slightly to keep from banging it on the next-higher platform. There were seventeen tiers above us, no ladders between tiers. The men who were doing the cleaning apparently managed it by monkeying up from one staging to the next. Kam had already disappeared into the shadows above me. I took a couple of deep breaths and began to climb.

I was still close to the side of the open archway. At first, I could hear Liu's singsong voice in animated conversation with the guards as they waited for the honey buckets to come down. Then, as I climbed higher, her voice seemed to fade until all I could hear was the night breeze and the solenoids clicking when the traffic light changed.

The scaffolding seemed flimsy. There were times when I thought the whole structure was going to pull away from the wall. Vertical supports creaked and swayed, the bamboo platforms sagged under my weight. As I mantled up from one stage to the next and my height above ground increased, I began to climb more slowly, clutching each hold tightly, resting often, with my cheek pressed to the wood.

The upper platforms were covered with dust from the cleaning operation. The breeze blew this dust into my eyes. I tried to rub it out with the heel of my hand. Kam was somewhere above me. He seemed to be able to climb without making a sound.

When I was eighty feet above the ground, I heard Liu start the truck and drive away. The easy part for her was over; the hard part would be coming back.

Don't worry about that now, I thought. *Worry about this.*

Tools had been left on the higher stagings, primitive sandblasting equipment, mortaring trowels, odd-looking wire brushes, long and hooked, with tapered ends. As I pressed myself up onto the eleventh tier and reached for the twelfth, I hit a metal stone drill with my hand. Before I could grab it, it rolled away from me. I watched helpless as it teetered for a second at the edge of the platform, then dropped into the void.

Christ, I thought.

The drill seemed to fall forever before I finally heard it hit the ground with a ringing clang. There were voices. An armed Pathet Lao guard came out from under the Arch, looked in the direction where the sound had been, then peered up at the scaffolding. I froze. The breeze tugged at his cap. He snatched at the bill, pulled the cap lower on his brow, then turned and walked back out of sight.

I finished the climb. When I pressed myself up onto the last tier, just below the jagged roofline, Kam was waiting for me. He had unslung his AR; I unslung mine. He pointed up at the roof edge. From somewhere behind it, I could hear faint sounds of laughter, the murmur of conversation and tinkle of glass.

"Men in building speak Chinese," Kam said quietly. "Maybe three, four men there. No guards this side. No lights in bonze cells."

"What's the roof surface like?"

"Stones fixed in tar. Make small noise under feet."

"Okay," I said. "I'll check the cells, you cover me. We'll circle to the right. Our intelligence says Toby's in pretty good physical shape. He should be able to walk, but he could need help on the scaffolding. If so, I'll lower him to you, one tier at a time."

Kam nodded his agreement. The sounds of the distant voices increased, carried by the breeze. "Could take men in building," he said. "Gun very quiet. Cannot be heard from street."

"No," I said. "Too risky. Too many things could go wrong. As long as they stay inside, we'll leave them to their rice wine."

"Be surprised in morning," Kam said. "Come out to see Toh-bas, Toh-bas is gone."

I have him the thumbs-up sign.

"Okay, brother," I said. "Let's do it.

The breeze continued to freshen, powdering dust into the air as we climbed over the roof edge onto the roof itself. Below us, the city stretched out in darkness to the sharp meander of the river, where the long sandbar presented its curve under the light of the moon. Our equipment was hidden in a reed swamp there, the dive tanks and canister. Across the river, on friendly soil, in a small fishing shack, Terry, Rajah Banerjee, and Little Pea waited by their radio to hear the next crucial number in our sequence of five.

Keeping low behind the battlement, I made my way to the bonze cell at the northeast corner of the Arch. The gravel roof felt sharp through the neoprene soles of my wet-suit boots; there was a slight crunching sound as I moved along. Kam stayed well behind me.

When I reached the cell, I crouched below one of the slit windows and listened. From inside I could hear the sound of a man snoring. Keeping flat to the wall, I circled to the door. The door was slightly ajar. I motioned to Kam I was going on. A wide path of yellow light showed through an open door in the large center building. The light reached to the roof edge. To avoid passing through it, I dropped down to the north-side scaffolding and crossed that way to the bonze cell at the northwest corner. Kam did the same, staying thirty yards behind me, rifle ready. The door to this cell was closed, but not bolted from the outside. I motioned to Kam I was going on.

The only light on this side of the roof was the light of the moon. I moved along quickly to the bonze cell at the southeast corner. The door was shut and bolted from the outside. I listened at one of the windows. There was no sound. I slipped the knife out of my leg sheath, used it to tap softly on the butt of my rifle. Using the POW code, I spelled the name Toby: *four-four, three-four, one-four, five-four*. There was no response. I tried it again, louder this time. I had scarcely finished before there was an answering series of clicks from inside the cell, same number of letters, different words:

H-E-R-E.

I felt a tremendous rush of joy, sliced through with apprehension. I went to the door of the cell, slid the deadbolts back. The door was heavy, the hinges not well greased. I opened it as slowly as I could. Whenever the hinges began to squeal, I would pause, then start again. I had slung the AR over my shoulder, resheathed the knife. I worked with the stealth of a safe cracker, opening the door of that cell. When the opening was finally wide enough, I went inside. There was a single chair, a cot, and a small table. Toby was standing near the center of the room.

He stood in a faint rectangle of light that came through the slit windows at the west side. He wore black pajamas; his feet were bare. He was tall, pale, slightly stooped, terribly thin. His hairline had receded; his forehead was high. His eyes looked very deep in his skull. He seemed confused by my presence, unable to talk. I told him who I was, that we had come to free him and take him home. He obviously hadn't recognized me in the half-light, the shape of my head concealed by the hood of the body stocking I wore, my features altered by the camouflage stick.

So I told him who I was, and he listened, and there was a pause before he answered, as if he was trying to keep himself under the right kind of control and not say anything that would be out of character for a man who had endured as a prisoner for four years, and whose maternal bloodline traced to Thomas Jefferson. When he finally did speak, it was in a soft, deep voice, and quiet drawl.

"Awfully good to see you," he said.

I started to reply when I saw his expression tighten and heard the soft crunch of a footfall behind me.

"It's okay," I said. "It's Kam. You remember Kam."

Toby shook his head.

When I turned to look, I saw the spirit medium framed in the door.

Chapter
TWENTY-EIGHT

He wasn't holding a jeweled dagger from Villay-Phone's this time. He was holding a light submachine gun. He told us, speaking his English well, to put our hands on top of our heads and come slowly out of the cell. We did that. I could hear Toby cursing under his breath. He said this one often came to torment him in the night. The spirit medium called over his shoulder toward the big building at the center of the roof. The breeze was blowing hard out of the west, and his voice carried on it. There was an answering call, but nobody showed at the door.

"Maybe they don't want to come out in all this dust," I said.

When the spirit medium heard my voice, he looked at me more closely. "That's right," I said. "We met at a funeral shop in Singapore. We've got an old score to settle."

"Best not shake a stick at him," Toby warned. "He's a sadistic bastard."

"Yeah, I know. I've seen his act."

"He does the killing for their number one," Toby said. "They had me watch the other day: a young man they thought had betrayed them. This one used a piece of sharpened wire."

"Yeah, I know," I said. "He killed Graham Melbourne that way. You remember Graham."

Toby swore.

The spirit medium looked nervous. A lividity of scar tissue showed at the corners of his mouth. His backup troops still hadn't arrived, and there were two of us, and I had the AR slung on my shoulder.

"No more talk," he said. "Go to the large building. Keep your hands placed where they are."

As he started to back that way, something moved along the upper right side of his chest. When he tried to brush it off, it moved on his hand. It was a red dot, the size of a small insect. He glanced to his right, toward the roof edge, saw through the dusty particulate there the thin red line of the laser. He shouted again, swung his submachine gun that way. Then Kam's rifle made its tearing canvas sound and the spirit medium fell in two pieces, making a lot less noise than a tree.

That one's for Terry, I thought.

I unslung the AR-180, put it on full auto, crouch-ran toward the center building. A Chinese in an officer's uniform had come out. He had a rifle, saw me, aimed it my way. I ticked off a burst, took him before he could fire, brass cartridges from the AR ejecting in a stream, slugs powdering cement. Then Kam and Toby were at my side, Toby with the spirit medium's gun.

"We go quick now," Kam said. "Make too much noise."

Toby jerked his finger toward the top of the center building, started to say something. A light had showed there. From somewhere inside, I could hear the chirping clicks of a field telephone being cranked. Men were shouting. I grabbed Toby's arm.

"Come on," I said. "You can tell us about it later."

We vaulted over the battlement on the east side, began our quick descent of the scaffolding. Kam went first. Toby didn't need any help. He slung the spirit medium's gun, swung down from tier to tier as if he could have gone on doing that for the rest of his natural life.

I stopped once on my way down, just long enough to use the squad radio. I gave Terry the number four, didn't wait for her to give it back. "*Mama-san,*" I said. "*this is Papa Wolf. We're on our way home, and we're hot.*"

Pamela's answer came back garbled and broken. There wasn't time to try again. Our position on the wall was too exposed; it wasn't going to take the guards long to figure out where we were. I racked the radio, dropped from that platform to the next. The bamboo made splitting noises under my weight; vertical supports threatened to pull away. Kam and Toby were already well down the scaffolding when the old truck lurched up Lane Xang Avenue, two Pathet Lao on bicycles in distant pursuit.

Liu didn't take any chances missing our side of the arch this time. She headed straight for it, swerved at the last minute, banged the wall as she came to a metal-screeching halt. Pamela opened the rear doors, radio in hand, ran for the passenger side of the cab. The men on the bicycles were a hundred yards away and closing. I could hear their shouts of alarm. There was rifle fire from the roof. Bullets stitched the road. Kam jumped to the top of the truck, crouched between the barrels, put a burst in under the archway. Toby jumped down after him, then me. Pamela was inside the cab now, shouting instructions to Liu in Chinese. The men on the bikes had sidearms and were using them, too unstable and far away to be accurate, but getting closer. I unslung my AR, switched on the laser.

"*Go! Go!*" I screamed to Liu.

Bullets spanged into the wall over our heads. I put the rifle on full auto, put the red dot chest-high on one of the bikers. When I squeezed off the burst, he flew from his bike as if snatched by a hand. I settled the red dot on the second man. Before I could fire, Liu crunched gears and pulled away, throwing my aim way off to the left. The second man jumped from his bike and dove for a hedge at the side of the road as we jounced and rolled under the archway.

Toby was lying flat on the cargo platform, firing into the right-side archway doors, emptying the box magazine of the spirit medium's gun in one long ear-splitting burst. Kam was firing into the left. When Toby was out of ammo, I took over for him, using the AR, brass cartridges pouring away. So far, the upper cornice overhang had protected us from the shooters on the roof. Now, as we came into view, they began to open up in

earnest. Bullets crack-zinged around us, clipped the top off one
of the barrels. Liu wheeled left around the traffic circle, sped up
a side road, quickly taking us out of range, and also away from the
river. I leaned down until I could see Pamela.

"Tell Liu we've got to get back to that sandbar!" I shouted.

"She knows that!" Pamela said. "We had to run a checkpoint
on our way in to get you! All the patrols will be alerted by now;
they'll expect us to make for the river!"

Vientiane, which had been so quiet, was now alive with
sound. The Teung were compulsive, not well disciplined. Sirens
wailed, vehicles rumbled through the streets. Men shouted to
each other, firing random shots in the night as they tried to
organize their pursuit. The noise they made covered the noise we
made. Liu knew her city. She drove with the lights out, lurching
through narrow alleys, speeding up dirt tracks, avoiding the main
streets and checkpoints. We flashed by the old White Rose, a
club where I had once done some interesting time. We went
away from the river for a while, then made a wide circle and
began to come back.

Kam and I had reloaded our ARs. I lay flat on the cargo
platform, covering our front. He covered our rear. Every time
we turned a corner, my heart stopped beating for the time it took
to be sure we hadn't run smack into a PL patrol.

Toby lay next to me, holding to one of the barrel straps,
empty machine gun in hand, as though if things came to it he
would use it as a club. In fits and starts, I told him about the
original plan, the dive gear and canister.

"If that bastard hadn't come out on the roof," he said.

"We'd have slipped in, picked you up, and slipped out," I
said.

"I'll need to contact someone with rank in the Agency as soon
as we're across the river," he said. "It's urgent."

"Campbell's in Thailand," I said. "Will he do?"

"Your father-in-law?"

"Yep."

"Great," Toby said. "Has Campbell been in on this?"

"All the way," I said.

Liu was on a dirt-road straightaway now, rolling fast. Steam
was jetting from the radiator. Pamela stuck her head out the
window to say the truck was losing gas. I leaned down so I could
talk with her, had to shout to be heard in the windrush.

"How far is the river?" I said.

"Six kilometers down this road," she said. "We'll come out

just below the sandbar. It's as close as we'll be able to get! This road isn't much used anymore! The Teung may not think of it at first!''

"Tell Liu to go for it!" I said.

"We'll let you off there! Don't worry about us! We have friends! We'll be all right!"

I didn't believe that. Neither did Pamela. If her cover on this mission wasn't blown, her friend Liu's certainly was—and that was a line of beads even the Teung could string.

We rolled on, spewing steam. We never made the sandbar. A mile from the river, just before the engine seized up, Liu swerved off the road into a concealing thicket of brush. The truck back-fired once, then stalled out in a stink of scorched metal. We worked quickly, the five of us, throwing branches and deadfall over the path the truck had made going in, brushing away the tracks in the road. From the southern outskirts of Vientiane, barely two kilometers away, we could hear shouts and the sound of jeep whine. Kam went out to reconnoiter. I looked at Pamela.

"Is there any chance at all of our swimming the river?" I said.

She shook her head.

"There are machine-gun nests on the levee," she said, "with overlapping fields of fire. The sampan patrols will be out with searchlights. The jungle along the river below here is impassable."

"Exactly where does this road end?"

"It goes to the river, then turns north toward the city. It used to go into the city, but the last segment was washed out three years ago by the monsoon flood. It ends now just short of the levee, near the place where I met you."

"If I understand our situation," Toby said, "the diving equipment can handle three people. Assuming we can reach it, would it be possible to make several trips?"

It was a good idea—ferry them across the river to Thailand one at a time: Pamela, Liu, and Toby. Banerjee could probably handle the problem of refilling the tanks. But even if we were lucky enough to get back to our gear, when I looked at Liu, I knew the plan, for her, would never work.

She was not a short woman, and she was very nearly as wide as she was tall: a roly-poly Chinese in baggy pants and shirt, with graying hair that hung in sweaty straggles around her face, arms and legs like sausages bursting at the seams. There was no way in the world she was going to fit in the canister. Pamela had already told me Liu couldn't swim.

As I looked at her, large tears welled from her eyes, rolling down her cheeks among the fatty creases.

"I did not drive well," she said.

Pamela put an arm around her, gave her an affectionate hug.

"You drove beautifully," she said.

"I've seen soldiers under fire," Toby said, "who didn't do as well."

Liu looked shyly pleased, peered up at the tall, emaciated, still courtly POW. I made the introductions. Toby said he understood all Pamela and Liu had done to help free him, and that he would be forever grateful.

"From here on we would only burden you," Pamela said. "We will leave now. There is a Hmong village in the mountains sixty miles north of Vientiane. We will be welcome there."

"They're gassing the Hmong villages," I said. "You and Liu don't have a future in Laos. As far as I'm concerned, we counted on three and now we've got five. When we cross the river, you two are coming with us."

"I absolutely agree," Toby said.

"You are very kind to us," Pamela said. "But this is not possible."

I was about to reply when Kam darted back into the brush. He said a jeep patrol was coming down the road. We took positions around the truck, staying low. Jouncing beams of light stabbed toward us through the dark, our shadows moving in the peripheral glow. The jeep passed us at a high rate of speed. There were two Pathet Lao soldiers in front; another manned a .30 caliber machine gun post-mounted in the rear. They swept out of sight, leaving a thick cloud of dust that blew off on the westerly breeze.

"PL between us and sandbar now," Kam said.

"There's an old water tower at the place where the road washed out," Pamela said. "They'll probably set up there."

I thought for a minute, tugging the lobe of my ear.

"How good is your network in the city?" I said.

"Very good," she said. "There are many people loyal to me. Most of them are not armed, but they are eager to help."

"How many could you bring down to the waterfront, say in the area along the south levee wall behind the sandbar?"

"The curfew ends at sunrise. After that, as many as you wish."

"As many as a couple of hundred?"

"Easily. More if you like. What would you want them to do?"

"Mill around down there. Look curious. The word will be out about what happened tonight.. They shouldn't have any trouble accounting for their presence."

"You want them to distract the soldiers?"

"That would be part two of the plan," I said. "A lot's going to depend on part one."

I switched on the squad radio, tried to get Terry. No luck in the canebrake. I tried again on the road.

"Sierra Echo, this is Papa Wolf," I said. "Do you read?"

"I read you, Papa Wolf," Terry replied. The tension in her voice was palpable.

"We're on the Georgia side of our air," I said, "outflanked and one klick east. We've lost our wheels and we've got extra baggage. Tell the Hmong we need a lift from his friend."

Terry was silent for a long moment, then came back on.

"That's a roger from the Hmong," she said.

Chapter
TWENTY-NINE

It took a long time to get to the river. We kept inside the brush on the left side of the road, took our turns breaking and erasing trail. When we reached the river, at the place where the road turned north toward the city, we turned south and went into the denser jungle there. We went as far as we could, which was not very far, and then went down into the reeds and cattails that lined the bank. The sky now was faint blue-gray; the stars had disappeared. There were ripples on the surface of the water, created by the breeze.

A quarter mile upriver, we could see the water tower where the Pathet Lao had set up their machine gun, just as Pamela had thought they would, their jeep backed up to the bank. The sandbar was just beyond them, and behind it the levee wall. Pamela had alerted her people. At sunrise, they would start to gather there. I had radioed our position to Terry; she had briefed me on the plan.

"Boat take big chance coming into shore," Kam said.

"They'll have to make it look good," I said. "I think they can do it."

"Little Pea say captain drunk most of the time. If captain is not drunk, he will not come, I do believe; and if he is, he will not find this place."

"We had to put our money on something," I said. "I'm glad to be putting it on Little Pea."

"I remember the Dooley boat," Toby said. "I went out with a nurse from it once. Her name was Cindy. She was from Idaho. I'd never been out with anyone from Idaho before. She was quite nice, Cindy was."

I smiled, put my hand on his shoulder. It was nothing but string muscle and bone. He looked at me.

"God, it's good to be with you people," he said.

During our march from the truck to the river, he had said again he had essential information to deliver to Campbell. I filled him in briefly on the things that had transpired since Graham's murder a week ago. He listened with the discipline of a trained intelligence officer, taking it all in, computing it, storing it with the rest of what he knew. He was moved when I got to the part about the disastrous raid on Quebec Bravo, and the body of the American soldier we had found in the fresh grave by the caves.

"His name was Tom Gannon," he said. "If I make it back to tell his story, he should get the Medal of Honor for what he's done."

"Not if," I said. "When."

We waited. The sky pinked up, the sun rose. We began to see traffic on the river, long-tailed motorboats, fishing vessels, small barges loaded with produce. Most of the traffic moved along the Thai side of the river. We sat in a swampy place, waist-deep in water. We didn't dare talk very much. When the sampan patrols passed, we didn't dare breathe. Kam and I would ease the safeties off our ARs, then ease them back after the patrol had passed.

"Beautiful weapon," Toby said.

"Real street sweeper," I said.

Otherwise, we sat and we waited. Liu looked miserable. There were leeches in the water; she had already pulled two from her wrist. The air was fetid, and alive with insects. Our faces streamed blood from the bites.

Pamela and Toby were stoic. Kam, who usually had infinite patience in a situation like this, began to fidget as the hours passed.

"Boat not come," he said finally. "We go in jungle. I find way south to place where we can swim across river at night."

"We don't have gear for the jungle," I said. "And Liu doesn't swim."

"We tie rope to her. Tow like canister. Be all right."

Kam smiled briefly at Liu as if to assure her he was only kidding, but I knew he really wasn't kidding, that he wanted very much to get out of this place.

"Pamela's people are all over that levee wall," I said. "Terry's got our position. I could risk calling her again, but if there was something wrong, I think she'd call us. I say let's give it a little more time."

"Boat not come," Kam said. "Captain tell Little Pea climb tree. Would rather be in jungle. Do not like being this close to water. PL brigade come anytime, go one-by-one search, find us quick." He was going to continue, but stopped suddenly and pricked up his ears. At first I couldn't hear whatever it was that had caught his attention, then I did, coming to us very faintly from the downriver distance: the *oom-pah-pah* and *ting-a-ling* of a high school marching band. Kam slipped through the reeds that way, peered out, came back wearing a lopsided grin.

"Trak wrong," he said. "Boat comes."

Pamela used her radio, alerting her people along the levee wall—calling one, who would pass her brief message on. They knew nothing of our specific situation, only that Pamela needed their help. There were hundreds of them, all ages and sizes, villagers and fishermen, shopkeepers and mama-sans: the good people of Vientaine. The Pathet Lao soldiers tried to keep them off the levee, but there were too many of them. They pushed onto the wall and peered out as the rag-tag black-and-yellow Dooley boat wobbled its way up the river—helium balloons tied to its stern, midget band playing their hearts out in the bow.

We crouched among the reeds, the boat two hundred yards away now and closing. The captain was either actually drunk or doing a masterful job of pretending to be. He zigged and zagged, never so much as to appear ridiculous, but enough to capture the imagination of the crowd. Soon they were laughing and shouting to each other with each wobble of the wheel. The captain responded with ducklike quacks from his air horn. The soldiers stood with their rifles slung loosely in the crooks of their arms, obviously bemused by what was happening. The boat made its unsteady way. The band played on.

"He'll keep wandering closer to this shore," I said. "When he's got a visual on us, he'll nudge the bank, reverse engines at once, and back off. We'll be boarding over the deck rail on the starboard side. We won't have much time. As soon as we're on board, we lie flat on the deck, keeping below the gunnel. We stay that way until we get word it's okay to move."

"I am very frightened now," Liu said.

"Toby and I will give you a hand," I said. "Kam will cover us. You're going to be fine."

"I was very frightened last night too," she said. "But I was also busy with my driving. To sit still here is much worse."

"You hang on," I said. "As soon as this is over, we're going to have one hell of a party."

When the boat was fifty yards away, I separated the reeds in front of us enough so we could be seen from the water. When it was thirty yards away, Pamela keyed her people on the levee wall. From their perspective, it was apparent now that the boat was going to collide with the shore. When it was fifteen yards away, they began to pour over the levee wall and onto the sandbar, as if to have a better look at the captain's misfortune. The soldiers tried to stop them, but the soldiers were quickly engulfed by the general melee and bedlam of noise.

The PL by the water tank swung their .30 caliber our way and hosed off a warning burst as the boat crunched into the reeds. It hadn't stopped moving before Toby and I were at its blind side, helping Liu and Pamela over the rail, climbing in after them, followed quickly by Kam. The PL fired another burst, exploding the balloons over the stern. The captain came out of the wheelhouse and made a low bow. It wasn't Kong; it was Banerjee, dressed in Kong's clothes. He stumbled back to the wheelhouse, reversed engines and began to back away. The band, which had stopped playing when the machine gun fired, started up again: a half-dozen very small men dressed in lederhosen and alpine hats. They were sitting on deck chairs facing the bow, sweat pouring off their faces, blowing their lives out into their horns: trombones and cornets, one tattered tuba, and a set of drums—all eyes fixed on Little Pea, who lay hidden on the bow deck, facing them, tiger suit and floppy hat, both hammers of his 12-gauge back. I smiled at him. He smiled at me.

Oom-pah-pah and *ting-a-ling*.

Chapter
THIRTY

Banerjee wobbled up the river a ways, made a wide turn, and wobbled back. When we were safely south of Vientiane, he peered down from the wheelhouse window and said, tips of his mustache twitching with excitement:

"Ready for a drink, boys?"

At that, we sprang from the deck with whoops and hollers, came surging into the main salon, where Little Pea was already popping tops off warm bottles of Singha beer. I had barely made it through the door before Terry was in my arms. We hugged each other so hard I thought our ribs would crack. I introduced her to Toby, and she flung her arms around him. We drank the beer. We poured it over each other. We pressed around Toby, poured it over him, began to chant, "Toh-bas!, Toh-bas!, Toh-bas!" The midgets picked up the beat. Banerjee quacked his horn. We kept it up, doing introductions on the fly, popping more beer, chanting and cheering, and shouting our joy over the success of the mission and Toby's safe return. Finally, out of sheer exuberance, Little Pea stepped out to the rail, thumbed the hammers back on his 12-guage, fired into the tops of the trees. The twin booms echoed up and down the river; Monkeys chattered, birds screeched. When he came back in, Liu, under full sail now, snatched the tiny Hmong to her ample breast with all the affection of a mother who has had to wait too long for a child. Toby grinned happily at the two of them. Little Pea, peering out from Liu's embrace, grinned back at the tall POW he had done so much to help rescue.

"Will have no man in boat," he said proudly, "who is not afraid of whales."

* * *

The party went on. When we docked along the wharf above Nong Khai, Toby, who had been very careful with his beer, took me aside and asked me how he could get in touch with Campbell. I told him he might be able to reach Campbell through Sakoon Panapong, gave him the code names and frequency to use.

"He's Adune's nephew," I said. "He's well connected with ISOC. If you can't reach Campbell, Sakoon himself should do. He's been with us from the start. He flew the chopper in the Quebec Bravo raid."

"Be sure to save me a couple of beers," Toby said on his way out of the salon. "It's been a long time since I had a beer."

He disappeared into the stateroom where Terry had set up the radio.

"I like him," Terry said. "You can see what he's been through, and you can see how he managed it: how quiet and strong he is; and how bright."

"He's a professional," I said. "He's the kind the past administration drove out of the Agency, and out of the military. Better not get me started on that."

She gave me a mock salute, put her arms around me again. She had on the green slacks and blouse, both wet now from the beer.

"Wish we could be alone," she whispered.

"Bet we could find a place," I said.

"I was sure I'd never see you again."

"I knew we were going to make it this time," I said. "I can't explain how. It's a feeling you get, like in a poker game when you know you're going to fill a flush, and you do."

"You should have seen the look on Little Pea's face when I relayed your message. He was ecstatic! He'd been terribly gloomy about not having an important part to play."

"Where's the original Captain Kong?"

"Sleeping one off in his cabin. Rajah trussed him up there so he wouldn't be a nuisance. The midgets agreed to go along, for quite a handsome sum."

"Looked more like a command performance to me."

She laughed. "Little Pea thought they might need additional incentive if things got dicey on the Vientiane side."

"Things got dicey enough," I said. "I'm glad all we lost were the balloons."

"I am too," she said.

I held her. We were standing by the open door of the salon, on the river side of the boat. The midgets were playing a repertoire of dance music, mostly American pieces from the '40s: "As Time Goes By," "I'll Be Seeing You," "Moonlight and Roses," all a little tinny, but nice just the same.

"Did Toby tell you anything about Major General Hua?" Terry said after a while.

"No," I said. "Toby wouldn't do that. Not unless he had to. Whatever Intel he's got, he'll deliver to the right people in the Agency."

"I wish Graham could be here. This was the moment he worked so hard for."

"As far as I'm concerned, he is here," I said. "He always will be. By the way, for what it's worth, the man who killed him is dead."

"Not Hua."

"No. Hua's lieutenant. The one who did the tricks with the skewering rod."

"It was Hua who killed Graham," Terry said. "He was the one who made it happen."

I didn't want to talk about Hua. Right now I didn't want anything to come between us and the fine euphoria we felt.

"Listen to the music," I said.

"It's pleasant music," she said.

"The one they're playing now was in a movie called *Casablanca*. Did you see it?"

"Yes. In Sydney. Graham insisted. It was a marvelous film."

"Wish we could be alone," I said.

"Bet we could find a place," she said.

The party mellowed down with the music. Banerjee brought out an enormous platter of sandwiches, then went off to settle affairs with Captain Kong. Kam and Pamela, who were not drinkers, sat in the salon, talking quietly to each other, speaking Chinese. Liu and Little Pea set up chairs on the bow, drank steadily, danced from time to time, kept the midgets company. Terry and I sat on the rail, sipped our beers, munched our sandwiches, watched the muddy river go by. After a while, Toby joined us.

"How'd you make out?" I said.

"They weren't able to locate Campbell; they're still trying. Colonel Panapong is on his way here to pick me up. I'll debrief with the Thai Security people."

"We just got you back," I said. "I'm not sure we'll agree to let you go."

He smiled. His feet were bare—callused enough to work a shovel.

"You look good, Matt," he said. "Camouflage stick and all. You look the way I remember you, as if the years hadn't passed."

"I got shaky for a while after the war went sour," I said. "After I lost Diana. Things are much better now."

"And Brian?"

"He's doing fine. Out of his coma, getting back on his feet. Still a way to go, but the prognosis is good. He's living in Paris this year, with a friend of Bob Coyle's."

"That's great to hear," Toby said. "I've got four years of everything to catch up on. The PL don't deliver the *Times*. Is my father, do you know if he's . . ."

"As far as I know, he's fine," I said. "Irascible as ever. He's been going head-to-head with Senator Talbot. Big investigation series on the nightly news. I'd score your father ahead on points."

"I'll be calling him as soon as I've been debriefed. He didn't give up on my situation, did he?"

"No way. He's used the station to keep the MIA issue squarely in front of the people. The major networks dropped it after a while."

Toby looked at me.

"Dropped it?" he said.

"Long story," I said. "You won't like it much when you hear it. It'll keep."

"When I heard the tap code outside my cell, I couldn't believe it," Toby said. "Not on top of that Arch. I thought it was one of them, having fun with the American the way they like to do. I wasn't going to answer at first. Even when you came through the door, I knew you were too big to be one of them, but I still couldn't believe it. I'd tried to escape so goddam many times. I'd always gotten caught."

"All over now," I said.

"There are others," he said. "I don't know how many. A lot died over the years. I don't know how the U.S.G. is going to handle my coming out. If they make much of it, there could be reprisals by the other side against the POWs in Laos and Vietnam who are still alive."

"Campbell's close to the top these days," I said. "He'll get the right input."

"I'm awfully sorry to hear about Graham," Toby said, addressing Terry. "He was a good friend and a fine officer. He always carried a picture of his kid sister. He was proud as hell when you won that title."

Terry smiled, brushed a beery strand of hair back from her cheek.

"He should see me now," she said. "I must look like the wrong end of a wallaby."

"Let's hear it for wallabies," I said.

"I'll drink to that," Toby said.

An hour later, Sakoon arrived. He arrived in an armored car, escorted by six military police on motorcycles. The convoy stopped long enough to pick Toby up, then sped away. After that, the party powered down. The midgets packed their kits and left by van for the Chaiporn Hotel in Udorn, where they had another engagement. Banerjee dropped Terry and me at Adune's villa, then drove on to his house, where his wife had invited Liu and Pamela to stay for as long as they needed a home.

"I get down on the world sometimes," Terry said. "Then I meet people like Pam and Liu."

"You should have seen the way Liu put that truck up against the Arch when she came back for us," I said. "Just like shaking a hip."

"Speaking of hips," Terry said.

"Yeah," I said. "I know."

We were in my old room at Adune's villa. Pushpinder had changed the sheets and linens during our absence. It was now two-thirty in the afternoon. We had told Pushpinder we would show up out by the goldfish pond for cocktails around six. That gave us three and a half hours.

Terry didn't pull me out of the shower this time; she got in with me. We stayed there a long while. The water was piping hot and never ran out. We soaped and shampooed, rinsed off, soaped and shampooed some more. Then I kissed her, standing under the soft spray, and she kissed me back hungrily, our bodies warm and slippery where they touched, our need too urgent to measure in the slow taking of each other, our connection muscular and quick under the christening flow of water, Terry's release almost simultaneous, long and shuddering and mutual with my own.

That night, I sat on the edge of the bed in her room, gently stroking the small of her back. The moonlight was bright where it came through the window. She lay on her stomach, cheek resting on her arm.

"I don't know why I like that so much, but I do," she said.

"It's all part of the Eberhart feel-good theory," I said.

"You Eberharts," she said.

"The theory gets complicated after a while," I said. "But at first, all it calls for is a stroker and a strokee."

"The strokee has all the fun."

"Not so," I said.

"I only meant at first," she said.

"I think Pushpinder is wise to us, don't you?"

"He certainly left us alone at supper."

"Showed us to separate rooms when we arrived, though."

"Well, he does have to keep up appearances."

"I'm going to keep them up tonight," I said. "These beds weren't designed for a couple of big guys like us."

"I'm not a guy," she said. "I'm a girl."

"Big, though," I said.

"In all the right places?"

"Every one."

"Should I come for you in the morning?" she said. She smiled when she said it.

"We could meet in the shower," I said.

"I've never had it off in the shower before," she said. "It was quite remarkable."

"They say the only place you can't make love is on top of a picket fence," I said.

"No truth to that, of course," she said.

"None whatsoever."

"I think I love you," she said.

"Sounds qualified," I said.

She thought for a moment.

"I really don't think I could live on a farm in Virginia," she said.

"Wait till you see it," I said.

"Am I going to?"

"I'll spring for your tickets. We can stop in Paris on the way."

"I love Paris," she said.

Chapter
THIRTY-ONE

Campbell woke me up at six-thirty the next morning. He rapped on the door of my room, asked if he could come in. I said sure. He had a four-day beard and pouches under his eyes, was wearing a pair of dark slacks and a flowered short-sleeved shirt.

"I flew to Bangkok," he said. "I went to Caesar's Palace, hired a room and two Eurasian girls, ordered in a supply of food and liquor, and screwed myself blind."

"Hey, Campbell," I said softly, "you don't have to explain anything to me."

"Yes, dammit, I do," he said. "I jumped all over you in '75, after Diana was killed and the war was lost, and you were drinking and debauching your way across Europe. Frankly, I came close to losing respect for you over that. You were a highly disciplined man, one of the best pilots we ever put in the air, and there you were suddenly letting it all go. I knew you had your reasons, damn good reasons, for doing what you did; but somewhere near the measly bottom of my soul, I couldn't forgive you. Could not. I never told you that, did I?"

"No," I said. "But I pretty much guessed that was the way you'd feel. Most of what I was doing then wasn't particularly forgivable."

Campbell folded his arms.

"You had your reasons," he said, "but in spite of that, I never really understood. Now I do. When I learned what Midge had done, I almost came apart. I kept myself from doing that by working even harder than I had been on finding Toby and getting him out of Laos. What had been a worthy cause became an obsession. Then, when the Quebec Bravo raid failed and we lost those men, something snapped. I had to let go. I couldn't maintain the steel anymore. So I understand what happened to you in '75 because in a much smaller way I've finally been there myself. Am I making it sound ridiculous?"

"No," I said.

"Sakoon's people rousted me out of Caesar's Palace yesterday, flew me back to Udorn. We've got a problem. I hope you're ready to go to work."

I smiled.

"*Two* Eurasian girls?" I said.

"I'm not that old, dammit," he said. "I can still get it up when I have to."

"You don't mean two at the same time?"

"Oh Christ," he said. "Get dressed, will you? We're meeting downstairs, same room as before." He started to walk out, then came back. "You all did a terrific job bringing Toby out," he said. "I was a damn fool about that."

"You made it happen," I said. "You and Graham."

He seemed pleased I'd said it.

"I talked to the President this morning," he said. "I goosed hell out of him. Now that we've got one of our men out alive, maybe he'll start doing something about the rest."

"How are they going to handle Toby?"

"They're convening a top-level interagency group security meeting to decide that. They wanted me to come back for it. I told them no, I was too busy here."

"Has there been any fallout from the Vientiane mission?"

"So far nothing more than an increase in jeep and sampan patrols. The PL may think Toby and your team are still in Laos."

"That beard looks good on you," I said. "Maybe you should let it grow."

He rubbed his jaw.

"Think it would put me one up on the tennis pro?"

"I think you're already one up on the tennis pro."

Into the shower again, then into the slacks and safari shirt. Whistled a lot and hummed. By the time I got to the second living room, the rest of the group had already assembled there: Campbell, Terry, Sakoon, Toby, Kam, and Little Pea. There was a breakfast cart with tea and coffee, scrambled eggs and bacon, slices of melon, and sweet rolls. I helped myself to a fair amount of everything there was. I felt good, rested up, ready to meet the day. Every time I looked at Toby, I grinned. He had on a tan suit that fit him pretty well, looked as if he had already gotten back some of the weight he had lost. The meeting would be his.

We took our seats; he faced us, standing. When he thanked us again for what we had done his voice broke, and the muscles knotted and unknotted in his jaw before he was able to go on. He never looked away.

"As some of you already know," he said, "I was the only passenger on an Air America reconnaissance flight from Phnom Penh that crashed in southern Laos on 12 November, '74. The pilot was killed. I was captured by members of a Pathet Lao battalion at the site of the crash. I was held prisoner by that battalion for three and a half years. Then, in April of this year, a group of dissident soldiers deserted the battalion, taking me with them. We trekked north and west into the Quebec Bravo sector, where the dissidents established a permanent camp. I was the only Caucasian prisoner. In late June, a Hmong prisoner was brought into the camp. He remained there for three weeks before he managed to escape while on a wood-gathering detail. I was never allowed to talk with this prisoner and was not able to identify him. I now understand his name was Sisani, and that he was killed in action during the Quebec Bravo raid."

Toby paused here long enough to sip from a glass of water, then continued.

"Seventeen days ago," he said, "the dissidents who were holding me captured an extremely debilitated Caucasian prisoner who stumbled into camp from somewhere north of the Nam Yang River. They put him into the same cage where I was being kept. For the first three days, the man was delirious with fever and unable to talk. I did what I could to help him, but the PL would not share the few medical supplies they had, and there was not much I could do.

"On the fourth day, the man's fever broke, and he was able to talk. It was difficult for him because he was very weak, and his throat was badly abscessed. He talked off and on for the next five days. He told me his name was Tom Gannon, that he had been a Green Beret major in charge of the engineering section for a Special Forces and CIA team. The team had worked with the Royal Laotian Army, building Lima sites in the Plaine des Jarres. Gannon was captured there by the Pathet Lao in the spring of '72 and was eventually moved north to a POW camp at Muong Sai.

"One year later, this camp was taken over by a renegade PRC major general named Hua Hai-ling. Prior to 1970, Hua had been in charge of constructing the Chinese road spur from Muong Sai to Pak Beng. During that period, he had also developed a plan to invade Thailand, using the road as a supply line.

"In October of 1970, when the Thai government saw the road had reached a point only sixteen nautical miles north of their border with Laos, they became sufficiently threatened to conduct an impressive military exercise they called 'Air Chandra,' using Thai and SEATO group aircraft; and to start construction of their big Air Chandra base at Chaing Lae.

"This reaction by the Thais persuaded the Chinese to abandon the road project at Pak Beng. Major General Hua's troops, numbering over a thousand men at the time and including a construction battalion, an infantry battalion, and an antiaircraft company, were pulled back into Yunnan Province. Hua himself was ordered to return to Peking. There he fought bitterly to have his invasion plan reinstated. When this failed, he returned to Laos and carried on the work, without the sanction of his government. About two hundred of his men remained loyal to him. He ran opium out of the Golden Triangle to finance their operations, formed strong alliances with the Pathet Lao in northwest Laos, used American and other POWs as forced labor to help construct a tunnel complex running south of the Mekong River at Pak Beng sixteen miles to the land border with Thailand. The tunnel took five and a half years to complete. If Tom Gannon hadn't managed to escape and tell us about it, none of us would know it was there."

Toby paused again to sip some water. We were all silent, waiting for him to go on.

"There were initially twenty-seven American POWs being held by Hua. Most of these were pilots and navigators of American aircraft shot down over Laos in the '60s and early '70s. Some, like Tom Gannon, were men from the Special Forces. There were also Lao POWs, most of them from the Hmong tribes. These numbered about forty when the tunnel project first began. Many of them subsequently died, or were executed by Hua.

"Tom Gannon was the ranking officer among the American POWs. He was an exceptional leader, apparently by main force of his personality and his extraordinary ability to endure the worst kinds of physical deprivation. He was eventually kept in a cell inside the tunnel complex with four of the other Americans: a Green Beret captain by the name of Jackson Gage, two Navy pilots, and one Air Force navigator.

"This group began excavating an escape tunnel, using tools they managed to steal from the main construction project. Their goal was to create a passageway through the floor of their cell thirty meters to the wall of one of the ventilator shafts that serviced the tunnel complex.

"It took them two and a half years, from the time they started, to reach the ventilator shaft. Once they had broken through its wall, Gage was able to chimney sixty feet up to the top of the shaft. There his way was blocked by a heavy iron grate. He and Gannon were the only ones still strong enough to chimney up the shaft. They took turns doing that, using a broken hacksaw blade to saw through the grate. This effort began last June, and took five months to complete.

"One day last August, while Gage was working in the shaft, he saw a private jet aircraft fly low over the Pak Beng area, heading southeast. The identification sequence on the rudder indicated the plane was out of Singapore. When the same aircraft returned later that day, Gage, using a handcrafted reflector, tried to signal to it. He and Gannon did this on two other occasions, once in early September, then again later that month."

"*Gray,*" Terry breathed. She was sitting next to me. All the color had gone out of her face.

"He must have picked up their signal," I said. "At least saw something that looked out of place."

"And Hua's people must have seen the Sabreliner," Terry said. "Hua decided to get rid of both pilot and plane, then steal the flight logs to be sure Gray hadn't picked up on the tunnel complex."

"That had to be it," I said.

Campbell looked at Toby.

"Please go on," he said quietly.

"By now," Toby continued, "all but five of the American POWs had died from poor nutrition and the brutal conditions under which they were forced to work while constructing the tunnel complex. It was agreed by the five remaining prisoners that Gage and Gannon should make a break as soon as they were able to cut through the grate that was barring their way out of the shaft. Work was nearing completion on the tunnel. Most of the surviving Hmongs had already been executed by Major Hua. The Americans were sure they too would be executed once their usefulness to Hua had ended.

"Five months after they began sawing through the grate, Gage finally broke through. This was during the early daylight hours of 24 October, after their shift of work in the tunnel had ended. To protect the three Americans who were still alive, but too weak to chimney up the shaft, Gannon gagged them and tied them to their cots. They would tell Hua they had been betrayed by the two who had escaped.

"The escape was made in the late afternoon of that same day. Gannon and Gage themselves were in severely weakened physical condition by this time. They had no weapons, no decent supplies, no shoes, no sure method of finding their way through the jungle. They were pursued at once by a PL patrol with two Chinese advisers sent out by Hua to bring them back. On the second day of their escape attempt, this patrol found Gage and Gannon while they were drinking water from a jungle stream. The patrol opened up with AK-47s. Gage was killed. Gannon managed to get away. Five days later, he stumbled into the Quebec Bravo camp, delirious with fever."

Toby glanced at Campbell, as if to double-check whether or not to carry the story any further than this. Campbell nodded that he should.

"Without substantial men and material from the PRC," he continued, "Major General Hua knew his plan to invade Thailand could never succeed. He needed an equalizer. At the time he returned to Laos from Peking, the Russians and North Vietnamese had already begun a preliminary program of gassing the Hmong villages to eliminate their resistance to the Pathet Lao. Hua purchased about forty canisters of the gas from a North Vietnamese depot supply sergeant with whom he had previously trafficked in drugs. He recruited three Chinese technicians who had been trained in chemical-warfare research, set up a laboratory inside the tunnel complex, and began experimenting with various kinds of nerve gas.

"Eventually, using a light airplane, an AN-2, he began to spray the gas on several Hmong villages in the area of his operations. At first, the gas was crude, and took a long time to kill. Hua and his technicians kept refining it, however, until it was finally sophisticated enough to kill instantly on exposure. Once he had achieved this, he began to stockpile a large supply of the gas, in canisters, inside the tunnel complex, along with delivery systems and protective masks for his men. He intends to launch a surprise attack against the Thai Air Chandra base three nights from now."

"Good God," Terry said.

"Is all this coming from Gannon?" I asked.

"All but the launch date. I got that indirectly from Hua, during my time at the top of the Arch."

"Isn't he liable to change his plans now that you've escaped?"

"I don't think so, for two reasons. First, he has an agent in place at the Air Chandra base. As long as the base is not put on alert, Hua will assume the situation is normal.

"Second, Hua doesn't think I know about his plans. I convinced him Gannon had only mentioned the surviving American POWs and Hua's name; that otherwise Gannon had been much too ill to talk. I flattered Hua by being familiar in close detail with his reputation, from his tour in Tibet through his early work on the road. He's susceptible to flattery, if it's not too obvious. I remembered his CIA file very well.

"When that PL patrol showed up at Quebec Bravo, with its two Chinese advisers, I worked hard persuading them they should take me to Hua. I wanted to try to interest him in the kind of person I was. I thought if I could get into his presence, I might be able to challenge him intellectually, massage his ego, arrange a way by doing that to escape. His ego is substantial. He said that on the night of 18 November—that is, three nights from now—he would take his place as one of the most imaginative military tacticians in the history of Asia."

"Oh boy," I said.

"From what Tom Gannon had told me, it was easy enough to tie that date to the attack on Air Chandra. Armaments there include Scorpion tanks, Saracen APCs, 105mm and 155mm howitzers, and UH-1B assault helicopters. Air Chandra personnel include an infantry division, special forces battalion, and an aviation company. The base has a formidable radar-directed air-defense system, including 40mm AAA guns and Hawk missiles.

"Once Hua controls that base, he controls the entire north half of Thailand. His own troops are seasoned combat veterans, fanatically loyal to him. He'll be joined by every Thai insurgent in the surrounding provinces. They'll consolidate their hold on the north, then sweep south to Bangkok. I expect Hua assumes once the government in Peking sees what he's managed to do on his own, they'll reauthorize the original plan and back him up with the full military might of the PRC. Hua told me he had already established strong communist cells in Burma, Malay, and Singapore. He wants the whole region—just as the Japanese did in the '30s."

"In any case," I put in, "what we're saying here is, that tunnel complex has to go."

"I believe that is correct," Sakoon said.

I looked at Toby.

"Do you know if our three guys are still in there?" I said.

"According to Hua," Toby said, "they are."

Chapter
THIRTY-TWO

Pushpinder came in at that point to say Campbell had a long-distance call on the scramble line in Adune's private office. While Campbell was out taking the call, Sakoon set up an easel display that had been sketched by ISOC from the close description Tom Gannon had given Toby of Hua's tunnel complex. Toby used a pointer as he explained the drawing. The drawing was a large vertically oriented rectangle. He started at the top.

"Here," he said, "is the town of Pak Beng. It lies on the north bank of the Mekong River. The river runs on an east-west line where it passes Pak Beng. In this area, the river does not constitute a border with Thailand. The border here is a land border, also running on an east-west line, sixteen nautical miles to the south.

"Major General Hua began his project by building a submerged bridge that would allow him to move men and matériel from Pak Beng, across the Mekong. The Mekong at the site of the bridge is a third of a mile wide. They only used the bridge at night.

"Once the bridge was in place, Hua established a camouflaged road thirty meters across the flood plain to the place where he would begin his tunnel. The place he chose was a large natural limestone cave that went over a thousand meters down into the north side of the karst mountain you see here. The mountain has an elevation of thirty-three hundred feet, and is pocked with smaller caves and strategic outcroppings.

"There were four stages to Hua's construction project from this point. First, in and around the smaller caves above what was now the tunnel entrance, he established a defense capability with concealed gun sites. These included one 57-millimeter, one 37-millimeter, and three ZSU-23-4s. This ordnance was salvaged from the original road-defense system. From their height advantage, once sited, the guns could elevate their barrels against an air attack, or depress them against a ground attack. Hua also revetted a Fire Can acquisition and tracking radar van. In the

158

van, his fire director would be able to receive target information, altitude, speed, and direction from the acquisition radar, then feed it to the tracking radar that would tell his gunners where to aim and how to fuse.

"Once this defense capability was in place, Hua proceeded to the next phase of his project. Using a mixed labor force of Chinese, PL, and POWs, consisting at times of as many as eight hundred men, he constructed the first and most difficult segment of his tunnel complex. This segment was two miles long and a quarter mile wide, and was roughly patterned by Hua after the North Vietnamese underground complex at Tay Ninh. It included an operations center and barracks, the experimental laboratory, a truck park, ordnance depot, the POW cells, and eventually the storage vault for the gas canisters. This complex took two years to complete.

"Once the main complex was in place, Hua began constructing an assault tunnel that would run fourteen miles from the end of the main complex to an exit point across the land border with Thailand, and within light-artillery range of the Air Chandra base. The assault tunnel was designed to accommodate a convoy of twenty jeeps moving in single file, each jeep towing a 105-millimeter howitzer. The howitzers were to fire the gas shells. The assault tunnel took three and a half years to complete.

"Once the assault tunnel was in place, Hua proceeded to establish firing sites for the howitzers. On the night of the attack, a small, well-armed squad of commandos, equipped with protective masks, would exit from the tunnel and infiltrate to positions around the Air Chandra base perimeter. They would be joined by Hua's undercover agent there, who would advise them of any unanticipated problems. When these commandos were in place, Hua would bring his convoy of jeeps and howitzers from the main complex, down the assault tunnel, and into their firing positions. On Hua's command, the gunners would put a barrage of a hundred of the gas shells into pretargeted areas within the base. As soon as the barrage was over, the commandos would storm the perimeter, killing anyone who had managed to escape the gas, and would secure the base. Assuming ordinary atmospheric conditions, the gas would dissipate within two hours—or about the time it would take the main body of Hua's invasion force to arrive."

When Toby was through, I looked at the rendering, then at him.

"Gannon got his knowledge of the tunnel complex by having

to help build it," I said. "Do you know how he got this much detail on the invasion plan itself?"

"Directly from Hua," Toby said. "As the leader of the American POWs, with advanced training as an engineer with the Green Berets, Gannon interested Hua. Hua knew what he was doing was brilliant, and he wanted a man like Gannon to say so. Gannon played to this. You have to remember these two men were in relatively close quarters, working under extremely difficult and physically hazardous conditions for over five years. Most of the troops involved in the project were nowhere near being close to Hua in intellectual capacity. Gannon was."

"How well defended is the assault tunnel where it exits in Thailand?" I asked.

"Gannon was never allowed to work on the last three miles of the assault tunnel," Toby replied. "Neither were the other Americans. The effective range of the gas-firing howitzers is about seven miles. That means the tunnel could exit anywhere within a twenty-five-square-mile area and still put the howitzers within range of the Air Chandra base. The terrain we're talking about is rugged as hell: karst pinnacles, mountains, winding rivers, hidden valleys, jungle canopy. An infantry division could search for years and never find it. And even if they did, it's too narrow to storm. A handful of men with grenade launchers could defend it for a long time."

"The strategic target is, of course," Sakoon said, "the main complex that makes up the first two miles of the tunnel. This is where Hua's troops are billeted and the gas is stored. Major Gannon believed there were two practical ways to eliminate this target. One was by means of a conventional air and ground attack. The other was to use a couple of fighter planes to dive-bomb a trench that would divert water from the Mekong River into the tunnel. The first two miles of the main tunnel and the first mile of the assault tunnel have a one-degree downpitch. Major Gannon estimated the force of water coming down that much grade from a trench roughly fifteen feet wide by twenty feet deep would be enough to take out most if not all of the post-and-beam shoring in the main complex. Without the shoring, there would be a massive cave-in.

"These matters aside," Sakoon continued, "the presence of the three American POWs within the main tunnel complex complicates the situation now faced by my country. I hope you will understand that while the prime minister is sympathetic regarding this matter, it is, for him, not the essential consideration.

Assuming the story told by Major Gannon to Mr. Porter is true, Thailand faces an imminent threat to one of its most critical military facilities. The Air Chandra base is not equipped to engage in chemical warfare; nor are the other ground forces that we have available and that could be moved into position in time to counter Major General Hua's attack.''

"Where's the ball on your response right now?" I asked.

"The matter was debated by the highest officials of my government throughout most of the night. There was sharp division over how much credence to give Major Gannon's story. He had obviously suffered great deprivation. Several ranking members of the cabinet advised the prime minister to verify that story through regular intelligence channels before taking any action at all."

"With all due respect, that's ridiculous," Toby said. "Nobody who spent five minutes with Tom Gannon would doubt the truth of what he told me. I spent nine days with him. The detail he passed on to me and that I have now passed on to you and your intelligence people couldn't be more persuasive. If you and your government don't act quickly, I think I can assure you you're going to lose Air Chandra."

Campbell, who had come back from taking his phone call, broke in.

"I don't think we have to brace Sakoon about this," he said. "Sakoon personally happens to believe Major Gannon's story is true. So does Mr. Adune, who met with the prime minister in Bangkok last night."

"There were others in the cabinet," Sakoon continued, "who also believed the story to be true. They recommended an immediate air strike against the main complex, using Major Gannon's plan to flood the tunnel. This, of course, raised the problem of the three Americans. There was also a concern that if the strike was made by the Royal Thai Air Force, the ruling government in Laos would almost certainly consider it an act of war, thereby giving the Vietnamese an excuse to retaliate against us on behalf of their allies."

"Okay," I said. "Then what you're talking about is a clandestine strike: no markings on the planes; no identification on the pilots. Keep the number of planes to a minimum. Get in, get the job done, and get out."

"Precisely."

"Which brings us right back to the POWs," I said.

Campbell fielded that one.

"The prime minister has conditionally agreed to authorize a two-pronged raid on the tunnel complex," he said. "One objective will be to liberate the three Americans, and any other prisoners who might still be there. The other will be to destroy the complex itself, using Major Gannon's plan to flood the tunnel."

"What's the condition?" I said.

"That the operation be conducted jointly by ISOC and the CIA. I've just talked to the President. He's agreed."

"Outstanding," I said.

Campbell smiled.

"We'll have two helicopters with volunteer crews at our disposal," he said, "plus two F-model F-5s. I told the prime minister you flew the F-5. I do have that right, don't I?"

"Bet your life," I said. "All I need is a brush-up."

"Good," Sakoon said. "We'll give you one this afternoon."

Chapter
THIRTY-THREE

At ten a.m. we adjourned our meeting to the air base at Udorn. There we assembled in the big briefing room that had been built by the USAF's 432nd Tactical Reconnaissance Wing in the '60s. Until the war ended in 1973, hundreds of F-4 pilots had filled these same movie-theater seats, finding out what their next targets would be. I had been here myself, several times in those days, flying up from Ubon to attend briefings for consolidated, multiwing air strikes. The same iguana-type gecko lizard was crawling behind the briefing panels on the big stage, popping its throat bag, making a noise that sounded like someone with a falsetto voice saying, "*Fuck you, fuck you.*" This lizard had broken up more than one briefing during the war.

We had been joined by the two Thai helicopter pilots who had volunteered to fly the mission. Kam would lead the team on the ground. Sakoon would command our fighter-bomber attack. ISOC had also provided a young Thai captain to give us the Laotian Air Order of Battle. He would brief us on the routine intelligence

Thai Security had collected since 1975 from Comint, Elint, reconnaissance flights, agent reports, and satellite photos supplied by the United States. He was businesslike, obviously had no idea why this unusual briefing had been called, gave no sign of curiosity. Pointer in hand, maps and overlays pinned to the sliding panels behind him, he stood on the stage, under a large color portrait of the king and queen of Thailand, and began.

He said at the present time there were 40,000 Vietnamese troops strategically placed in Laos, with several hundred Russian advisers and technicians to handle the sophisticated equipment such as PT-76 tanks in the Plaine des Jarres, and the ten MiG-21 jet fighters based outside of Vientiane at Wattay. Pak Beng was 140 miles from this base, well within MiG intercept range. The Lao air-defense system, though rudimentary and underequipped, did have border radar coverage that scanned from Vientiane to the Golden Triangle. This meant Pak Beng was under radar surveillance. Depending on how quickly they reacted to our blips, MiG intercept time from Wattay to Pak Beng could be less than twenty minutes.

Sakoon and the chief helicopter pilot asked a number of questions. The captain answered these questions, then left the room. Sakoon set up another easel display, this one a large-scale rendering of the main tunnel entrance and operations complex. As Toby reviewed them, Kam copied the diagrams into his green field message book.

"The cave opening which provides entrance to the tunnel," Toby said, "is thirty feet wide. It's camouflaged by two doors of slotted bamboo, covered by natural vegetation. The doors swing out when they are opened. There is a single guard post outside the entrance, just beyond the sweep of the right-side door. The post consists of a slit trench manned by two Pathet Lao with AK-47s.

"The POW cells were one of Hua's first necessities as he began to widen the cave and construct his complex. They are located three hundred feet inside the doors, along the left wall of the cave. There are six cells in all. The first is a large communal cell where the Hmong prisoners were kept. The next five are smaller cells, where the American prisoners were kept. Gage and Gannon made their escape from the last of these five cells, as you go deeper into the cave. We can assume that this cell is no longer used, which would put the three remaining Americans in one of the first four. The cell doors are identical to those Hua installed in the bonze cells on top of the Arch: solid steel, with deadbolts on the outside. There are usually no more than a couple of guards in this area of the cave. The bulk of Hua's troops are billeted a half mile farther into the actual tunnel.

"Assuming we will have the advantage of surprise, a small raiding party should be able to eliminate the guards, free the prisoners, and bring them out. The team should be well equipped with smoke and frag grenades, and timed satchel charges to cover their retreat from the cave."

Kam asked Toby a number of questions, then Sakoon took us to the map room, where he selected a table and laid out a plastic bas-relief map of the Pak Beng area.

The terrain was as rugged and threatening as that of Quebec Bravo. The jagged karst afforded advantages and disadvantages. The advantage was in favor of the helicopters. They could fly at low level up a valley formed by the Nam Nguen River south of Hua's karst mountain. This would keep them under the line-of-sight radar of both Hua's and the Lao air-defense nets, and was probably what Graham had done on his surreptitious flights over the country. Our two choppers wouldn't be exposed until they skirted the west side of the mountain and popped around to the north.

The disadvantage, Sakoon explained, worked against the F-5s. We would have to make our trench-bombing runs due south, pulling up sharply just short of the mountain. Also, unlike the choppers, we would not be able to refuel at Muang Ngop. The strip there could not handle fighter aircraft. Even carrying fifty-gallon tip tanks on each wing to give us extra fuel, the distance to Pak Beng—274 nautical miles—plus our overall weight load would give us a scant eleven minutes over the target before we would have to return to Udorn. To gain even this much time, Sakoon and I would have to use a hi-lo-hi flight profile: in at high altitude; strike at low altitude; out high to conserve fuel. There was no way we could avoid being picked up by the radar nets as we flew over the Thai-Lao border.

Sakoon laid out the mission in detail. The F-5s would have two jobs to do. First we would have to draw fire from Hua's gunners on the karst mountain in order to pinpoint their positions, then knock them out so the choppers could come in. Second, once the POWs were out, we would have to lay our bombs in a pattern that would dig a trench from the mouth of the tunnel to the Mekong River, creating a water hammer that would collapse the tunnel shoring.

The helicopter force also had two tasks. They would accomplish these by dividing into two teams. The A team would eliminate the guards outside the gates and in the forward part of the cave, free the POWs, put down the smoke and satchel charges, and bring the POWs back to the waiting choppers. The B team would lay a series of six-foot magnesium canisters in a line from the mouth of the tunnel to the river. Once ignited, these canisters—referred to as Mark-6 Markers, or "logs"—would glow cherry-red for twenty minutes, giving Sakoon and me visual reference as to where we should place our bombs. The choppers would land on the narrow flood plain between the mountain and the river.

The F-5s Sakoon had chosen for us were F models, two-seaters with twin 20mm cannons mounted in the nose. We would each have a full load of 560 rounds for these cannons. We would also have a 2,000-pound Mark-84 bomb on the center-line station under the fuselage, a 1,000-pound Mark-83 bomb on each inboard wing station, and one CBU-24 cluster-bomb unit on each outboard wing station. The CBU is a clamshell canister that can be dropped from a dive-bomb run. At a preset altitude, the clamshells open up, spreading hundreds of grenade-type small bombs into the target area. We would each have a backseater whose main function would be to call out altimeter readings and airspeeds during the bombing runs, freeing us to concentrate solely on the admittedly hazardous night dive bombing.

Since neither the jets nor the choppers had terrain-following radar—or any other kind for that matter—we would have to fly the mission visually, by moonlight. If the MiGs bounced us, they would probably do so about the time we were climbing off the target and heading home. At that point, we would be two or three minutes from the border. It was a calculated risk, but we were willing to gamble that the MiGs, flown almost certainly by Russian pilots, would not pursue us into Thailand. If they did, they would know that the Udorn squadron would vector up and intercept. The choppers, with their extremely low altitude and maneuvering capabilities, would be able to utilize the karst terrain to evade pursuit.

Our final problem was buying as much time as possible for Kam and his two teams on the ground before the main force of Hua's troops came boiling up the tunnel in a counterattack. We decided to do this by performing a standard heli-borne assault into a hot LZ. As soon as Sakoon and I had knocked out the big guns, the choppers would come in with all the noise and shoot-

'em-up they could muster. The door gunners would be shooting their M-60s, Kam's troops would be popping standard and concussion grenades, each chopper would play the old ammo-dump-exploding tape at full volume over skid-mounted speakers. Sakoon and I would be in the F-5s, screaming around overhead, giving Hua and his men the impression they were under attack by a full-bore invasion force. The ruse wouldn't have to work for long. Kam's estimated time on the ground for both his teams was five minutes.

So that was it, or at least I thought it was until Terry, who had been extremely attentive during the long briefing, looked at Sakoon and said, "I want in on this. The man you're going after is the bastard who killed my brother."

She said as far as she was concerned she was well qualified to handle the back seat in one of the F-5s. She said she had earned the right to do this by serving as copilot for Sakoon, under fire, during the Quebec Bravo raid, and by performing successfully as our RTO on the Vientiane mission. She said if the worst happened and her plane went down, her presence in the cockpit would underscore the image we were trying to create that the raid was a covert operation carried out by mercenaries from several governments, and not a provocation against the Laotian government by the Thais. She said she was perfectly willing to risk her life to help rescue the POWs and end once and for all Hua's ambition to occupy Thailand by force. She spoke persuasively, with obvious emotion, but under good control. When she was through, Sakoon looked at Campbell, and Campbell looked at me.

"I'm not the commanding officer here," I said.

"We'd like your input just the same," Campbell said.

"If you're asking me whether or not I think Terry can do the job, the answer is yes. If you're asking me whether or not I think she should go, the answer is no."

"Do you realize how *infuriating* that is?" Terry said. Her eyes were throwing amber sparks. I felt the blood throbbing in my neck.

"I was asked for my opinion and gave it," I said. "As I pointed out, I am *not* the commanding officer here. If you're going to press your case, you'll have to press it with Sakoon."

"I understand your feeling, Colonel," Sakoon said. "And while it is not one we share, I do respect it. As for me, I have flown once before with Terry, in combat, and, if she wishes, I shall be happy to have her in my plane."

It had been graciously said. Terry shot me a look of triumph. I gave her a short nod. Would I have felt the same if it had been Jillion Leggett? Yes, I thought. And no. When Jillion and I had first met in Phnom Penh, combat had been a fact of life for both of us—me as an air attaché in a city under siege, her as a war correspondent. Terry and I had met in the plush environs of Singapore, the Long Bar at the Raffles, the custom interior of her brother's jet. Maybe it was this distinction as much as anything that ruled my feeling here.

Sakoon was about to speak when Little Pea stood up. He had his tiger suit on, stood very straight, jungle hat in hand. His childlike features were filled with emotion.

"Sir," he said, addressing Sakoon. "Excuse me, sir. I have listened carefully to everything Toh-bas has reported to us this morning at your uncle's house; and now I must say this: My family lived in a village in the mountains west of Muong Sai, and it was here they and my brothers were killed by the yellow rain. Now we say the bad mens who did this killing are in the place below the ground, across the river from Pak Beng. I too wish to go with you to bomb these mens. You will see I am all okay, for I have flown with Shit Hot many times and have no fear."

Sakoon smiled, then looked at me.

"Colonel?" he said.

"It looks like we've got our backseaters," I said.

Chapter
THIRTY-FOUR

The F-5 is a light tactical jet fighter manufactured by Northrop Corporation in Los Angeles. The F model is a two-seater, one seat behind the other. The plane is needle-nosed, with stubby wings and a sleek silhouette. The twin engines are built side by side into the rear fuselage.

The F-5Fs Sakoon and I would fly were parked in an isolated alert hanger the USAF had built, during the war, on the southeast corner of Udorn Air Base, near runway three zero. Outside the hangar were the two UH-1H helicopters that would insert Kam's strike team to rescue the prisoners.

Senior-level maintenance and armament people were on hand to prepare the airplanes for the covert mission. All the equipment we were using, including our clothing, would be completely sterilized: no identifying markers or labels to indicate a country of origin; planes, choppers, weapons, all miscellaneous gear selected in part because they could be found worldwide and were not unique to Thailand.

Sterilizing the mission in this way would give the Thai government plausible deniability on the diplomatic front with Laos, though the Lao government would know perfectly well our flight had originated on Thai soil with at least the tacit approval of the Thai prime minister. By carrying out the raid the way we were, the level of provocation was reduced, and the Lao government had a way to save face. We had no way of knowing to what extent that government might know or approve of Hua's operation.

Terry and Little Pea went off with the personal-equipment people at Udorn to get familiar with the G-suits, helmets, parachutes, and rocket catapult ejection seats that would be part of their backseat realities in the F-5. Campbell and Toby went with Kam to meet and brief the twenty-man volunteer team of Thai Special Forces who would carry out the ground mission. Sakoon and I suited up, climbed into one of the F-5s, and took off on my brush-up flight. Strapped in the front seat, I pushed both throttles forward then outboard to kick in the burners, and felt as if I'd been strapped to a rocket.

The F-5 was no Piper Chieftain or Rockwell Sabreliner. It was airborne in less than two thousand feet, accelerating so fast I had to keep pulling back on the stick to let the gear and flaps get up before the airspeed was too high. When they were up, I eased forward on the stick slightly, gained best climb speed, and in less than two minutes had leveled at 30,000 feet.

What an airplane! I strained and surged against my shoulder harness, stretching in pure joy, then began all kinds of steep turns, reversals, rolls, and dives through Mach 1, the speed of sound. I was singing and humming, body vibrant and alive. I threw that airplane all over the sky. In the back seat, Sakoon was laughing at my exuberance. Once, when I had about six Gs laid on, he grunted through the intercom, "Well, now that my mask is down, I think I'll have a smoke." At another point, when I had just come back through the Mach, reversed, then pulled into a high-speed yo-yo against an imaginary MiG, he broke into the old Nellis chant: "Fangs out, stick aft, hair on fire, and press on into a bat turn." I never did find out what a bat turn was.

I had flown the F-5 in 1966 out of Bien Hoa with the Skoshi Tigers commanded by Bob Titus. I had been detached for a month from my F-100 squadron, the 531st, to fly twenty-five missions with the Tiger evaluation program. Now I had a chance to fly it again, and I loved it.

When I settled down from the sheer exhilaration of being turned loose in a responsive fighter, Sakoon put me to work on the checkout. We were flying almost clean, no heavy ordnance or fuel tanks slung under the wings as there would be on our attack mission. We carried just a small rack with practice bombs and a full load of ammo for the 20mm cannons.

We did stalls of all kinds: high-speed and low-speed, power on and power off, clean and dirty, straight ahead and turning. Then Sakoon gave me some emergency procedures, followed by single-engine maneuvers.

From there we flew to the air-to-ground gunnery range to do some dive-bomb runs. I needed to refresh myself on how it looked to fly a square pattern, called a box, around a target, then roll into a forty-five- or sixty-degree dive-bomb run. We spent our time first flying the box pattern, then a wheel where I'd circle after pulling off, finally a random pattern where I could roll in from anyplace I chose around the target.

Out of twelve bombs, my scores ran from one bomb 600 feet short at six o'clock from the target (I pickled too soon) all the way up to three shacks, or bull's-eyes. After bombing, I entered the strafe pattern. The ball ammo, used in practice, kicked up dust as the slugs impacted the ground after tearing through the eight-by-eight panel I was shooting at. I made radio calls like "Tiger lead in, right and white," then would hear the range officer clearing me in hot.

From the range, we went back to Udorn, where I shot some simulated flameout patterns, single-engine approaches, several touch-and-go landings, and one full stop. On one approach, Sakoon unexpectedly chopped a throttle, forcing me to react to a simulated engine failure. It worked out. The small, needle-nosed jet had plenty of thrust with only one engine operating.

When we finally debriefed, Sakoon said my procedures were okay, but I was overcontrolling and ham-fisted. I knew why. I was rusty, excited, and eager to show Sakoon I was neither.

*   *   *

Kam and his ground assault team, including the chopper pilots, crew chiefs, and door gunners, had been billeted in crew quarters behind the alert hangar. The rest of us had been given rooms in a quarantined building near the Officers' Club. Sakoon, Terry, Little Pea, and I met in a private dining room at the club, grabbed a quick supper, then back to the F-5s for a night training flight on the gunnery range.

As we were driven to the planes, in a flightline van, Terry and Little Pea talked enthusiastically about the day they had spent with the personal-equipment people. The two of them had put on parachute harnesses, been hung from the rafters, taught how to release the seat survival kit and how to jettison their silk.

In the ejection-seat trainer, they had been taught to raise either armrest to blow the cockpit canopy, then squeeze either exposed trigger to eject from the aircraft. They were shown how the G-suit would inflate automatically in proportion to the amount of G-force the aircraft was undergoing. Finally, they were given a demonstration in an altitude chamber that showed them how to handle their oxygen masks, and what to do in case of rapid decompression at high altitude.

They were dressed now in their green flight suits, G-suits, survival vests with rations and radio, parachutes on their backs, helmets in hand. They both looked eager, but apprehensive too, under the yellow glare of the flightline floodlights. Terry, who had said little to me during supper, now stayed close to Sakoon. I felt a twinge at that, but only a small one. The love affair I was having right now was with the F-5.

Once our backseaters were strapped in, Sakoon and I fired up and took off. We took off ten seconds apart, with the moon in front of us. Sakoon turned left after his gear and flaps were retracted, throttled back a few percent so I could join up; then we climbed out into the starry sky, heading for the gunnery range. I was tucked in tight formation, just off Sakoon's left wing, light on the star. I felt comfortable and settled. Little Pea seemed happy in the back seat.

The planes were loaded now with the same type of ordnance we would use against Hua's tunnel complex. When we reached the range, we each made two passes as we would do in the target area, dropping our CBU to simulate taking out the guns Hua had sited on the mountain above the cave. Then, in a log-lit rectangle prepared by the range crew, ninety feet long, we worked to dig a trench with our heavy bombs. On my first pass, I stopped paying attention to Little Pea, who was calling out my altimeter and airspeed readings. I pressed too much to line the gunsight pipper up just right and released too low. The range officer reported that the bomb had gone long, 300 feet at twelve o'clock. Worse, Sakoon came over the radio to say if this had been the actual mission, I wouldn't have cleared the karst mountain on the pullout.

"Oh, sir," Little Pea said through the intercom, sounding sad.

"My fault," I said. "I pressed. Let's try again."

I made more runs down the chute. He called out the readings. We worked together to sharpen the routine.

"Looking good," Sakoon said. "You cleared the mountain that time."

"You're all heart, Panapong," I said. "How's your back-seater?"

"Doing well," he said. "She wants to fly the plane."

By the time we had dropped the last of our bombs, the range officer reported we had dug a trench over sixty feet long and ten feet wide in the hard gumbo of the range. Not bad, first time around. The soil would be softer in the flood plain by the river; each bomb there would blow out a larger crater. We had set our fuses for a quarter-second delay after impact, allowing the bombs to penetrate several feet into the earth before exploding.

Flying back to the base, we did some formation tactics, alternating the lead. I could see the outline of Terry's helmeted head studying me intently when I was on Sakoon's wing, or he flew mine. When he finally did let her take over the controls, I noticed she was pretty smooth.

You Aussies, I thought. But I didn't say it. Things weren't that good between us right now.

Sakoon porpoised his plane, indicating I should drop just below his jet wash, then took me through some in-trail acrobatics. That's tricky stuff at night, but I was on a high now and had no trouble staying in position. After that he waggled his wings, dipped the right one sharply, telling me to join up on his right wing in close formation. As soon as I had, we turned again for Udorn.

At nine p.m. we met in the map room, where Campbell and Toby had fabricated a sandbox model of Pak Beng, the river, Hua's submerged bridge, the karst mountain, and probable gun locations. Kam and his men had already studied the model. They would spend the daylight hours tomorrow on the gunnery range, conducting a simulated raid, coordinating their A and B team efforts, agreeing on contingency plans. Campbell announced the actual mission would launch tomorrow night.

"That gives Hua another twenty-four hours to move up his schedule," I said. "I understand the value of practice, but maybe we should get the job done tonight. There's still time."

"We considered that," Campbell said. "We've decided the gamble of one more day is worth taking. You and Sakoon need some rest. Kam's operation is critical and has a lot of constraints. What they'll do on that gunnery range could make a significant difference for them. We think Hua will stick to his 18 November date unless he has good reason to believe we're wise to him. ISOC agrees."

"We have to assume he's getting regular reports from his undercover agent at Air Chandra," Toby said. "The situation there is normal. No alert. No company of police sweeping the adjacent border. No unusual recce flights. We've even got King Bhumibol and Queen Sirikit scheduled in for a visit tomorrow to review the troops."

"Excellent," Sakoon said.

"It's a calculated risk," Campbell said. "One we feel we have to take. Hua has spent five and a half years preparing his invasion. We don't think he's going to be easily panicked into pushing his timetable up."

Sakoon reviewed the air attack. He said we could pretty well disregard the 57mm gun. It was slow-firing, effective only against high-flying aircraft. The 37mm might give us some trouble, but his main concern was the three ZSU-23 guns. Each of these had four barrels which could put out 1,000 rounds, for a total of 4,000 rounds, per minute. I had seen them literally saw a plane in half, and while I was respectful as hell of what they could do, I was eager to go nose to nose with them again, and I felt confident we could take them out.

Our basic plan was to fly to a point five miles short of the target area, in formation at high altitude, navigation lights on. At this point, I would turn my lights out and drop back in extended trail to Sakoon's F-5. He would bring his lights up to Bright-Flash, dive at the karst mountain from the east, fire a few rounds of 20mm to wake up the gunners, then pull out north, exposing himself to their fire. As he climbed to bomb altitude, about 13,000 feet, he would go blackout.

Meanwhile, I would be diving at the guns that were shooting at him, dropping CBU on the muzzle flashes. Sakoon would then roll in on the guns that were firing at me, coming from any direction he felt best. We would alternate passes, keeping in constant radio contact to coordinate our timing. Terry and Little Pea would work the airspeed and altimeter gauges, keeping us off the karst.

Once the guns were out, Sakoon would radio the choppers to come in. It would take them five minutes—with luck, less—to grab the POWs, put down the magnesium logs, and take off. As soon as they were clear, Sakoon and I would dig our trench, working from the mouth of the cave to the river. Besides the guns, there were two other dangerous aspects to the flight. First, we'd be making the CBU dives carrying all our heavy bombs, which made for shuddering pullouts. Second, on the trench-digging runs, since we could only roll in north to south, our pullouts would be right in the face of the karst.

And then, of course, there were the MiGs from Wattay.

"It sounds like an altogether enjoyable evening," Sakoon said, by way of summing up.

"You love it," I said.

He smiled.

"I believe this is true for both of us," he said.

And it was.

Before I turned in, I stopped by Terry's room. She was already in a pair of pajamas, sitting on her bed, studying the F-5 Dash-One Manual and pilot's checklist.

"You looked good up there tonight," I said, "when Sakoon turned it over to you."

"Thank you," she said.

"What did you think of the airplane?"

"It's a beautiful plane, exciting to fly. I've never flown anything that fast."

"Bomb runs bother you?"

"No."

"I had some trouble coordinating at first. Then Little Pea got my act together and we did fine. How did it work with you and Sakoon?"

"Fine."

There was an awkward silence.

"Look, Terry," I said. "Tonight was the fun part; tomorrow night's for real. Being hacked is no way to go in."

"How do you expect me to feel?" she said. "You made it clear to everyone you didn't want me along."

"That's right," I said. "But you're part of the mission now.

That decision's been made. If you think an apology's called for, consider that made too.''

"There's no need to apologize."

"Then why do I feel like I'm standing here in a very chilly breeze?"

She shook her hair back, gave me a fair half-smile. The pajamas were the shorty kind, lemon-yellow with rust-colored cuffs. Her legs and arms were tanned and long, cheekbones high, amber eyes were familiar: wide-set and flecked with gold.

"I'm sorry about the breeze," she said.

"People get hurt on missions," I said. "Sometimes they get killed. I wouldn't want either of those things to happen to you."

"I really wouldn't care," she said. "So long as they happen first to Hua."

Chapter
THIRTY-FIVE

The next day passed with agonizing slowness. We slept in our separate rooms, ate when we felt like it, pestered Campbell and Toby for every scrap of new intelligence that came in through ISOC and their own sources in the CIA. There wasn't much. New check points had gone up around Vientiane. The ferry service from Nong Khai to Tha Deua had been temporarily suspended. The king and queen of Thailand had arrived with the usual ceremonial flourish to review the troops at Air Chandra.

In the base exchange at Udorn, Terry found her picture on the front page of a copy of the *Straits Times*, dateline Singapore, three-column head:

BEAUTY QUEEN SISTER OF MURDERED
EXECUTIVE STILL MISSING

The story reviewed the events, insofar as they were known to the reporter, beginning with the crash of the Sabreliner, then Graham's death at the hands of unknown assassins, the incident in the funeral shop on Sago Lane (attributed by Police Inspector

Kim to a war between rival cults), concluding with the sudden and mysterious disappearance of Terry Melbourne.

"Nice picture," I said.

"My hair's long in it," she said, glancing nervously around the exchange. "I don't look like that now, do I?"

"Better get your sunglasses," I said. "And your hat."

At eleven-fifteen p.m., Kam stopped by my room to say goodbye. The choppers were due to launch at midnight. He had on a well-worn tiger suit, and an AK-47 slung over his shoulder.

"This time we're doing it right," I said. "You on the ground and me in the air."

"Like old days," he said. "I go out, find enemy, tell you where to bomb."

"No one ever did it better than you," I said.

At midnight, I heard the choppers leave. They would land at Muang Ngop to refuel—just as we had on the Quebec Bravo raid—then take off again, picking up the Nam Nguen River this time, following it to the place where it intersected the Mekong, then turning west for Pak Beng. The rivers would give them advantages in navigation and a safe path of constant elevation to fly between the karst mountains and under the Lao radar net. The disadvantage would come as they approached Pak Beng. Outlined in moonlight against the river surface, they would be easily seen by Hua's gunners on the north face of the mountain, above the cave. Sakoon and I had to ensure that before the choppers arrived, those guns would be silenced.

Shortly before two a.m., we suited up and were driven in the flightline van to our airplanes. No one spoke, not even Little Pea. We were all alone now with our private thoughts. Campbell and Toby, who would monitor the mission along with officers from ISOC's high command, shook our hands and wished us good luck.

The van stopped between the two F-5Fs parked in the alert hanger, a cavernous concrete half-barrel open at each end and well lighted by huge floods on the ceiling. Each needle-nosed warplane was loaded with nearly three tons of olive-drab ordnance slung under the wings. Two Thais stood by each plane: a crew chief and an armaments man. The line chief stood in the center of the hangar, saluting as we climbed out of the van. These men had obviously worked hard preparing the aircraft for a mission they knew nothing about. If they had any feelings about the presence of a female crew member, they didn't show them.

The crew chiefs put our parachutes in the ejection seats and our helmets on the front canopy bows. Then they followed Sakoon and me as we preflighted our airplanes: pulling gear and pylon pins, checking bomb and CBU fuse settings, generally looking things over. The planes were immaculate.

Terry and Little Pea stood by watching. When our preflight was finished, Sakoon and I walked over to them. We all shook hands and wished each other luck. Briefly, Terry and I embraced.

"Take care, Matt," she said.

"You too," I said.

And that was it. Little Pea and I climbed into our seats and strapped in. The crew chiefs started the two MA-1A starter units that would give us 42 psi of air to rotate our turbojet engines. Each unit was run by a miniature jet, causing a reverberating roar. The noise dampened as I put on my helmet. I did my Before Start cockpit checks.

"You read?" I asked Little Pea on the hot mike intercom when I had finished the checklist.

"Roger, sir," he replied.

"Tiger Two, check in," Sakoon transmitted through his UHF.

"Two," I responded.

"Fire up," he said.

I twirled my forefinger at the crew chief, who opened the valve shooting air to my engines, left one first. Then the RPM reached ten percent, I pressed the starter button and moved the left throttle to the idle position. The engine gave a comfortable rumble as the ignitors touched off the JP-4 fuel in the burner cans. The engine stablized at fifty-two percent. I checked oil pressure and exhaust-gas temperatures in the green, Left Generator light out, and started the right engine.

I completed the Before Taxi checks, trying out systems—moving the controls, speed brakes, and flaps—then received the okay signal from the crew chief.

"Ready to taxi?" Sakoon said.

"Ready," I said.

Our crew chiefs and armament men gave us the thumbs-up sign, and the line chief saluted as we taxied out, Sakoon first.

I lined up next to his airplane, on the runway. He had his formation lights on, nav lights at Dim-Steady. Mine were on Bright-Flash. I turned on the red rotating beacons mounted on each side of my rudder. We did our Before Takeoff checks and closed our canopies, the signal we were ready. The air was turbulent and hot behind our two F-5s as we ran our engines up to one hundred percent.

Sakoon released his brakes and started to roll. His afterburner eyelids opened and, after a second, long cones of white-red flame shot out of the twin tailpipes as his burners ignited. The roaring sound was loud even with my helmet on and the canopy closed.

"Ready to go, Little Pea? Seat pins out?"

"Ready, sir," he replied.

At that, I released the brakes, moved the throttles outboard to ignite the burners, and started the long takeoff roll. At our gross weight of nearly 20,000 pounds I would need 7,400 feet of ground roll to achieve takeoff speed of 160 knots.

We bumped along on the uneven runway, slowly accelerating. At 155 knots, I pulled the stick full aft to raise the nose wheel from the ground. We lifted off cleanly at 160. The airplane was a bit sluggish until the gear and flaps retracted. I joined up on Sakoon; then we turned and climbed out due west for our first leg. In just fifteen minutes, we would swing north to Pak Beng.

"Luck," Toby transmitted from the command post.

"*Kop kune,*" Sakoon replied, which in Thai meant "Thanks."

I flew a loose formation so I could relax. We would be over the target at 0310, thirty minutes from now. As the weather forecaster at Udorn had promised, the night was clear except for a few buildups with cloud-to-cloud lightning well to the north. The moon was nearly full, and so bright we could have flown without nav lights.

We leveled seven miles up in the thin air, making position reports to no one, aware we were being tracked by Brigham, the radar site at Udorn. The controllers at their scopes didn't know our mission. They had instructions to monitor but not contact our flight.

I was snug in the cockpit, attached to my craft by two hoses, three wires, lap belt, and shoulder harness. You don't really get into a jet fighter, you put it on. Without conscious thought, I moved the controls here or there to stay in position. I felt steady, and ready to engage; adrenaline pump primed for combat. I thought of the failed Quebec Bravo mission, the ambush on the ground, the ten good Hmongs who hadn't come back; how finally I was now in my element. Above all, I thought of the three American POWs we were about to snatch from Hua.

When we reached the Thai-Lao border, Sakoon reduced power and started down. "Switches up," he transmitted. I acknowledged, then reached to the top left of the instrument panel, moved my Armament Mode selector to Bomb and flicked up the Left Outboard Store switch. I rechecked my gunsight on, proper mils depression dialed in for bombing, then turned all the cockpit lights down to a dim glow to keep reflections from the front windscreen.

A rapid-fire burst of Lao came over Guard Channel into my headset. Little Pea keyed his mike, unkeyed, then keyed again, answering in halting tones. There was a back-and-forth exchange. We were into Lao airspace and being challenged. Little Pea would try to stall the radar scanners for as long as he could. Sakoon switched to another channel, checked that the choppers were getting into position, told them we were on schedule. He brought them back to our frequency as Little Pea finished his chatter with the Lao air-defense controllers.

"What did they say?" I asked.

"I don't think they believe me, sir," he said. "They want to know my unit. I tell them I have now an aircraft emergency and cannot talk."

Sakoon switched his lights to bright-flash, the signal he was ready to descend and dive on the guns. I dropped back in trail, turning all lights off, placing my Master Arm switch on. We were now at an altitude of 20,000 feet. Below us we could see the jagged jungle karst.

Another burst of Lao came over Guard Channel.

"Sir," Little Pea said, "they have ordered us to turn toward Vientiane; and they are bringing up their MiGs."

"Tell them you're flaming out," I said. "Then break the transmission."

"Yes sir, I will," he said.

I hoped that might buy us a few more precious minutes, that by then Vientiane would lose us in radar ground clutter. Sakoon was already well into his dive. I was diving behind him. To make sure Hua's gunners saw him, he had switched on his rotating beacons. The first cherry tracers were floating toward him. That stream was quickly joined by a second. I was at 13,000 now, keeping my eyes fixed on the muzzle flashes, trying not to follow the tracers, just zero in on their source. By feel, I rechecked all the switches on, pushed the throttles up to one hundred percent, then punched the transmit button on the right throttle.

"Two in, LA to Atlanta," I radioed. In case the men in Hua's tracking van were onto our frequency, Sakoon and I had a simple code to tell each other what direction we were diving from and pulling out.

"Clear," Sakoon replied.

From outside, the sound of the dive I was making would be an earsplitting scream. Inside my helmet, it was little more than a rising rush of wind. I could see the mountain clearly now where it rose above the river. The mountain was black and karsty, the river silvery under the moon.

I pulled the nose farther down from a diving turn, rolling wings level when the pipper in my gunsight reticle was just short of where I had pinpointed a gun. I was in a sixty-degree dive. Little Pea began calling out my altitudes in 1,000-foot increments, and our airspeed as it built up to over 500 miles per hour.

The ZSUs had opened up. Their garden-hose streams of cherry balls floated up in a converging arc that looked as if it would impact right between my eyes. I knew from experience this was an optical illusion. Soon they would diverge and look as if they were bending away at nearly right angles—the ones that wouldn't score, that is. If they didn't appear to bend away, I'd better do something about it, jink the aircraft around, change direction and altitude. Not so easy to do when you're coming down the chute with a load of "dumb" bombs and want to put one smack on a target.

As had been true with every combat mission I'd ever flown, time became distorted, things moved in slow motion. The tracers came up so lazily I felt I could slip between them.

I had my pipper square on the target as Little Pea called out 5,000. I thumbed the button on the control-stick grip. As soon as I felt the left CBU canister separate I pulled sharply but carefully back on the stick, got about five Gs, and rolled left to pull away to the north.

"Two off left to New York," I told Sakoon.

"Roger Two," he said.

The remaining CBU on the right outboard station gave me what's known as an asymmetrical configuration, which means your aircraft is unbalanced and you can't quite roll it the way you want to.

As I shot up from the karst mountain, the 37 opened up. A clip of seven exploded orange and white just inside my turn. When they are that close, you feel it in your gut. Fly to the burst is the old rule of thumb. That will work once or twice with a dumb gunner, since they don't traverse or elevate in order to

blast the same airspace twice in a row, unless they are trying to
box you. I decided these guys were smart. Good thing. A clip of
five 57mm blasted the same space in black-and-red explosions,
scattering lethal shrapnel scores of feet in all directions.

"They're pretty good!" I told Sakoon.

"Roger that," he said. "Looks like you nailed one. I'm in
from Oregon to Florida."

"You're covered."

I was passing the target area to the north. I could see my CBU
going off. The hundreds of small bombs were twinkling ground
explosions that cut off a ZSU as it began firing at Sakoon. The
gunners were now awake and then some. Secondary explosions
caused by touched-off ammo lit up the black karst ridge. The 57
kept firing at me. I saw their method. The 23mm rapid-fire ZSUs
would shoot at us as we rolled in and off; the slow-firing heavy
37 and 57 would open up when we were higher, circling to dive
again.

I pinpointed the two remaining ZSU sites, selected right External Store, rolled in, punched the mike button.

"Two in, Chicago to Houston."

"Roger. Lead's off."

More Lao came over Guard Channel, then someone speaking
guttural English. It was the flight leader of the MIGs that had
been vectored up from Wattay to intercept.

"You are violating Laotian airspace," he said. "You must
identify yourself at once, or we will shoot you down."

My backseater handled that one. At the top of his voice, he
shouted into the mike: "*I am Shit Hot's cousin, Little Pea, and I
have come to bomb!*"

"You copy that?" I radioed Sakoon.

"Roger," he said. "*And* the intercept. We'll carry on."

His CBU was cooking off the second 23 site, so I eased my
pipper over to the remaining one. The fire stream coming up at
me was so heavy and concentrated they must have been burning
their barrels to pudding. The 37 gunner opened up behind them,
knowing they probably couldn't get a hit, but trying all the same
to unnerve me and throw off my aim.

My adrenaline was full up now. A nose-to-nose gun duel will
do that every time. This was my life. What I'd been trained to do
and had done for over twenty years. As I screamed down the
chute another clip of 37 went off in front of me, lighting up the
sky. They had fuzed for 6,000 and I had to fly through it; too
late to jink around. The glare nearly erased my night vision, but

I pressed on, knowing by the time I went through the smoke, the shrapnel would have fallen out.

"Five thousand!" Little Pea shouted.

I pickled and pulled out, grunting in my mask against the sudden influx of gravity force. A full clip of 23 went off around us. The plane shuddered as I jinked away; then that gun went off the air as my last CBU canister sparkled all over the black karst and blew it up.

But the 37 was still on me and tracking good.

"They're shooting at you, Two," Sakoon said in a laconic voice. "Do tell," I panted, slapping my bomb-heavy plane around, trying to twist away from that persistent 37 gunner. Sakoon had one CBU canister left, I had none. We both had the cannons. The 37 and 57 had to go.

"You hit?" Sakoon asked.

"Negative," I replied. "How's your passenger?"

"Passenger's fine," Terry said. "Tell Little Pea I love him!"

If that one didn't boggle the MiG flight leader's mind, nothing would.

"Lead's in," Sakoon said.

"Roger, Lead. Take whichever one you see; I'll take the other."

He rolled in after the 57 that was now shooting at me. Knowing the 37 would put a clip in front of him, he shallowed his dive to thirty degrees and put his CBU right down the gun barrel. The thing blew, sending pyrotechnics crazily into the night sky: orange bright, and red. As Sakoon pulled off, I rolled in to strafe the last gun still shooting: my old friend the 37. I flipped up my Gun Select switch and changed my sight depression in the turn. The gunner tried to bracket me. I went in at thirty degrees, dove low, laid a two-second burst—a hundred rounds—of mixed-load Armor Piercing and High Explosive Incendiary right into the middle of that big gun. As I pulled off, I glanced back to see the secondaries. The last site was out of action.

I hope you're enjoying this, Hua, I thought.

So far, our show had taken exactly six minutes. Act One was over. Time for Act Two. We had five minutes remaining.

Sakoon and I orbited north at 5,000.

"You're cleared in, Taxi," he told the choppers.

"Roger," the lead pilot said.

I could see them clearly outlined against the river nearly a mile below as they popped around the karst and started toward the site of the tunnel. The reflection from their blades made them look like twin whirlpools of silver. As they approached their target, I could see tiny muzzle flashes as the guards in the slit trench opened up with their AKs.

"You're taking ground fire," Sakoon said.

"Roger the ground fire," Taxi Lead said.

The door gunners from each chopper were hammering streams of return fire from their machine guns. Seconds later, both choppers were on the ground. I could see back-and-forth firing. Then a phosphorous grenade exploded in a white burst of streaming smoke tentacles to one side of the action. *"Hit the smoke! Hit the smoke!"* I heard Kam yell over his radio. He had thrown a WP grenade into a position Hua must have set up after Gannon had escaped from the complex.

"Roger," Sakoon answered. He was closest and rolled in. He sprinkled the marked target with his twin M-39 20mm cannons. The ground fire dwindled away.

"Alpha team is inside the gate," Taxi Lead said.

"Roger," Sakoon said. "Give us some light."

Seconds later, one by one, the magnesium logs began to light a path from the tunnel mouth to the river. We watched as the cherry-red rectangle grew.

"Alpha team is out!" Taxi Lead called excitedly. "We got 'em!"

The two choppers peeled up and away.

"Shall we dig a trench?" Sakoon said.

"Yeah," I said. "Let's do it."

One after another, we rolled in and started bombing: first the 2,000 pound centerline bomb, then each inboard 1,000-pounder, dropped in three passes each. This time we had to roll in north to south, but could pull off east or west. Either way, we were always heading toward the mountain on the run-in. The mountain was 3,300 feet high. We pickled our bombs at 4,500 feet, then pulled up sharply in front of the karst, passing over it at about 500 feet before rolling left or right. We started the trench, working from the tunnel mouth to the river's edge so that the last bomb would bring the water in. If the water came in first, it would absorb the impact of the following bombs.

I was rolling in as Sakoon started to pull off west from his second run. Suddenly, twin streams of cherry tracers spurted up directly under him as he came through his lowest point.

"Lead's hit!" he transmitted. A long tongue of flame shot from the tail of his F-5, as if he had engaged his afterburners to help him get away. I punched my transmit button, asked if that's what he had done.

"Negative!" he said.

"You're burning pretty bad then!"

"Cancel that gun, will you?"

"Roger, Lead! Are you going to return to base?"

There was no answer. I continued my run, raising the nose, setting up my switches to strafe the ZSU site that had come back up. Hua must have run in a second crew and gotten a couple of barrels working. They shot at me, but I took them out. I still had a 1,000-pounder under my right wing. We were close to Bingo fuel, the minimum level remaining that would get us back to Udorn.

I pulled off west, looking for Sakoon and Terry.

"What's your position, Lead?" I asked.

No answer.

"Tiger Lead, this is Taxi," I heard the chopper pilot say. "You got to punch out? Give us your coordinates, and we'll pick you up."

No answer.

"Lead, where are you?" I transmitted again.

Just as I did, I saw a big rolling fireball on the west end of the karst mountain.

The kind an airplane makes when it goes straight in.

Chapter
THIRTY-SIX

"Ahhh no," Little Pea said over the intercom. There was traffic on UHF Guard Channel as well: The MiG flight leader repeating his demands, sounding much too close; the Lao air-defense controller; our own guys in the choppers:

"Tiger Lead, Tiger Lead, this is Taxi, do you copy, over."

"Taxi," I called, in a flat voice, "this is Tiger Two, Tiger Lead bought it on the karst. You'd better go home. We've got MiGs inbound."

All this taking place in seconds, no time for emotion, no time to dwell on what had happened to Terry and Sakoon. I had one bomb left, one less now than we needed to do the job, and the cherry logs were almost out.

I couldn't help looking at the burning wreckage scattered along the karst as I pulled off from taking out the gun. I climbed north, then rolled in to put my last bomb where I hoped against reasonable hope it might link our trench with the river. I'd have no way of knowing unless I saw the river surface swirl across a darkness of ground shadow toward the cave.

There were no more guns. I came in full blower, jet engines screaming, at sixty degrees and 520 miles per hour. Little Pea called off the altitudes and airspeeds. I put the pipper where I thought it should be and released at 4,000 feet, just skimming the silent karst as I pulled out over the burning wreckage on the west ridge. I didn't want to look at it again. I was low on fuel and the MiGs from Wattay had to be close; but I circled north anyway to see if by some stroke of luck my last bomb had done the job.

It hadn't. The river flowed in its regular course, a twenty-foot lip of earth still in place.

"*Goddammit!*" I shouted. The words weren't out of my mouth before tracers were suddenly flicking past my canopy and Little Pea was screaming over the hot mike, "*MiGS! MiGS!*" and I was instinctively rolling left, sucking the stick into my lap, trying to turn inside the MiG pilot as his tracers began to slam home, tearing into the rear of our plane and left wing, red and amber warning lights glaring up from the instrument panel as I pulled tighter and tighter, just off a high-speed stall, the F-5 clean and light now, responding like the flick of a dart as I saw the tracers begin to slide under me and knew I had outturned the MiG pilot who was doing his best to shoot me down.

I never did air-to-air during Vietnam; only air-to-ground. I never knew the intensity of concentration, the pulsing red-line fury, the tightening quick circle of death miles above the earth, where everything a man has learned joins in a single blunt expression of necessity and rage printed in flame across the circuits of his brain: *Shoot the cocksucker down!*

In bright moonlight, I rolled and pulled up into the beginning of a yo-yo. This caused the MiG pilot to overshoot, and for an instant we were canopy-to-canopy. I saw his helmeted head fixed in my direction, saw the speed brakes open on his delta-winged craft as he tried to slow his ship to stay behind me. I cobbed the throttles, pulling higher; he tried to accelerate and follow. I reversed over the top, pulled down inverted, rolled out 200 feet behind him and let go with my cannons. I was panting as I squeezed the trigger. Behind my oxygen mask, I could feel my face contort into a rictus of hate as I thought of what had happened to Terry and Sakoon.

The MiG pilot broke sharply right, diving toward the karst. I released the trigger, following him down in close trail. I was on him and was going to stay on him until one of us was dead. We had about five seconds before we'd both slam into the mountain. It was enough.

Pipper in place, I squeezed the trigger on the B-8 stick grip. The twin 20s thudded in tandem, everything I had left in the gun bay going up his tailpipe. When the HEI and API impacted the hot section of his engine, he exploded so violently we were flipped upside down, diving through flaming fragments of the MiG. My helmet slammed once hard against the canopy; I heard Little Pea grunt through the intercom. For a second, I was badly disoriented. I held in the stick, completed the roll, and pulled as hard as I could for what I prayed was the sky.

One MiG down, but there had to be two; the second was probably trying right now to maneuver behind us.

"Little Pea!" I shouted. "Check our six o'clock!"

"I am trying, sir!"

"Do it! Do it! Are we clear!?"

"Yes, sir! I think we are!"

"Keep checking! That guy's number two is up here somewhere!"

"Roger, sir! I will!"

My cockpit was full of acrid smoke as I shot between a saddle in the karst, then skyward. The MiG had impacted Hua's mountain in a fireball of blinding light, strewing metal fragments along the flood plain, where they now lay steaming on the dark gumbo soil. I hit the Ram-Dump switch that opened valves in the cockpit to the outside air, switched off all nonessential equipment to try to stop any electrical fires. I was getting only eighty percent RPM from the left engine, had lost my left generator and utility hydraulic system. The plane felt a little out of rig, but not too bad—smoke clearing rapidly from the cockpit. I had turned south, keeping my eyes peeled for the second MiG. We had no more ammo to fight him. Less then three minutes had elapsed since the first MiG had opened up on us.

Then Little Pea was screaming it again—"*MiGS! MiGS!*"—and I was cobbing the throttles and screaming back, *"Where?!"*

"Left! Left! On the left!"

I jerked the plane up and over, preparing to split-S for the deck, hoping I could make the Thai border before the new guy had a chance to fire. In the instant before the pull-through, I caught a glimpse of the other plane: not a MiG, not a MiG, but a blacked-out F-5 cruising low and slow; right wing, engine bay, and fuselage damaged; jagged tears in the skin, scorched by fire; most of the upper radio antenna blade shot away.

"Sir!" Little Pea cried. "It is Terry and Colonel Sakoon!"

I grinned in disbelief, snatched the throttles back, rolled level, waggled my wings in the join-up signal. As the shot-up F-5 slid closer, I heard the last half of a broken transmission over the UHF.

". . . wounded and can barely talk," Terry said. "Do you copy, over."

A thrill went through me at the sound of her voice. I could see her in the rear cockpit, looking my way; Sakoon in front, helmeted head tipped back.

"Say again, Aussie." I grinned.

"Oh God, Matt! Do you read me now?!"

"Loud and clear. Your antenna's gone. You'll have to stay close. Are you all right?"

"Yes. Sakoon's wounded. I'm flying the plane. We've lost our right engine."

"How bad is he?"

"Pretty bad, I think. He says his shoulder is torn up."

"Did he run that second MiG into the karst?"

"Yes."

"Beautiful," I said. "Can he talk?"

"He goes in and out. He says he's passing the lead to you. He wants us to carry on."

"Roger that. Hold steady as you are," I said. "I'm going to take a look at your ship."

I slid down and under the crippled F-5. It seemed to be handling fine with one engine. Sakoon's last bomb was still slung under the left wing.

When I came back up, Terry said, "Were you able to finish the trench?"

"Negative," I said. "You want to make a pass?"

"I don't see how I could."

"Have you got a pickle button on your stick?"

"Is it the small red one on top?"

"That's affirmative. Ask Sakoon if his switches are still set up to bomb."

She was off for a moment, then came back on.

"He says they are," she said. "He wants us to make the run. But Matt, he's only half conscious, and I can't see the gunsight from here."

"I'll take care of the sighting," I said. "You stay on my left wing. We'll use a standard box pattern. Do you remember that from the practice flights?"

"Yes. I think so. . . ."

"We'll go in at thirty degrees. I'll offset my pipper to the right to compensate for the distance between us. When I tell you to pickle, you press the button, then pull out. There's plenty of moonlight. We've got a good strong horizon."

"How close do I have to be on your wing?" she said.

"A lot closer than you are now. Say five feet."

"God," she said.

"You'll have to hold it close all the way down," I said. "We can go home if you'd rather."

"*Balls to that*," she said.

I grinned, turning on my formation lights.

"Close it up, Two," I said. "We're heading north."

We were well past bingo fuel. Sakoon must have known that when he had urged us to make the run, must have known too that the G-forces in the dive might kill him. So press on into a bat turn. You're all right, Panapong, I thought. You've got the stuff.

We came back over Hua's mountain, leveling at 12,000 feet. The Lao air-defense controller was going very high-decibel now, trying to contact his MiGs. They were off the air. No indication as yet he was vectoring up another flight. Since Hua's guns were down, I left my formation lights on to make things as easy as possible for Terry. With Sakoon wounded, and Terry flying single-engine, I would keep my airspeed lower than normal through the dive. The night sky was clear and bright except far to the north, where clouds bulked up and occasional flashes of lightning showed.

"Check in, Terry," I said.

"Here," she said.

"Sakoon with us?"

"I don't know. I think so."

"We'll make a shallow turn, then start the dive."

"What's our altitude and airspeed on release?" she said.

"Forty-five hundred and three-fifty," I said. "You got that, Little Pea?"

"Roger," Little Pea said. "Forty-five hundred and three-fifty."

"Read the needles and call them exact."

"I will, sir."

"Check seat pins out."

"Seat pins are out, sir."

"Seat pins out, Terry?"

"Affirmative," she said. "But Sakoon won't be able to bail out."

"If it comes to it, you go," I said. "He'd want it that way."

"I won't leave him," she said.

No time to argue.

"Keep it tight," I said. "Five feet."

I adjusted my gunsight to allow for the shallow angle of dive and lower airspeed; I would make the compensation to allow for Terry on the dive roll-in.

"Close it up, Two," I said.

"God," she said. "I'm not steady. I'm trying to be, but I'm bobbling."

"Settle down," I said.

"Keep talking to me."

"Remember," I said, "you're going after the son of a bitch who killed your brother."

"Don't let me miss," she said. "Don't let me."

"You're drifting," I said. "Close it up. I won't be able to watch you once we're into the dive. You ready, Little Pea?"

"Ready, sir."

I went into it from way out as smoothly as I could, the moonlit river clearly visible below, the narrow flood plain, the rising karst. As we went into the dive, Little Pea started calling out the numbers; altitude first, then airspeed.

"Seven thousand and two seventy-five."

"Keep 'em coming, Little Pea. Terry, you okay?"

"I'm getting too close to you; am I too close?"

I shot her a glance down the slant of my wing, saw her helmeted silhouette in the rear cockpit, Sakoon slumped over in the front. Her airplane, which had been tight and close, had begun to yaw, the nose of the F-5 drifting away.

"Get off the left rudder," I said.

She eased off it, brought the nose of her plane back into true parallel with mine.

"Six thousand and three-ten," Little Pea said.

"God, Matt!" Terry said. "I can't hold it! I'm all over the place!"

"You're a good pilot!" I said. "Fly the goddam plane!"

I couldn't look at her now; I had to keep the pipper in place: twenty feet to the right of that last lip of earth.

"Five thousand and three-twenty," Little Pea said.

"You're on your short count, Terry," I said.

"Matt!" she said. "I can't do it!"

"Keep it close!" I said.

"Forty-five and three-fifty!" Little Pea said.

"Pickle! Pickle! Pickle!" I shouted.

I gave Terry a second to respond, then laid in four Gs on the pull, banking up over the karst. I thought I could feel the F-5 shudder as the bomb went off below us. I glanced back and down. The lip of earth at the end of the trench had disappeared under a mushroom of dirt and smoke and flame.

An instant later, I saw the river sweep sideways, sending a silver ribbon of water toward the mouth of the cave.

Chapter
THIRTY-SEVEN

We joined up at 26,000, best we could get, heading south, sucking on oxygen. Neither of the F-5s had cockpit pressurization now, and it was cold five miles above the earth. The altitude would help conserve what little fuel we had. Terry was still too far off my wing for her UHF to work well.

"Close it up, Two," I said.

". . . get it?" she said, as she slid in. She sounded out of breath.

"Say again?"

"Did we get it?"

"Bet your life."

"I felt the bomb let go, but I couldn't see where it hit; I was too busy trying to keep off the karst. Did we really get it? Did we put the river into the cave?"

"You scored a bull's-eye," I said. "A couple of hours from now and the Mekong south of Pak Beng should begin to look like a trout stream."

"Then Hua is finished?"

"He is if Gannon had his figures right—and Gannon's been right about everything else. How's Sakoon?"

"Not good. He was conscious right after the dive, but I've lost him again."

"What's your fuel?"

"Nine hundred pounds."

"That's going to put us just about thirty miles short of Udorn when we flame out."

"You too?"

"Afraid so."

"Can't we put down at Air Chandra now this is over? It's a lot closer."

"Won't work," I said. "The longest strip they've got is three thousand feet. We need at least six thousand."

"I'm not punching out," she said. "Not with Sakoon the way he is."

"That narrows the options," I said.

"Can we glide in from thirty miles out?"

"I'd say so."

"I've never landed an F-5 without power," she said.

"Unless I've missed something," I said, "you've never landed an F-5."

"Well, I'm going to," she said. "You'll have to tell me what to do."

I talked her through a low-speed controllability check to see if structural or internal damage would cause any problems during landing. Northrop builds a tough airplane. In spite of the hits it had taken, Terry's F-5 was handling well. We had just finished the check when Campbell came up on frequency, transmitting from the Udorn command center.

"Tiger Flight, Tiger Flight, this is Delta One, do you copy, over."

"Roger, Delta," I said.

"You're on clear channel, Tiger."

"We'll be discreet."

"Advise your situation."

"Tiger One has passed the lead. He's WIA; his backseater is in charge of the aircraft. We'll both be flamed out on approach. We'll need the field ready for a double emergency."

"Understand, Tiger Flight. Crash and Rescue alerted. How do you plan to come in?"

"In formation," I said.

There was a moment of significant silence. Then Campbell came back up.

"Very classy," he said.

The runway we would be using at Udorn was nearly two miles long and 300 feet wide. I would keep Terry on my wing. She was an accomplished pilot, very cool, and had taken well to the F-5. There were a few things to cover first. I told her to stick her seat pins in, disconnect her survival kit and parachute, keep her lap belt and shoulder harness tight. I told her to steer straight ahead after touchdown, to pull her drag-chute handle immediately, that I'd keep out of her way. I told her that on the landing rollout, her brake pressure would deplete and she should get her aircraft stopped as quickly as possible.

The Thai supervisor of flying came on the radio and reviewed the emergency procedures we'd be using: how to get the gear down, glide airspeed, the compensations required by the fact that our flaps and speed brakes would not be operating. He wished us good luck, said we were to maintain our current radio frequency, that Brigham radar would get us into position for the approach.

Terry's airplane dropped back suddenly as her engine flamed out. I chopped my throttles and popped the boards so she could catch up. We were now at 23,000 feet. I lowered the nose to establish a 250-knot glide speed. Then my engines flamed out, first one, then the other. I keyed my mike, transmitted to Udorn.

"Fire's out," I said.

"Roger, Tiger Flight. This is Brigham. How do you read?"

"Loud and clear, Brigham."

"Very good, Tiger. We have you twenty-nine miles west of Udorn on the two six eight radial. Our height finder says you are descending through twenty thousand."

"That's a tally, Brigham."

"Very good, Tiger. Take up a heading now of zero eight five degrees. We're positioning you into a flameout pattern for runway three zero."

"Roger, zero eight five for three zero."

"You'll be landing at a field elevation of five eight four. You'll have ten thousand feet of concrete to roll on. Wind is from the west at three knots, slight crosswind from your left. Your altimeter setting is two niner niner five. We'll put you over the runway at twelve thousand, heading three zero zero."

"Roger, Brigham. We thank you."

He did as promised. Two miles below, our runway was clearly

visible, two parallel rows of bright lights. I began a thirty-degree bank to the right in the first leg of the flameout pattern, trying to be extra smooth so as not to jar Terry or overtax our flight-control hydraulic pressure, powered now only by our windmilling engines. If the pressure dropped too low, the controls would lock up and the F-5 would crash.

"Looking good," I said to Terry.

"I'm not worried about this part," she said. "I'm worried about down there."

"Take it easy," I said. "You're doing fine."

We hit the downwind at 9,000 feet, then base at 6,000, where we lowered the gear, using the emergency extension system. With the gear down, I had to lower the nose to keep up a pattern glide speed of 220 knots. Our descent rate, out of necessity, was high—4,500 feet per minute. Just before touchdown, Terry and I would have to flare the airplanes to break the high sink rate. Doing that also rapidly bleeds off airspeed. A few feet above the runway, we would have to find the thin line between a stall and a plane-crunching slam-down.

"Okay, we're on final now," I said.

"I'm tensing up," she said. "My hands are slippery."

"Take it easy," I said. "You're doing fine. Altitude twenty-five hundred now, maybe two miles to go. You're looking good. Little Pea's keeping an eye on you, right, Little Pea?"

"Yes, sir," he said, very quiet now.

Ahead, through the frosty windscreen, I could see the rows of crash and rescue equipment lined up outside the runway boundaries. Their engines would be idling, lights and beacons off so as not to distract us.

We came over the end of the runway, fifty feet off the ground, airspeeds indicating 200—high and hot under normal conditions, but it would give us a safety margin for what we had to do.

I eased down, searching for the runway.

"Controls!" Terry shouted. "They're locking up!"

"Hold what you've got! They'll come back!"

"Negative!" she said. "It's not building!"

"It will!" I said. "Hold what you've got!"

I slammed the F-5 down, popped the drag chute. Terry overflew me, locked in attitude, blown by the light crosswind almost to the edge of the strip. No time left. She was seconds away from a stall. One wing would drop, causing the plane to cartwheel in a disintegrating wreck down the runway. I kept steady pressure on my brakes, tried my best to talk her in.

"Okay, Terry," I said. "Land it now. Set her down."

"Jesus!" she said. "I can't! The controls are frozen!"

"Try them again! They'll come back!"

"I don't have enough!"

"Do it!" I said. "Get it down! Get it down!"

She dropped one wing, drifted back toward the center of the runway, rolled level about five feet above the ground, slammed down, bounced back up. "Jam the stick forward!" I shouted. She was already doing it. The plane hit nose wheel first, porpoised once, then stayed down. "Pop your chute!" I shouted. "Go easy on the brakes! Keep her straight! Keep her straight!"

The chute came out. She skidded left, then right, burning up runway, but slowing all the while, stopping finally thirty yards short of the runway end.

"Christ," I breathed, sweating and wobbly, coasting to a halt well behind her, crash trucks surrounding me, foam turrets pointed at the plane, others charging down to reach Terry and Sakoon.

No fires. Everything fine.

"Check in, Little Pea," I said. "You all right back there?"

No answer. Just a very faint clearing of the throat.

"Little Pea?" I said.

"Sir?" he said.

"What's your situation back there?"

"I am well, thank you."

"That Aussie's some pilot," I said.

"And woman," Little Pea replied.

"That too," I said.

Chapter
THIRTY-EIGHT

At three o'clock that afternoon, I stood with Campbell and Toby next to a USAF C-141 hospital ship on the ramp at Udorn. The engines were idling; the three American POWs who had been rescued from the tunnel complex were already on board. They were in serious condition but, according to the flight surgeons, were expected to survive. I had only had a glimpse of them as their stretchers were carried on board, terribly gaunt men with plasma and IV tubes running into their arms, medics and MDs hovering around them.

"I was luckier," Toby said. "The bastards who had me were nasty enough, but they weren't as bad as Hua."

Campbell smiled. He was clean-shaven, had on a sharply pressed three-piece suit, high-polish shoes, looked more like himself than I had seen him in a long while. He and Toby would accompany the POWs to Hickam Air Force Base in Hawaii, then go on from there to Washington. Midge had agreed to meet the plane. She and Campbell would spend a week together on the Eastern Shore. Their reconciliation was not a *fait accompli*, but it was definitely in the air.

"Nice bit of news just in from ISOC," Campbell said. "One of the recce flights out of Air Chandra this morning spotted a large number of Hua's men pouring out of the tunnel exit. The observer called in a Thai Special Forces company. They took over two hundred prisoners without firing a shot."

"No gas?" I said.

"Hell no," Campbell said. "Apparently most of Hua's men hadn't had time to put on their pants. The gas was there, though: six jeeps already in the assault tunnel, each towing a 105-millimeter howitzer armed with a gas-firing shell. The Thais had to wade through a lot of rubble and water to reach them. The main complex was completely destroyed."

"What about Hua? Was he taken prisoner?"

"No, I'm afraid not. The Thais have sent a demolition team in to destroy what's left of the assault tunnel. They'll take a lot of photographs first, also bring out several of the gas shells as hard evidence of what was going on. It will be up to the Lao government whether or not to excavate the entrance to the complex. I suspect they'll decide to leave well enough alone."

"So we'll never know for sure about him," I said.

"Not necessarily," Campbell said. "A couple of the men who were captured by the Thais are Chinese who claim to have had rank in Hua's organization. They've already fingered his man at Air Chandra—a captain in Special Operations. They may be able to confirm Hua's death. They're being interrogated separately by ISOC."

The copilot of the C-141 stood in the door of the big transport, indicating it was time for Campbell and Toby to board. Toby and I embraced.

"Matt, thanks for everything," he said. "We'll be in touch."

"After you've gotten reacquainted with your family," I said, "come on down to Cedar Run."

"Count on it," he said. "Thank Terry again for me. And all the others."

"Will do," I said.

He turned and climbed the stairs to the waiting plane. Campbell watched him proudly, clapped me on the shoulder.

"I made up a limerick about Toby when he first came with the Agency," he said. "Like to hear it?"

"Sure," I said, whereupon my father-in-law recited the following:

> "Young Porter is a man who can't fail,
> His credentials cause colleagues to pale:
> For unlike you and me,
> He has a degree
> From Harvard, and Princeton, and Yale!"

"Not bad," I said.

Campbell smiled happily.

"And you finally got a MiG," he said.

"Right," I said feeling smug. "Sakoon got one also," I added.

"Right," Campbell said, "And without a gun."

"Pinked," I said.

Campbell laughed. "Take care, Matt," he said. "You'll see Brian before I will. Give him my love."

"I'll do it."

"By the way, I got a call from Bob Coyle this morning. He says he's got a problem he wants me to look into."

"Whatever it is," I said, "don't tell me about it."

Campbell laughed. It was his old laugh, deep and rich, rising above the engines of the plane.

"So long!" he said from the top of the stairs. "See you soon!"

I watched the C-141 take off, then caught up with Kam out by the alert hangar where the damaged F-5s were parked. He was still in his tiger suit, had the AK slung over his shoulder.

"*Chum rip seur*, my brother," I said.

"*Chum rip seur, Lōk*," he said.

"You wouldn't call me Matt," I said.

He smiled shyly and shook his head.

"Where will you be heading from here?" I asked. "Back to the ranch?"

"Yes," he said. "I talk to Mr. Adune. I say we need number one good man to help run the guard camp at Khao Wah. I tell him right man for this is Little Pea. He say very good, okay."

"Great," I said.

"Little Pea go off to Banerjee's place to say goodbye to Banerjee, and to Pamela and Liu. I wait here on base, see if news come about Thais who got shot up on the Pak Beng raid."

"Campbell said there was one KIA?"

"Yes. Three more hurt. One bad."

"Sakoon's going to be okay," I said. "Terry's with him at the hospital. The first bulletin said he was critical. That's already been upgraded to stable."

"What you do now, *Lōk*?"

"I'll be leaving in the morning for Bangkok, then on to Paris. I'll spend Thanksgiving there with Brian and Whiskey, then I'm off to England. British Aerospace wants me to do another article on the Hawk. I told them fine, so long as they let me fly it. After that, I'll be going back to Cedar Run."

"Terry go with you?"

"I don't know," I said. "We haven't gotten that far. We're meeting later today at Adune's place."

Kam was silent for a long time. When he finally looked at me again, his expression was melancholy, almost wistful.

"Maybe world be better place some day, *Lōk*," he said. "Men like you and me not need to carry guns. Do hard work in sun. Make love to good woman. Eat rice and beef, drink tea. Enjoy what is left to share of this part of wheel of life."

"That would be my wish," I said.

"And mine," he said, "I do believe."

That night, Terry and I stood talking in the hall between our rooms at Adune's villa. We had arrived at the villa separately, me in a base taxi, she in Sakoon's Jaguar, which had been parked at the base. We had had drinks and supper out by the goldfish pond, just the two of us, with Pushpinder doing the serving. I had on my slacks and safari shirt. Terry had on the same white jumpsuit, big hoop earrings, and stack of bracelets she had worn the day after Graham's death. The light in the hall was soft. Through the open windows, we could hear the wind chimes sounding in the courtyard.

"If the mission hadn't been clandestine," I said, "you'd be decorated for valor."

She smiled.

"There were times when you were awfully harsh with me up there," she said.

"I get that way," I said.

"I'm glad you were harsh," she said. "I'm glad we made it back."

"I'm standing here trying to think of a way to ask you to come to Paris with me," I said. "I've been trying to think of a way all night. I guess I've got a hunch you're going to say no."

"It's not that I don't want to go," she said. "But I called my solicitor before I drove out here. He's practically lost his mind since we left Singapore. He says they need me desperately. There are papers to sign, checks to clear . . ."

"Sure," I said. "I understand."

"I've been thinking about something all day, something I wouldn't have considered before. I think I'd like to try running Gray's business. Just for a year. See how it goes. What do you think of that?"

I smiled.

"With you running it," I said, "I think it'll go fine."

"Thanks," she said.

We were silent for a moment.

"Will you come visit me again?" she said. "Someday, I mean."

"Sure," I said. "We've still got some champagne to drink at Sentosa Lagoon."

"I'm sorry about Paris," she said.

"Paris will wait."

"I really did want to meet Brian; and that nurse you told me about—Nurse Whiskey, isn't it?"

"Whiskey it is," I said.

Terry looked at me, eyes shining, face framed by her closely cropped hair.

"It's been good, Matt," she said. "It's been really good."

"Take care of yourself," I said. "You're one hell of a lady."

We stood in the hall, holding on to each other, close and silent, for a long while.

"Goodbye," we said finally.

Goodbye.

Chapter
THIRTY-NINE

Three weeks later, Nurse Whiskey and I sat on the open terrace of a brasserie at Honfleur on the Normandy coast of France. The late-afternoon sun laid sharp shadow spikes onto the quay from the masts of the fishing boats tied in the Vieux Bassin. A December breeze blew in off the ocean, swirling up the waterway. Whiskey shivered, rolled down the sleeves of her wool sweater, which was the same steel-gray color as her hair.

"Want to go inside?" I said.

"Why?" she demanded in her gravelly voice. "You cold?"

"No," I said. "I'm fine. I thought maybe you might be cold. You want another Calvados?"

"I want everything they've got behind that bar," she said. "I'll start with another Calvados. Make mine a double this time. If you're going to sit here with me, you better have a double too."

I laughed, caught the eye of our waiter, ordered the drinks.

Whiskey's real name was Wilma O'Neill. She had been a top surgical nurse in the Army, had served under combat conditions in both Korea and Vietnam. She had taken personal charge of my son, Brian, at Walter Reed Hospital and later at the Swiss clinic. When Brian had finally been released from the clinic two months ago, Whiskey had accompanied him to the 16th Arrondissement in Paris, where Brian had chosen to live under the roof and general guardianship of Dominique Fabray. I had told Whiskey about the Chinese Spur, all that had happened, including the fact—recently reported to me by Campbell—that Major General Hua's body had been found by the Thai demolition team, in the rubble that blocked the first mile of the assault tunnel.

"I'm not thinking about Hua or his tunnel, I'm thinking about POWs," Whiskey said. "When we were told they were all home in '73, I believed it. Then Garwood came out in '79 and now your three . . ."

198

"Four, counting Toby," I said.

"God," she said after a pause, "Do you think there are more?"

"Yes," I said, "I do."

"Any proof?"

"Not yet. Toby and Campbell are working on it."

I lit a Caporal, shielding my lighter from the breeze.

"Okay, Whiskey," I said. "You've heard my story. Let's have yours. What went wrong between you and Dominique?"

"It was water and oil from day one," she said. "For one thing, *Madame* Fabray wouldn't speak English to me. She'd speak it to everybody else, but never to me. I always got the French: '*Voolay-voolay-voo*'; all that bushwa. I don't speak French. I don't understand French. I don't want someone talking French at me, who damn well knows how to speak English."

"Okay," I said. "Okay. What else?"

"She treated me like a servant. '*Voolay-voo donut mwah uhn varre doo tay.*' Know what that means? I looked it up in the kid's dictionary. 'Would you bring me a cup of tea.' Jesus Christ, I said. Let her get her own fucking tea!"

I laughed.

"I don't know how you managed to keep all this to yourself during my visit," I said.

"I didn't want to spoil Thanksgiving for you and the kid," she said. "All he knows right now is I'm tired and I'm taking a vacation trip with you. You think I didn't bawl these brains out the night before we left? I've been with him every day for three years, gave him every shot of medication he ever had, cleaned the shit out of his drawers, walked him a step at a time out of that room. I love him like he was mine."

"He looks great, Whiskey," I said. "We had a couple of pretty good talks; first time we've been able to do that since he was hurt. He still carries a chip on his shoulder about me, wants to blame me for what happened to him and his mother; but I think the chip's smaller now than it was. He even says he might come to Cedar Run for a week at Christmas."

Whiskey shot me a hard look.

"You had any second thoughts about me coming there to live?" she said.

"No way," I said. "There's a room with your name on it. There has been since I bought the place. You move in when you feel like it, stay as long as you want."

She took out a handkerchief and blew her nose. The sound was like the horn on a freighter.

"You didn't make out so good on this one, turkey," she said. "You started out with Miss Cosmos/World, and you ended up with an old broad like me. Terry sounded right for you. What happened?"

I shrugged.

"Terry couldn't have lived at Cedar Run," I said, "any more than I could give it up. There was probably more to it than that, but that by itself was enough."

Whiskey gazed across the quay, chin in hand, sharp blue eyes thoughtful and steady.

"Miss Cosmos/World, huh," she said.

"Right," I said.

A moment later, Major Wilma O'Neill, U.S. Army, Retired, reached up and patted her steel-gray hair.

"You should have seen me thirty years ago," she said. "I could have been a contender."

ABOUT THE AUTHORS

Berent Sandberg is the pen name for the writing team of Mark Berent and Peter Lars Sandberg.

Berent is a retired combat fighter pilot who served with high distinction in Vietnam, Laos, and Cambodia. Sandberg is a novelist and short-story writer.

The two first met in Arizona during the early 1960s just before Berent went to fight in the war and Sandberg left for Washington to demonstrate against it.

The Chinese Spur is the third book in their Matt Eberhart series. The first two—*Brass Diamonds* and *The Honeycomb Bid*—are also available in Signet editions.

Exciting Fiction from SIGNET